HOARDER

ARMANDO D. MUÑOZ

Hoarder

This is a work of fiction. All of the characters, organizations, and events portrayed in this novel are either products of the author's imagination or are used fictitiously.

ISBN: 978-1519695338

ACKNOWLEDGMENTS

A number of individuals have helped to bring this book to life and are deserving of thanks.

Special thanks to Tori Pulkka for that crucial suggestion that my *Hoarder* story would work well in novel form, and for many more useful suggestions along the way.

Special thanks to Kevin Mangold, who had to live with my hoarder mindset as I wrote this, and for his editing.

For all of the reading and support, thank you John Heller, David Reynolds, Gregg Majeski, Marti and Melanie Kanna, Rebekah Nichole, Rhyd Wildermuth, Steven S. Wright, Lesleh Donaldson, Shane Lukas, Sareth Ney, Ron Williams, and Louis Buchhold III.

And thank you mom for teaching me to clean my room and pick up after myself.

For Kevin Mangold.

1

Something about the dark suburban street gave Ian the creeps. There was a sense of displacement that he was not used to, and it seemed kind of silly, really. He was fifteen, and he shouldn't have been bothered by the dark, or a sense of isolation, or a strange neighborhood at night. Okay, so it was many things giving him the creeps, but he sure as hell wasn't about to show it, especially to his brother, Keith. Not that anybody could see his face in the shadows beneath his hoodie. Not that anyone was looking.

He was only three miles from home, and two and a half miles from school. But go past Hacienda Heights and the freeway, and he might as well be in another city, or another country. Add the isolation and darkness and it might as well be the moon. Ian and Keith didn't live in a ghetto, but it was an urban area with schools bordering the freeway. There were people driving and walking at every hour of the night, along with noise and neon lights on every block. Buses, sirens, and shouting, all night on school nights. The noise was a nuisance, but also a reassurance that the world was busy and the better for it.

This suburban street should have felt like a safer area, but Ian found it more threatening. He wasn't afraid to be out after dark in his neighborhood, so why here? It was too dark, with far fewer streetlights, no marquees or billboards, and no bus stops. Stranger still, it was only a quarter past ten, prime time hours, and yet the majority of homes had all of their lights off. Could a whole street really go to bed this early?

This neighborhood probably saw a lot less crime than he was used to, which the lack of bars on any windows confirmed. Yet Ian had a chilly suspicion that if he did find himself screaming as he was being stabbed to death on this street, the one porch light that was on would turn off in response.

Except for the three others he was pedaling up the street with, there was nobody out. Not one car had passed them for five blocks. Ian tried to convince himself that this was a good thing. Nobody out meant no witnesses. Plus, they were camouflaged by the night. All four wore dark pants and oversized black hoodies. Their hoods were up, draped over long billed black baseball caps. All safety reflectors had been removed from their bikes. Hunched over as they pedaled, you couldn't even tell that one of them was a girl. They looked like generic hoods invading a rich neighborhood, a gang of thugs with criminal intent. They were conspicuous for their class, but again, there were no eyes to judge.

The lead bike barely held Keith, Ian's seventeen-year-old brother. Keith was hunched over as he struggled to handle a bike that he outgrew two years ago. Following side by side behind him were Dani, the girl, and the six-foot plus giant of the bunch, Will, the only one wearing a backpack, which was black like their clothing.

The three bikers in the lead were all seniors, and a close-knit trio who shared many of the same classes. Ian tried hard to keep up with the older kids, tonight on this street and daily in the high school halls.

Will looked more mature than his years, partly due to his hulking size and mustache, which his mother made use of by sending Will on frequent cigarette runs. Ian gave off the opposite impression. With his diminutive frame and hairless face, Ian looked more like he was in middle school. Ian could accept that, you just had to live in the genes you were given. Height was a hand-me-down.

Ian couldn't understand why size was such a rich subject for teasing by his brother, except that's just what older brothers do. Ian could be Will's size and Keith would still have something over him, the perceived maturity that comes from a higher grade level. Never mind that Ian's high A's topped Keith's low B's. Pointing that out might get him a sock in the arm, and Keith could certainly hit harder.

Dani frequently teased Ian, too, but that he was happy to take. She did it to get his cheeks to flush bright red; *putting on his boy rouge* she called it. Ian was realistic enough to keep his crush on Dani in check. She was a senior. He was a sophomore. His brother had a better shot with Dani, but she didn't show interest in Keith, Will, or any guys at school. Dani didn't want to date guys, only hang with them. Most every male at school had a thing for her, and Ian considered himself extremely lucky to be among the few she spent her free time with.

The further up the street they traveled, the more expansive the properties became, divided by foliage instead of fences. The homes were set further back from the street, increasing in size and stories. The trees followed the trend, extending their height and expanding their canopies. Branches engulfed many of the streetlamps, shielding the light. The road ahead became darker still.

Keith's bike slowed and veered to the right, and he signaled with his right hand for the bikes behind him to do the same. Keith took his bike onto the sidewalk, stopped, and got off. His ass hurt from the seat that was too small for him, but he was thankful he hadn't trashed his old bike. At least he still had something to ride. As his friends followed onto the sidewalk behind him, Keith walked his bike onto the lawn of a completely dark colonial house, pushing it up to the wall of hedges that bordered the far left side of the property.

The hedges stood over seven feet tall, flat on the top and neatly trimmed on the side. Smaller ornamental bushes were spaced every ten feet along the hedge. There were no lights in the yard along this dividing side, and the growth provided varying shades of darkness. Keith had counted on this, and he stowed his bike into the first pocket of black that the hedge and bushes provided. Dani, Will, and Ian stashed their bikes in a line beside Keith's. From the street or sidewalk, all of their bikes were virtually invisible in the dark pocket of the yard.

Free of their bikes, Dani and Will turned to Keith, the architect of this covert operation. Ian turned instead to the tall house. The porch light was off, along with every light inside. The house loomed like a silent sentinel far back in the yard. Ian was the first to voice doubt about his brother's well-laid plan.

"You sure nobody will see us?"

"There's nobody here. They're either on vacation or gone for the season," Keith assured his brother. He stepped away from the house, nodding toward the street. "That's not it. Come on."

Keith walked out of the yard, followed by Dani and Will, who adjusted the straps of his backpack. Ian hesitated and looked back at the dark house, making sure they weren't being watched. There was nobody watching.

The four hoods stepped around the dividing hedge, stopping at the edge of the next yard. The hedge was completely overgrown on this side. The yard around it looked like it had not been landscaped all year, perhaps not for many years. The long driveway held a disturbed carpet of leaves, with a partial bald spot stained with oil near the house where a car was frequently parked.

"That's it," Keith announced.

"Missy's house," Ian elaborated.

Ian had to laugh quietly to himself as he viewed the house. Of course their destination would have to be the most Gothic and decrepit structure on the block. Missy's house stood two towering stories, reminding him of an ancient cathedral. All of the houses around it were dwarfed by its size. The paint was peeling, looking neglected for decades.

The porch light was on, as was apparently every light inside the house, visible only in slivers. Every window was covered, a few by heavy drapes, two with foil, others with construction paper, and one appeared to be blocked by wooden boards nailed up on the inside. Light escaped between the boards and through a knothole.

Ian's silent chuckle was a defense mechanism to quell his unease. All four friends viewed the house ahead with foreboding. With their hoods up and their eyes on Missy's house, none of them knew it was shared.

Keith worried whether he had every detail down to get in and out, with his prize, without detection. Keith had never orchestrated a breaking and entering before. He was more concerned for his companions when it came to discovery. He wanted to take the lead, and he intended to take the fall in the event of an interruption. The *unlikely* event, Keith tried to convince himself.

Dani looked at the house with a frightened sense of finality. The past six endless weeks of worry would have an end in what she would find, or not find, inside Missy's house. Heroic vindication or grim acceptance were the only two possible outcomes. Dani was terrified to find out which it would be, but eager to get inside and put an end to this whole sad ordeal in her life.

Will's worry had to do with his sour sentiments toward the home's owner. At least he assumed she was the owner, rather than a renter. She had been living in the same house for decades, so rumor went. He guessed not rumor, since she had been inside that horrible looking abode all eighteen years of his life. After that long, he figured she should be the owner by default.

Will was the only one of the four to have had multiple interactions with the home's owner, all of them negative. You can't reason or argue with crazy, and it was his unfortunate lot in life to have to put up with Missy's epic hassles for far too low of an hourly wage. There would be great satisfaction in getting good dirt on her, and possibly bringing about her downfall. But if she caught them, damn, he knew they were triggering a whole storm of crazy. Make that a category five hurricane.

Ian was the last minute addition to this criminal expedition, and he had initially been excited to go along. Once he became aware of his brother's plan, he knew there was no way he'd miss out. Keith shouldn't have to do this alone. Ian was involved, too, because he saw this as a conflict between families. Keith and Ian had always been the Have-Nots. Just look at the compact apartment where they lived. Now here they were in this opulent suburb, to take back what was theirs from this horrible Have.

Ian had grown up with a curious lack of fear, and this mission had not phased him in its planning. Which was why the epic case of the creeps Ian currently felt was so jarring to him. He had fought for his place to be here, and now looking upon Missy's house, inside its walls was the last place he wanted to be. Not that turning back was a consideration. Where his older brother went, he went.

Beneath their intimidating black hoodies, all the more threatening for being in a pack, these hoods were not thugs; they were just innocent faced kids from any working class neighborhood in America. It was an unfair chain of events that had brought them to their current position, but theirs was a journey for justice. They were young, but they were not dumb. They were just desperate not to be victims anymore.

2

Keith was the first to pull back his hood. Mounted on the bill of his black baseball cap was a small spy camera. Now that they had reached their destination, it was time to start gathering video evidence. Dani, Will, and Ian followed Keith's lead and dropped their hoods, uncovering the spy cameras mounted on the bills of their black caps.

Whatever footage they eventually released would have to be carefully edited to remove their identities. Video evidence could also be used as back-up insurance, as an assurance that they would not reveal Missy's crimes if she didn't reveal theirs. However, meeting Missy was not a part of their plans, if they could get in and out fast enough.

Keith, Will, and Dani pulled small handheld video cameras out of the big front pockets of their hoodies, because one could never have enough footage or angles in today's uploading age. None of these cameras was a phone or personalized device, nothing identifiable whatsoever. All serial numbers had been scrubbed off.

Ian's presence had not been counted upon and he was left without a hand cam. Ian was still grateful to Will for the baseball cap cam he had been provided. Will was an active skater and videographer who tried to record all of his gravity defying feats, and perhaps more profitably, his gnarly falls. The bloodier, the better for selling.

Over the past two years, Will had cleared six thousand selling his spill videos to shows like *Most Shocking: Banged Up Boneheads 2* and *Whacked Off Sports* (actually *Whacked Out Sports*, but he was a teenage male, so whacked off always came out of his mouth). He got fifteen hundred dollars per clip, and he invested it in more and smaller cameras to fasten everywhere for more dynamic shots. Every one of his cameras was employed in their mission tonight.

The eyes and lenses trained on Missy's house numbered fifteen. Ian felt the need to voice his doubts. "You're certain she's not home?"

Ian's question was aimed at his brother, but it was Will who replied, "I'm sure. She never misses the Tuesday night late sale, ten p.m. sharp."

"And she lives alone?" Ian inquired to anyone.

Keith replied this time. "She must. I've never seen anybody else go in or out."

"She shops alone, too," Will added.

Ian wasn't assured. "But you've said she buys a ton of food."

Will had his own theory. "She has a hearty appetite. She's as big as an MMA fighter. She loves her food as much as her sales."

"And she's not married?" Ian asked. Will looked revolted at the thought and countered, "Who would marry her?"

Ian figured Will had a solid point. Who would marry the local witch with the scary house except for a warlock? And if that were the case, he'd be a part of the legend. Plus, Ian doubted Missy would want to give up her eerie last name, which also fed into her mythic reputation. Something like Creeperskin, or Crepitus, or Hagalina. "What's her full name?" Ian needed reminding.

"Ms. Missy Wormwood," Will had the misfortune to know all too well.

Keith smirked at the irony. "Perfect name."

Ian pulled up his sleeve to look at his watch. It was 10:04 p.m., just a few minutes after the start of Missy's weekly shopping frenzy. He should have been relieved, but he wouldn't let his guard down. "What if she comes right back?"

"She won't. She always shops until midnight, at the earliest. One thirty to two is her usual check out time," Will said.

Keith bristled at Ian's incessant questioning of his plan. He had spent nearly two weeks putting together this operation, and he was confident they would succeed. There was only one variable so far, his younger brother's participation, and he hoped that wouldn't be his plan's undoing. And since when had Ian become so doubtful of his older brother anyway, who he usually idolized and followed dutifully? He had to quell this mutiny now. "If you're so scared, Ian, you shouldn't have come."

"I'm not scared," Ian challenged back. He hoped the look on his face wouldn't betray him. And he wasn't scared he tried to convince himself. He was just creeped out a bit. A lot of bits, maybe.

"Why did he come?" Will chided Keith about Ian's presence.

"He said he'd tell mom if I didn't let him tag along," Keith reluctantly admitted.

Dani grinned at the simplicity of Ian's plan, and while she was concerned that no trouble should come to the kid, she was glad to have him there. "That old ploy. Always works, doesn't it?" Dani winked at Ian.

Ian's creeps didn't prevent him from cracking a grin. She was right. Ian would not tell this to his brother, but he and Dani were secret co-conspirators. They could understand each other and had a connection the others did not. Ian was happy to keep it his little secret, and he knew that most guys would do anything to have his closeness to one of the most desired and unattainable girls at school. Ian had never seen Dani wink at anyone else.

Keith didn't see Dani wink at Ian, but he was getting frustrated at the delay caused by their tag-along variable. It was long past time for him to take back what was his. "Let's get out of the open."

Keith started into Missy's yard, and Will, Dani, and Ian followed him. Keith stayed close to the unruly hedge, keeping their advance cloaked in the shadows. Once they were beside the house, Keith led the others across to the walls, keeping them out of the open as they headed back.

Ian looked at the covered windows beside him. The next window he passed was covered with heavy curtains. A gray cat sat on the windowsill, so still Ian thought it might be a fake. The cat's eyes followed him, proving it had life. Ian was disturbed to know they were being watched, even if the eyes were feline. Missy's house was filled with kitty spies. Ian was also disturbed by the unhealthy look of the cat. All of its bones could be counted beneath its gray, nearly hairless skin. Ian didn't stick around long enough to add them up.

Keith looked back at the three he was leading. "Over here." Keith passed a few untrimmed bushes against the house and stopped on the other side. Will, Dani, and Ian stopped beside him, and they all looked down at a rectangular basement window.

Brown construction paper was taped over the inside of the window, glowing from the basement light behind it. The kids crouched down in a line before the low window, filming it without obstructing each other's lenses. Near the bottom of the window, there was a seven-inch tear in the construction paper, the result of weather and wear, with a flap hanging down.

"There it is," Keith said as he filmed through the gap in the window covering. His crew leaned in with their cameras, looking at the limited interior through their viewfinders.

Through the tear in the construction paper, the blue striped handlebars of a bike were visible in the basement below. The clutter around the bike was indiscernible from their limited vantage point.

"My stolen bike. Disappeared off my porch twelve days ago," Keith announced with satisfaction that his friends could see it for themselves. Dani saw the handlebars, but she was not familiar with Keith's bike, so she had to ask the obvious. "You sure it's yours?"

Keith wasn't bothered by Dani's doubt; he welcomed her questions, whereas he was annoyed by his brother's inquiries. "The stripes on the handlebars, my dad did those. That was the last gift I got from him before he split."

"I thought you hated your dad, for running off on you guys," Will said.

Hate was too soft of a word for how Keith felt about his father. Words like *father*, *dad*, or even his name Roland were not terms that he would attribute to the man now. In Keith's mind, he was only *Asshole*, or *Coward*, or *Selfish, Loveless Motherfucker*, names that started with a capitol letter. He could think of a hundred other derogatory names for the man who had gone to work six months ago and decided to never come home. No note, no goodbyes, nothing but a secret new start for himself and endless questioning grief for his family. So Will was right, but it was hate Keith felt entitled to harbor. His brother and mother were entitled, too, but whether they chose hate or forgiveness, he didn't know.

"I do," Keith replied, "but it's my history, not hers. And I'm taking it back."

Dani chimed in again. "Why not report it to the police instead of breaking and entering?" Ian nodded in agreement with her.

"How do I tell them I found it here? By creeping in her bushes?" Keith questioned in answer. Everyone understood the necessary risk.

"What led you here?" Dani was curious to know.

Keith's mission at Missy's house had begun as schoolhouse rumor, coming from a trusted source. "When I put out the word my bike was swiped, Megan told me in the library she saw Missy walk by the week before last, pushing a bike with blue stripes. A day I was also at school while my bike was on our porch. She has a car. What does she need my bike for?"

Nobody had a good reason they could think of. Will offered a theory anyway. "She uses them for toothpicks."

Keith thought that was funny, but he wouldn't laugh and make light of their dangerous situation. He felt responsible for his friends, and he would even be fine if there was desertion among the ranks. He felt inclined to offer an out to doubtful Dani with sincerity. "I'll understand, Dani, if you don't want to go through with this."

Keith had not noticed that Dani was even more grim and committed to this recon mission. "Oh, I want to. I have to."

Ian could tell Dani was not saying that out of bravado. "What did you lose?" he inquired.

"Fiddlesticks, my cat. Six weeks ago," Dani said, and it still wounded her to say it. Ian winced at her pain. He knew Dani had been grieving for many weeks over her lost cat. Only now did he connect that unfortunate event to their current location, and the idea that her cat might have been snatched shocked him. A cat was worse to lose than a bike because a cat was warm-blooded and reliant on its owner. Keith might miss his bike, but the bike would never miss him back.

Keith added fuel to Dani's fear. "She's a crazy cat lady, too. I've seen a bunch of them on her property. Wild, feral cats. One of them clawed me last night."

Ian thought of the emaciated kitty spy in the window they had passed and knew his brother was right. Keith held up his left hand for proof. There was a white bandage on top, saturated with blood in the center.

Ian had been doubtful of Keith's initial explanation for the hand dressing this morning, that it was the result of slamming his hand in his locker door. That was the kind of clumsy move that Keith might make, but he knew his brother hadn't been wearing a bandage after school yesterday. Now he knew the reason for his brother's lie, and considered it justified.

Will did not want Dani to get her hopes up, since he had painful, personal experience with this in his youth. He would always remember lil' Sheba, the Shih Tzu who had split the first and only time he had left the front gate open when he was eight years old. He'd always wondered what had happened to that lil' shithead, and he equated the feeling with the pain Keith harbored from his father, to a much lesser degree, of course. "Cats run away, Dani. All animals do."

"Fiddlesticks was fat, he couldn't run anywhere. I think somebody lifted him off our porch." Dani's conviction that Missy was the culprit stemmed from proximity; Dani lived on the same street as Keith, and thieves often revisited areas they knew were good for raiding.

Ian was inclined to believe in Dani's suspicion. Missy had a well-deserved reputation among young and old alike. Her behavior had raised her to the level of neighborhood legend, the lady most likely to be seen as the local Boogeywoman by the little ones and *that insufferable bitch* by any adults unfortunate enough to have crossed her path. "She gets around. Kids in my class have stories about her taking things," Ian added to the legend.

Will had his own stories to tell, far more than his current company, about the neighborhood witch. "She shoplifts, too. She's the town klepto."

"She ever take anything from you?" Ian asked Will.

Will nodded. "Yeah, my virginity. That was her in that dark room at the farm party."

Nobody laughed out loud, but they all found that funny, even Ian, who was the only one of the group who had not been at that legendary party. Dani belted Will in the arm playfully. They all needed a laugh, and Will could always be counted on to cut the tension at just the right moment.

There was a rustling nearby, in the bushes to the left of Dani. "Shhh," Dani instructed the guys.

Everyone stood still and silent. They heard more rustling, relocated to the bushes to the left of Ian. Ian looked over as branches began to shake. A gray haired cat leapt out of the bush, claws out, with a hiss of attack. Ian dodged the feral feline by an inch. An inch more than his brother had.

"Shit!" Ian exclaimed. Apparently, Missy's kitty spies also acted as a clawed security force. They would do well to keep on guard for this threat. Hopefully, Dani's cat Fiddlesticks had not been indoctrinated into Missy's violent kitty cult.

Ian watched the cat run off toward the back of Missy's house. Will slapped Ian on the back, startling him a second time. "Almost had your first shave there, Squirt." Ian flipped Will off, but he smirked while doing it.

"I think I just turd my pants," Ian admitted.

Keith was done with interruptions. "Let's get what's ours, and evidence, and get out. Before we get rabies." Rabies had been on Keith's mind since his wounding at these bushes last night. He didn't want anyone to know the cat's attack had also involved its teeth; bubbly feline saliva had mixed with his blood.

Keith tried to open the window, pushing up, then in. The window was locked and wouldn't budge. Keith expected as much; he had tried the window the night before with the same result, right before he had been clawed. Will slipped off his backpack and unzipped it. He took out a crowbar and handed it to Keith.

Keith wedged the end of the crowbar beneath the window. He pried on the handle, but the window did not budge. Keith leaned toward the glass, looking down through the tear in the paper more closely. He noticed a revealing new detail.

"She nailed it shut."

Keith zoomed in with his handheld camera. He focused in close-up on the heads of two bent, askew nails sticking up from the inside window frame. Dani and Will stuck out their cameras to film the same disturbing detail. Ian didn't have a handheld camera to film, but he did add a suggestion.

"We can find another opening. The cats have to get in and out somewhere. I could squeeze through a doggie door."

Keith shattered the basement window with a quick jab of the crowbar, also shattering his brother's suggestion. He knocked out the glass around the frame and tore at the paper behind it. They were all hit with a blast of old, dusty air escaping from below. Dani equated it with a belch in the face from a sickly old man, her graceless grandfather in particular.

Ian looked around nervously from the noise. Not even the cats were watching. Ian looked up at the windows, which were covered and absent of eyes.

Keith handed the crowbar to Will, who put it into his backpack. Keith pulled his handheld camera back and leaned in through the shattered window frame. He wanted to look inside with his own eyes first, and the third eye attached to the bill of his cap.

Dani, Will, and Ian all leaned in around their leader, eager to know what else was inside. Keith was taking longer than expected, and his hesitation was heightening his friends' suspense.

Keith was offended by the smell. The air below had been trapped without circulation for decades. However, it was Keith's eyes that were assaulted the most. What he witnessed inside the basement was shocking, and although he thought he had planned everything down to the last detail, he had not planned for this. He had never seen anything like this in his life.

Keith feared that their mission was going to become terribly complicated, and fast. Suddenly, he couldn't breathe.

3

Ian leaned forward, intending to shake his brother's shoulder, when Keith pulled out of the window. Keith sucked in a deep breath of fresh air, requiring it before he could address his friends. "We were wrong. She's not a klepto. She's a hoarder."

The H-word set off a red alarm in Ian's head. He had seen enough on the subject, thanks to cable television, to know that most hoarders suffered from a high level of crazy. Compulsive hoarding was classified as a serious mental disorder. Those shows were fascinating to him, plus they were high in gag inducing shock value, all the more disgusting in high definition.

Ian wondered what kind of hoard Missy's house held. Did she collect random stuff and garbage, diving in dumpsters for her treasures? Maybe not, since she shopped at Will's store regularly. Was she a collector of one certain thing, like artificial pigs or frogs or bikes? With a chill, he realized that she did collect cats, the live kind. Animal hoarders almost always indulged in animal cruelty, usually unknowingly. Ian suddenly had a disturbing image of the basement below covered in a furry carpet of rotting cat carcasses. He banished the image from his head, but not before he considered how that carpet might smell.

Despite the alarm that hoarding triggered, Ian felt a distinct excitement at seeing a hoard firsthand. The appeal of going inside Missy's house was akin to a visit to an abandoned house in the woods, the kind that kids would dare each other to go into amid rumors of past deaths within its walls, in the hopes of finding a blood stain, or better yet, a stray skeleton.

"For real?" Ian asked his brother.

"It's bad in there. Careful of the glass." Ian could tell from Keith's tone that his brother was not joking.

Keith moved aside and Dani, nearest him, moved in. Dani's head entered the window frame, looked from left to right, and pulled out with a grimace, her nostrils flared. "Gag me. It smells in there. What is that?"

Ian was eager to see and smell for himself and offer Dani an answer. "Let me see."

Dani scooted aside so Ian could move in. Ian took a deep breath, and then he stuck his head through the shattered window frame to see inside the lowest level of Missy's house. It was a sight more vivid than the highest definition.

Ian looked inside Missy's basement for less than twenty seconds, but the peculiar details he saw numbered in the thousands, and was numbing to his eyeballs. There was not one square inch of floor visible. Keith's bike stood atop a few feet of refuse, mostly moist collapsed boxes and leaking garbage bags. Haphazardly thrown throughout the basement were over one dozen more bikes, maybe two dozen, from kid to adult sizes; overturned lawn chairs and patio furniture; garden tools, including rakes and hoes and shovels; a lawnmower lying bottom blade up; rusty scrap metal; empty animal cages, topping the bikes in number; a plastic Christmas tree with tinsel on the branches and Easter baskets spilling pink and green plastic grass; a broken plastic backyard play set and a punctured kiddy pool.

These were Ian's first impressions of the basement's contents, and had he looked longer, he would have picked up countless more curious details and patterns among the hoard. Witnessing this hoard wasn't just hard on his eyes; it was an assault on all five of his senses. The smell was a noxious blend of too many horrible elements, like mold and sewage and spoiled meat. Unable to hold his breath, he opened his mouth and found the rotten air had an offensive, acrid taste. Ian's throat, sinuses, and ears throbbed in tandem from the environment invading his system. Looking up into an exposed light bulb, he could see the swirling stew of particles choking the basement, and now aware of them, he could feel the terrible air caressing his skin like a diseased hand.

Words like *leprosy*, *e-coli*, and *ebola* flashed through Ian's mind. The moment he would banish one disease, another one would fester to the surface. Goodbye *cholera*, hello *malaria*.

A white cat darted over some overturned furniture to Ian's right, startling him before it disappeared behind more junk. Ian glanced up at the exposed pipes, broken and *repaired* with peeling tape and fabric. One broken pipe appeared to be wrapped with an extra large pair of lace panties, soiled with brown water that dripped down onto a pile of soggy, crumbling boxes.

Ian pulled his head out of the window, eagerly gulping in the refreshing outside air. His face was pinched with disgust. "It smells like toxic black mold, and sewage, too. There's a pipe leaking brown stuff."

Dani accepted Ian's assessment; she had seen the basement for herself. Keith questioned his brother, "How do you know what toxic black mold smells like?"

"It's all through the basement and boiler room at school," Ian confessed.

Keith was caught by surprise. He had been going to that school years longer than Ian, but he had never explored its forbidden underground. Keith was kind of impressed that his kid brother had the cojones to go behind any closed door he wanted, regardless of the rules. Perhaps Ian was a good choice to have along on this expedition. Ian's confession begged another question. "What were you doing in the boiler room?"

"Avoiding class, what else?"

"Let me see," Will said eagerly. Ian moved away from the window as the biggest of the group moved in.

Will stuck his head though the window frame, looked around, and inhaled the atmosphere. He started to choke on the thick basement air and pulled out. "There's mold and poop in there, but there's something else. It smells like dead things, dead rats, or some kind of rotting meat."

Ian didn't like Will's phrase *dead things*. Dani was more bothered by the word *rats*, and although Will had described them as dead, Dani knew they didn't start out that way. Keith knew that dead things were inevitable in a hoard the size of Missy's, and he only hoped that Fiddlesticks was not numbered among them.

Ian imagined being down inside the basement, within the hoard with its smothering air, and he came up with an alternative to Keith's plan. "Why don't you just lift your bike out and we'll split?"

Before Keith could respond, Dani answered for him. "I want to go in. I saw a cat in there. Maybe Fiddlesticks' in there."

Ian accepted Dani's answer, and he knew the others would, too. Dani was going in no matter what the group consensus was, and none of the guys wanted her inside this house without offering their protection.

Will could not contain his excitement. "I want to see this freak's house now. Who knows how much of the town she's stolen."

Keith finally answered his brother, with irritation. "Just head back home. You can watch our videos later."

Ian wasn't given a chance to offer a retort. Mindful of any residue glass around the edges, Keith lowered himself feet first through the window frame and dropped out of sight into the basement below. Keith's voice called up to them. "Dani next!"

Dani did not hesitate, following Keith's lead and lowering herself into the basement, with the aid of Keith's helping hands below. Dani's eyes locked with Ian's, and she dropped out of view.

Will moved ahead of Ian, eager to enter enemy territory. He dropped his backpack through the window first into Keith's waiting hands. Then Will took the plunge with a cry of "Geronimo!"

Ian was the last to move up to the window frame. "I'm coming down."

"Wait," Keith called up to him, "take this first."

The front tire of Keith's bike rose up to the window. Ian took hold of the spokes and the striped handlebars, pulling the bike out of the basement. He leaned the bike against the bushes, out of sight from the street. Ian moved back to the window.

"Make room for me."

"There isn't room for us," Keith called up.

"Too bad."

Ian followed the others through the window into the dank, lowest level of Missy's house.

Had Ian known what was going to transpire, and who was going to expire, in such a short amount of time, he would have put a stop to this mission. He could have simply told mom about his brother's cockamamie plan, and gotten him grounded. That wouldn't stop Keith, who would probably climb out his window in defiance. Ian could have stolen all of their bikes tonight, committing the same crime of which they were accusing Missy. Only Keith wouldn't be stopped by lack of transportation; he would have walked the few miles in his stubbornness. Ian could have broken both of Keith's ankles with a sledgehammer, now that would keep him from walking to Missy's house, and that would have also been a mercy to them all.

As Ian lowered himself into the basement, he really had no idea how quickly the world could come crumbling down on top of them, like a cardboard box collapsing beneath a massive, unstable, twenty ton hoard.

4

Keith's hands grabbed onto Ian's waist, helping him down onto the uneven, elevated floor of garbage. The ground gave another inch when Ian's shoes landed on it. Keith, Dani, Will, and Ian stood cramped up against each other in the space previously occupied by Keith's bike. They all looked around, stunned by their surroundings. They had already been swallowed by the hoard.

"I thought it smelled bad up there," Ian began, and decided not to finish once he tasted the acrid air again.

"The air smells poisonous," Will warned. He was no expert on the subject of toxic fumes, but he was convinced of it nevertheless. He trusted his instincts, and he wished he had the foresight to bring a gas mask, or four.

Dani found a flaw in Will's warning. "It's not poisonous to the cats, or Missy."

Will did consider himself an expert on Missy, and he thought his theory stood. "She's not exactly a picture of good health. I've seen her dripping sores up close."

Ian found himself looking less at the hoard and more at the wasted structure that contained it. Simple contact with the hoard was enough to warp walls. There was not one inch of exposed wall or ceiling that was unaffected by discoloration, wetness, or mold saturation. More amazing still were the rotten holes in the soggy structure, creeping black fuzz growing out of them.

"There's so much mold in here," Ian stated.

"We won't be here long enough to be affected," Keith replied.

Ian thought his brother was wrong about that. Ian had felt the ill effects of this noxious atmosphere when he first stuck his head into the house and breathed it in. Granted, Ian knew he was sensitive and allergic to just about everything. But even a modest dose of poison was still poison. This was like getting limited exposure to radiation. You might not feel it now, but it could sure fuck you up in the future.

While the three seniors filmed the potentially stolen junk around them, viewing it more on their cameras' flip screens, Ian continued his structural inspection. It wasn't just the mold that posed a danger. He was surprised there were lights on down here, showing every stark detail of this garbage pit. The bare, hanging light bulbs had mold and webs on them, and one was hanging within splashing distance of a broken, dripping pipe. Missy's place was a house fire waiting to happen, and Ian was highly uncomfortable being inside such a massive firetrap. Fire moved fast, but humans in the hoard could not. That's why hoarder houses were so frequently condemned.

Keith didn't consider the house that had Ian's full attention; his focus was on its contents. He was still fuming over the theft of his bike, and he made sure he got footage of every bike held in this basement. He knew exactly how all of the other bike theft victims felt. It stung.

"Looks like every missing bike in the neighborhood can be traced back here. And missing toys."

"She doesn't have any kids. What would she need a bunch of toys for?" Dani questioned.

The answer was obvious to Will. "To play with. She talks in an annoying child's voice, and has a matching IQ." Will imitated Missy in a squealing girl's pitch. "Oh lookie-loo! It sparkles! I'll buy all of them!" Will waved his hands in enunciation, just as Missy did.

Dani spotted a white cat slinking across the basement. She was the first to step up and out of their pit, trying to forge a path through the hoard toward the animal. "Here, kitty," Dani cooed.

Keith wished Dani had not stepped out first, since he thought he should lead, but he also knew there was no controlling her. Keith and Will stepped out of the pit and forged a different path through the basement hoard. Before Ian would follow, he had to inquire, "Where are we going?"

"Pussy hunt," Will replied, "You'll like it."

Ian didn't like anything inside this oppressive basement. Keith looked back at his brother and instructed him, "Follow me."

Ian took a big step up to get out of the pit. The refuse he stepped onto collapsed with the shattering of hidden glass beneath. Ian pitched to the side, his right hand going out to brace against the wall.

Ian's right palm hit the wet wood and punched right through it, his hand disappearing into the soggy structure up to his wrist.

"Aww fuck!"

Keith didn't see Ian's fall, but he responded immediately to his cry and reversed course.

Dani forgot about the white cat and turned along with Will.

Ian pulled his hand out of the wall, which had the consistency of black butter. Dozens of large cockroaches scurried out of the hole that Ian left behind. Ian's hand was caked in black mold, wet wall mush, and more running roaches.

Revolted, Ian shook his hand, flinging off the wet rot and skittering vermin. He saw a mass exodus of cockroaches coming through the hole he had opened in the wall. Ian was their reluctant liberator, and he shivered. "Yuck!" was a simple word, but it was the only one that fit the situation.

Keith stopped backtracking when he saw his brother wasn't injured. "You okay?"

"I'm doing great." Ian flung more parasites off of his hand. Wherever they landed, they were quick to disappear into the nearest dark crevice. Worse than the roaches exiting the wall were the swirling particles of mold spores, or *hoard spores* as Ian thought of them, certain to set up camp inside of him.

Ian spotted a blanket caked in its own funkiness and bedbugs. He grabbed it to wipe off the muck, the little brown bugs scattering as their home was invaded by human hands.

"We didn't need to break a window. We could have punched our way through the wall," Ian observed.

"Be careful," Keith instructed his brother. He hoped his younger sibling wouldn't defy his instruction. He wasn't trying to be a dick; he was genuinely concerned for Ian's safety inside this house of collapsing crud.

Keith moved back into the path behind Will. Ian followed his brother. He didn't want to play hero or comedian, move an object unnecessarily, and start an avalanche that would jeopardize their safety. He tried to follow his brother's footsteps exactly.

Dani was relieved to see Ian on the move again behind the others, and she shifted back to resume her search for the white cat. She felt a sharp stab to the back of her neck, and she gasped. The guys turned to Dani as she spun around.

The open blades of hedge clippers stuck out of the hoard. Dani could see a bead of her blood on the tip of the dirty clipper blade she had backed into. She wondered if the tetanus shot she received in kindergarten would still protect her. In hindsight, she should have gotten a booster shot before attempting tonight's mission.

"Don't decapitate yourselves on these," Dani warned the guys. She squeezed around the protruding clipper blades.

While Keith was concerned with the other bikes he saw, Ian focused on the overturned, dirt caked animal cages. All of their doors hung open.

"What's she got all these cages for?" Ian wondered out loud as he came upon another one. Up close, he could see the cage wasn't covered in dirt; it was coated with dried crap. With the knowledge came the smell, and it revolted him.

"They're caked in excrement."

"I thought I smelled dead poop in here," Will added.

Dani grew angry from the observation. "Whatever was in them was abused." She knew that any animal living in its own waste was living in neglect, and she didn't understand how anyone could be so horrible as to allow it. The more she thought about it, the more outraged she grew, and to think of Fiddlesticks within one of those cages… Dani banished the thought.

Keith shifted his handheld camera from the bikes to the cruel cages that had captured the group's attention. In his camera's close-up, he noticed something worse than the caked crap. There were dried bloodstains and patches of fur on the bars, even a few scraps of flesh. Keith decided not to announce his discovery. He didn't want to distress Dani any further. She would see it all on the tapes later anyway.

Keith understood that their discovery of the cages upped the stakes of their expedition, and the power of their footage. Being a thief was terrible and a personal outrage for the victims, he knew that all too well. But an animal abuser was offensive on a far deeper level, and once discovered, they could not be allowed to continue. Keith was concerned that they were going to find worse than wild cats and filthy cages before this exploration was over, and now they were obligated to document every horrid detail and use it to bring Missy down on charges of animal cruelty. Missy was going to lose her animals, her house, and her precious hoard when this was over, thanks to their anonymous videos.

Dani made her way into a thin culvert in the center of the basement. Will, Keith, and Ian squeezed into the space with her. Keith looked around for an exit and couldn't find one. While he had planned for an invasion of this house, he had done so without a map or a floor plan.

"Where do we get out of here?" Keith asked.

They all looked over the piles of junk towering around them. Ian was the first to see it, and he pointed high to the northeast. "Up there."

Over twenty feet high in the corner of the basement, atop a steep mountain of stuff, was a four-by-four foot opening, the upper half of an open door. The door itself had been long removed, probably to allow room for more storage.

Discovering the basement door so high made Ian realize how deep they really were. This basement was twice as low as any house basement needed to be. This was more like the multi-level boiler room beneath the school, only moldier. The sheer scale of Missy's house made Ian feel exceptionally small, like one of the many rodents he shared this dwelling with. They were all interlopers inside Missy's massive mansion.

"Where's the stairs?" Will wondered aloud, since there were no stairs to be seen.

"They've been swallowed," Ian responded, and he was right. The steep slope of refuse that led to the door was packed down tightly, like a rocky slide. The white cat Dani saw earlier darted out of hiding and bounded up the incline, disappearing through the half door into the house above.

Dani squeezed around the guys, but Will didn't want her up front. "I'll lead," he said.

"No, my cat will run from all of you. I'll lead."

Dani led the guys through the shrinking culvert in the hoard. She hadn't gone ten feet before she had to stop. The path ahead was just over two feet wide, and directly above it was a pipe generously dripping brown water.

"Maybe we can climb around it," Dani suggested.

Dani saw three wooden chair legs sticking out to the right of the path. Dani grabbed onto the high shelf of a leaning, busted up armoire and stepped up onto a chair leg. The furniture pile took a startling shift, threatening to collapse on her and close the path.

Dani stepped back off of the chair leg and waited as the furniture settled. She knew climbing around the dripping pipe was no longer an option. A few drops of stink were better than a concussion or impalement.

"We have to go through it," Dani stated.

Dani pulled up her hood, and three more hoods came up behind her. Dani leaned her head down as she squeezed past the dripping pipe, not wanting any wastewater to hit the spy cam on the bill of her cap. The top of her hoodie took a few drops of the foul fluid, which saturated into the fabric.

Will, Keith, and Ian squeezed through the path, also getting baptized by the hoard house holy water.

"That's a sewer pipe," Keith commented.

"Tastes like it," Ian confirmed.

The path narrowed to just over a foot wide. Dani had to turn sideways to squeeze through the shrinking channel. Her knee bumped a loose bike tire, which shifted and caused a cardboard box wedged against the handlebars to shift down. The open box top faced Dani, revealing its long forgotten contents to her. She froze where she stood and Will bumped into her.

"Sorry. What is it?" Will asked.

"In the box."

Will looked down over Dani's shoulder. Inside the cardboard box he saw a web draped animal skeleton.

Ian and Keith could not see into the box from further back. "What is it?" Ian asked.

"Bones," Will replied.

"A dead rat?"

"I hope not."

Will spotted the handle of a broom and pulled it out of the hoard. The broom's removal caused more junk to shift and a fresh plume of dust to rise. He turned the broom to hold the dusty brush end and fished into the cardboard box with the handle, puncturing the carcass. It was as easy as punching through brittle paper.

Will lifted the cat mummy out of the box for all to see. Dani filmed it with her handheld camera but not her cap cam, since her head was turned away.

"Is that Fiddlesticks?" Will had to ask.

"No, my cat would be fresher. I'm liking this lady less and less."

Will got a whiff of the cat carcass, and it made his stomach lurch. He didn't think that an animal this deep into decomposition could reek this badly, but there was the proof dangling in his face. Will flung the carcass into the hoard and tossed the broom after it.

The broom landed out of view, but their ears told them it triggered a chain reaction. They heard metal clang together, followed by wood banging against wood, followed by a long paper rip, followed by glass rolling against glass, followed by a half dozen thuds on the floor, followed by glass rolling on wood.

"Cat's eye," Will guessed.

Keith instructed the group, "Don't disturb the hoard." He saw the hoard as a sleeping beast. Disturb it, and it might inflict a fatal bite.

The procession led by Dani reached the bottom of the steep slope beneath the basement door. Ian looked up at the exit, and then he looked higher at a wooden beam beneath the ceiling. The beam was packed with boxes and other stuff precariously balanced on top. The junk appeared four times wider than the beam supporting it.

"I hope you guys can climb," Dani called back to the others.

"Can you?" Keith called back.

"Follow me and find out."

Dani slid her handheld camera into the front pocket of her hoodie, letting it record without her hand on the controls. The guys pocketed their handheld cameras in the same fashion. Dani started her climb up the slide, using both hands to test the surface stability.

Keith followed Dani up. Will climbed up beneath Keith. As was always the case, Ian followed last.

"Good thing I grew up a tomboy," Dani commented as she scaled the garbage mountain with as much experience as the guys beneath her. Not that any of them were experienced with this kind of hoard climb. It was a slow and awkward ascent for them all.

"I knew you were a boy. Dani's short for Daniel, isn't it?" Will teased.

"You wish."

Dani had three quarters of the slope scaled when a large rat sprang out of the hoard and ran over her right wrist. Dani instinctively pulled both of her hands back, losing her grip on the surface. She began to slide down.

Keith looked up as Dani's right shoe landed on his face. His nose erupted with blood and he was knocked loose on the slope. Keith was momentarily thankful that Dani's shoe had missed the camera on his head as he slid down. He shouted, "Look out!"

Will saw Keith sliding toward him and moved fast. He gripped a table leg to the right and swung his body that way. There was a painful spike of pain against his upper back. Will looked over his shoulder at the edge of the wooden table he had just swung into. Keith slid down beside him, passing within a few inches.

Ian looked up at his older brother sliding down toward him. Ian raised a hand and caught the bottom of Keith's shoe, just hard enough to stop Keith's slide.

Dani's left foot punched through a discarded screen door, stopping her slide. Below her, Keith tested his grip on the slope and started to climb again. Will resumed his climb beneath Dani. Ian followed his youthful elders.

As she tried to dislodge her foot from the torn screen door, Dani felt something warm and furry brush against her buried left ankle. She panicked, evincing her gender for the first time with a high-pitched shriek.

"There's something down there!"

Dani's left leg thrashed as her foot sought freedom. There was another pass of warm pressure against her calf. Dani kicked her leg back and the screen ripped further. A black cat was even more eager for exit, leaping out of the screen and climbing over Dani's ass as it ran upwards. The cat's color was not lost on her.

Dani released a mad bark of laughter. "I love cats!"

The dislodged screen door slid to the left, where it disturbed a teetering stack of crushed boxes. The crooked box on top fell onto its side. The folded top flaps bulged outward.

Keith didn't know what was pressing for release within the tipped box, but he wanted everyone past it before it escaped.

"Keep going!" Keith cried out.

Second in line behind Dani, Will climbed past the bulging box top. As Keith came upon it, the folded flaps burst open. Unlabeled tin cans spilled out of the box, raining down onto Keith and Ian.

"Watch out!" Keith called down to his brother.

Keith held onto the slide with one hand as he shielded his head with his other arm. Ian looked up just in time for a tin can to bounce off of his face.

"Owww!"

Ian knew the can would leave a nice bruise. He wondered what food could possibly be contained within those cans to give them such weight, and he would have to be content with never knowing the answer. As the cascading cans decreased, Keith and Ian resumed their climb.

Near the top of the slope, Dani came upon a swinging ceiling lamp hanging in her path. She knew that meant the packed junk that made up the slope was at least five feet deep to put her in the lamp's path. Dani pushed the hot light draped with cobwebs aside so she could crawl past it. Once released, the light swung behind her, releasing dust and some of its brittle webs.

A wayward tin can, a late escapee from the fallen cardboard box, rolled off of the slope and hit a pile of garden tools. One weathered handle with splinters sticking out was knocked aside, and a rusty hoe careened down at Ian's head. Ian reached out and grabbed the handle, preventing it from scalping him. He threw the hoe behind him, and heard it slide down the slope.

Ian was left with wooden splinters in his fingers and palm, but he was in no position to pluck them now. He would have to dig them out later. He hoped that the handle had not been drenched in rat and cat piss (or people piss, there were those leaky sewer pipes overhead) or covered with mold spores, and then he admitted to himself that his slim hope was just a lie. Every item in this basement had been touched by toxic crud. Ian was eager to get home and break out the peroxide and Band-Aids. He wondered if they had enough peroxide under the sink to bathe in, him and Keith both.

Ian had broached the subject of gloves with his brother before departure. It was a valid question; why would they risk leaving fingerprints in the house they were invading? Keith's response had been convincing at the time. Getting caught red handed would never happen with his fail-proof plan, plus if Missy's house was as full of stolen goods as he knew it was, she would not risk bringing the cops in to investigate a stolen bike she had stolen first. Despite his trust in his brother, Ian thought he should have worn gloves anyway, if only to protect his flesh from germs and harm. Only none of them had known about the contaminated hoard beforehand.

Dani reached the open half door at the top of the slope. She was eager to climb out of this basement death trap. In fact, she could not remember ever wanting to be out of a room more in her life. She didn't want to think about the fact that there was certainly a lot more hoard to come upstairs. She'd see it soon enough. Missy's house was like a human Chinese finger trap; the deeper in she went, the more locked in she became as the walls seized in around her. Around them all.

As ridiculous a thought as it was, Dani figured this dangerous dump they found themselves swallowed up by and fighting against likely brought its creator great comfort. And then she was the first one fully out of the basement.

Will pushed his way past the hot lamp, taking more of its webs with him. Dani reappeared in the open doorway above him. She reached in for Will's hand, helping him out and onto another unstable hoard.

Relieved to see two of his friends out of the basement, Keith pushed past the swinging lamp. Will's hand reached down, to help Keith as Dani had helped him.

Ian had lost some distance behind his brother. He looked nervously at more shifting garden tools stacked beside him. A standing rake fell away from the other tools, starting an amazing upward domino effect that kept Ian transfixed, his head tilting up to follow it.

The rake hit a folded ladder, which was already leaning at an impossible angle. The ladder spun forty-five degrees and fell against a loose clothesline, which gave about five inches before pulling taut. The clothesline knocked loose a curtain rod that stood up vertically, balancing the overhanging hoard atop the high wooden beam.

Ian didn't register his brother shouting as he saw the ceiling hoard shifting out of place above. Boxes, bulging bags, appliances, and giant holiday decorations moved for the first time in years, sending down a rain of dust and rat droppings.

Keith reached through the door above, waving his brother on.

"Come on!"

Ian kicked into overdrive and scurried up the incline. The first falling box landed directly behind him and didn't stay there, rolling fast. It sounded full of bells as it jingled all the way down.

"Faster!"

An aquarium landed directly beside Ian and exploded. Colored gravel, glass, and a few goldfish skeletons flew at Ian's face, which he turned away. He still got a few neon nuggets in his mouth, but that was better than glass. He was nauseous to notice the gravel did indeed taste like fish. *Like sucking on a dead goldfish* he thought as he spit out the gravel and continued to climb.

A six-foot plastic Frosty the Snowman with lights inside took a headfirst dive off of the high beam. Turned amateur wrestler, Frosty performed a piledriver into Ian's back, knocking him flat. Ian was not down for the count, and he kicked Frosty down the slope as he pushed past the swinging lamp. Pushed too hard apparently, as the bulb sparked and went out. Ian noticed the bulb remained unbroken, and he was thankful the sparks had not escaped their glass casing.

Keith leaned through the door for Ian, ready to grab his hand when he got within reach. Ian had his eyes firmly set on his brother ahead, so he didn't see what Keith saw. An enormous radiator was balanced atop the high beam, and it looked like it weighed a couple hundred pounds. Only it was no longer balanced, and it slowly tilted to the right.

"Hurry!"

Ian propelled himself up the slope as metal scraped against wood above him. He didn't waste a second to see what it was, nor did he see the radiator crash down on its side beneath his shoes. The massive impact shattered the stability of the entire slide as it rolled down.

Ian's hand clamped with Keith's as the ground beneath Ian shifted and sank. Keith yanked Ian through the door. In the basement beneath them, they heard the radiator hit a table half way down, and the cacophony stopped with a crack of wood. The radiator remained barely balanced against the same table edge that had jabbed Will in the back.

Ian, Dani, and Will looked down into the basement with relief that they hadn't been in the radiator's path. Keith's concern was on the added risk the collapsed path posed to them all. Leaving the same way had been considerably complicated.

"We'll find another way out," Keith instructed his followers, and he hoped it relieved them. He didn't feel relieved, that was for sure.

Only now that they had all narrowly escaped from the basement did they begin to assess their surroundings. As they looked upon their current room inside Missy's house, they were shocked and speechless. They had assumed that the basement was as bad as it gets, and they were so terribly wrong.

5

Missy was used to getting whatever she wanted at the Mega-Mart, whether it was her yummy-yummy food or her pretty-pretty clothes. And Tuesday night's weekly Late Bird Sale was Missy's most anticipated event of the week.

The Late Bird Sale always started at ten p.m., and Missy would march through the automated doors at ten p.m. sharp, sometimes with a "Kaw! Kaw!" to announce her arrival. She was Mega-Mart's most punctual and excitable Late Bird, and she saw the store as her own personal nest. Sometimes she would go "Tweet! Tweet! Tweet!" up and down the aisles until two a.m. or later. Later was partly due to the Mega-Gulps of soda she would consume as she shopped, literally gallons of sugar and caffeine slurped through a bendy straw.

All of the staff and managers knew Missy by name at the Mega-Mart, and they gosh darn well better, considering how much time and money she spent there. The staff was usually good about fulfilling her needs, but if there was a problem, usually from a new hire, Missy could lay a few eggs, and she wasn't afraid to break those eggs and make an omelet. The staff knew it was in their best interest not to get served one of Missy's Omelets.

Missy was quite accustomed to her weekly routine, which was why tonight's unexpected interruption of her program had her so panic-stricken. *It's not fair!* Missy thought as she coughed from the smoke and exited the store with a flood of fleeing shoppers.

The Late Bird Sale had started fine and on time. One reason she was so punctual was because she always wanted first pick, before other shoppers could get their grubby mitts on the Mega-sale products. And Missy often bought more than one of the same sale items. Sometimes she would buy all of them if it tickled her fancy. A Late Bird who wasn't early was apt to find the best pickings already picked over, and she didn't want to be the Dumb Bird in that position.

One of tonight's most sought after sale items was the two-liter bottles of Freshie's Fruit Punch, but that was too long of a name for Missy to remember, so she just thought of it as her Red. It was when she pushed her near empty cart into the soft drink aisle that Missy encountered that cheapskate, and cheap trash, Mrs. Cutter.

The big basket of Missy's cart was empty, but the top seat was filled with the latest tabloids. When Missy would pass the news racks on her way into the store, if the headlines screamed at her, she was likely to scream back. Missy parked her cart before the fruit punch sale sign, only the shelf was empty. Every bottle of Missy's Red was in the cart of that nasty woman. Missy was nice at first, and willing to negotiate.

"I need half of those," Missy demanded.

That Cutter woman had dared to laugh at her. Then Mrs. Cutter went on and on about her coupon counting and her shelf clearing rights, and to Missy, it all went in one ear and blew right out her butthole; it was all the same sound to her. Missy knew what kind of bird Mrs. Cutter was. *Cheap! Cheap!*

"I got first dibs. It's store policy," Missy announced with authority. She grabbed the binder overflowing with coupons out of Mrs. Cutter's basket and threw it on the floor. Coupons scattered like confetti.

"I hope you enjoy Missy's Omelet!" Missy gloated. "They're on special today, and you don't even need a coupon!"

Mrs. Cutter tended to the fallen coupons like they were a fallen child, and she let loose a tirade of dirty words that Missy was too much of a lady to repeat. With Mrs. Cutter's cart unattended, Missy grabbed the handle and pushed her Red away, leaving her own cart with the tabloids behind.

When Mrs. Cutter caught up with Missy in the front aisle, there was nearly a catfight between the birds. The store manager had to break it up, and because Missy was the longtime customer on a first name basis, she was granted the Fruit Punch Prize. Missy threw a "Cheap! Cheap!" over her shoulder as she went back to her serious business of shopping.

Three minutes later, nobody saw Mrs. Cutter in the home supplies aisle, lighting the EZ-Lite Logs with a fireplace lighter, both items on sale when bought as a pair. The logs lived up to their name.

When Missy saw the smoke rising from Aisle 8, she pushed her cart with urgency toward the nearest empty checkout lane. She reached out and grabbed about a half dozen bags of chips (all on sale) without slowing. Missy didn't have time to restock the tabloids she had left in her first cart, but that was okay because tonight's television schedule would keep her occupied.

Missy didn't have to see who started the fire to know who was responsible. She hoped Mrs. Cutter cooked her goose good in that barbeque. Preferably overdone.

Missy barked at the cashier to check her out faster, while the cashier's concern was on the smoke and self-preservation. Missy even pitched in and bagged the bottles of Red and bags of chips as fast as the cashier could scan them. Then the fire alarm went off and the manager's voice boomed over the PA, ordering an immediate cease to all sales and a nice and orderly evacuation.

Missy was not going to be denied her yummy-yummy snacks, which were her God given right. She grabbed the plastic bag handles and shouted at the cashier before he could halt the sale.

"I.O.U.!"

Missy flew the coop with the other shoppers, who were not leaving in a nice and orderly fashion as they'd been instructed.

Fire trucks and police cars were pulling into the lot as Missy headed for her car, carrying her grocery bags in triumph. She thought the rotating red and blue lights were pretty-pretty, but she wasn't going to stick around and voice her suspicion on the fire's cause. Missy had gotten what she wanted, as she was entitled, and Mrs. Cutter hadn't bought squat. Why, Mrs. Cutter could kiss her high turned tail feathers!

Missy had been in a rush to leave, and while she had gotten her snacks, she had forgotten to get cat food. She figured that was okay, she'd have to go to the store again soon, assuming it was still standing, to stock up on everything she missed tonight. Missy didn't realize that she had been coming up with excuses for forgetting to buy cat food for over three months straight, a new record.

Missy was suddenly eager to get home, her thwarted hours of shopping already forgotten. She was never home during these hours on Tuesday nights, and she was excited to find some new programs on TV that she would normally miss. It would be like a whole new night of television. How awesome was that?

Missy never knew what the Mega-Mart staff called her behind her back when she left following her weekly shopping excursions. Bird Lady was too kind, and Crazy Bird was not severe enough. They called her *The Vulture.*

Later it would become incorrect legend that The Vulture started the fire that night inside the Mega-Mart.

6

They were stuck in Missy's kitchen. Keith thought they were stuck like rats in a glue trap. Meanwhile, the real rats were not stuck at all as they darted from one fetid food source to another.

Will saw movement all over the place. For every rat, there were at least a hundred roaches. Neither vermin seemed particularly alarmed by their presence. Missy let the pests have free reign in her house, and they had no reason to fear humans anymore. Will thought that Missy needed better friends, the kind that didn't have an exoskeleton or carry the bubonic plague.

The next time Missy went shopping at the Mega-Mart, Will would have to tell her about any sales on rat traps, roach motels, or bug spray. There were an awful lot of gnats and fruit flies swarming around her kitchen. He was about to say something about it when a particularly juicy fruit fly flew into his open mouth. Will spit the nasty little bugger out and kept his lips shut.

It occurred to Ian that the current hoard they stood on was far less level than the basement below. If that was even possible, and apparently it was. This was the first time that Ian found himself nearly eye level with Will. What made this room so different from the basement was the fact that this room was used everyday. Which meant it was piled higher with mounds of ever growing and shifting garbage.

Ian noticed that the kitchen was considerably muggier than the basement below. It had to be at least fifteen degrees hotter in here, which wasn't a surprise; heat rose. Ian didn't think that Missy employed any heaters or air conditioners (where would she keep them?), but the hoard seemed to trap and hold the heat. It also explained the enormous petri dish that the house had become. Mold flourished in warm and humid environments.

Regardless of the heat, Ian felt a chill when he thought of how stifling hot the upstairs might feel, like Missy's Easy Bake Oven. He hoped they would find Fiddlesticks fast and not have to go upstairs and find out.

Dani covered her nose with her free arm as she filmed her surroundings. She was profoundly revolted by the smell of so much rotten food, and something worse – *dead animal* – which she didn't want to think about – *dead CAT! Don't think about it, just document it.*

Dani focused her camera in close-up on the filthiness around her. A half hour ago she barely knew what a hoarder was, and now here she was dissecting the details of a food hoard, a concept she had never before considered in her life. She was quickly becoming an expert.

Missy's menu was scattered everywhere, most of it partially eaten and moldy. From the food scraps on display, Dani knew Missy was not a healthy eater: chicken bones, pizza crusts, hardened donuts, sandwich cookies with the filling scooped out, French fries that looked as fresh as the day they were deep fried, a pie with one slice gone and black, putrescent filling spilling out (she thought the flavor might be deathberry).

Dani's attention moved from the food to the containers that held it. She noticed a preponderance of fast food wrappers, Styrofoam food boxes, TV dinner trays, and fountain soft drink cups. Every dish and utensil was caked with yesterday and yesteryear's meals.

Among the littered packaging, Dani noticed the familiar pictures and logos of unhealthy convenience foods that she shared Missy's fondness for, delicious junk like Kellogg's Pop Tarts, Hostess Twinkies, and Pillsbury Toaster Strudels. She wondered if she'd desire to eat another Twinkie or Pop Tart ever again. They had been psychologically spoiled.

"I want to puke," Dani warned the others.

"Use the sink," Will recommended.

"What sink?"

Will saw that Dani was right. A sink was not visible. Nor were the counters. There were only mounds of kitchen items beneath the high cupboards. One mound, over four feet high, was made up entirely of dirty dishes, as though the dishwasher had overflown. Directly beside the mountain of dishes was a mound of used utensils that had an even higher peak. It looked like every utensil in the neighborhood, perhaps the city, was stuck around a gigantic magnet. Many of the utensils were corroded with rust. The cupboards above were open, revealing shelves that were stuffed with garbage and covered in cobwebs. The cupboards lacked the contents they were made for, namely dishes and food.

Dani removed her arm from her nose. She remained nauseous but the urge to hurl had passed. Dani was more disturbed to realize she was getting used to the dead… the smell.

Dani led Keith and Will through the thinnest of culverts twisting around the mounds. Will wondered how Missy could maneuver through such tight spaces. She could barely be contained in the aisles of his store. Will realized he was probably conflating her size with her big personality, but the fact remained she was a massive and strong woman who moved with the grace of a buffalo.

Ian's curiosity kept him from following his friends. He turned to the object that intrigued him, Missy's refrigerator. The front of the refrigerator and the handles were smeared with food. Taped to the doors in overlapping patches were messy delivery menus with fingerprints in Missy's favorite sauces, some of which smelled spicy. Multi-colored letter magnets were assembled to spell YUMMY YUM BOX.

Ian had seen enough television shows on hoarders to know that the best parts of their hoards were usually inside their bathrooms and within their refrigerators. And by best, Ian meant the most totally disgusting and gag inducing parts. Ian knew Missy was disturbed, but probably not a serial killer. Still, he expected to find some seriously disgusting heads inside her refrigerator, heads of decomposing lettuce.

Keith looked around, just in time to stop his brother.

"Don't open that!"

Ian's hand froze a foot from the refrigerator door handle, which was caked with a substance that resembled yellow cottage cheese with black bugs in it.

"I have to."

Ian was not going to let Keith deny him the satisfaction of seeing the grossness inside Missy's refrigerator. He grabbed the handle, and as his fingers sank into the funk, he realized it probably *was* yellow cottage cheese with bugs in it. He yanked the door open, and immediately regretted giving in to his curiosity.

Ian's error was in not considering all of his senses first. On television, he was only seeing inside those rank refrigerators. In person, the blast of rotten, warm air that hit his face was enough to make him swoon. He briefly thought of a giant monster with poison breath blowing in his face. Not only could he smell and feel the spoiled air, he could taste it. Many new species of mold were invading his system to fight for destructive dominance.

As the refrigerator door opened, dozens of little cockroaches swarmed out around every edge. Some of them ran around the handle and onto Ian's fingers, causing him to let go and shake the bugs off. So Missy's minions included the roaches, no surprise there. They were only protecting their queen, her palace, and their never-ending feast.

The door settled into full open position, jostling just enough to cause some contents on the inside shelves to fall and slide out. Everything inside the refrigerator was glistening and wet, also like the inside of a monster's maw. As for the patches of quivering green fuzz, those were the monster's cavities.

Everything inside the refrigerator was bathed in a sickly yellow light. At least that was working, because the cooling system was not. The shelves were packed with food that had transformed through fermentation. All packaging had erupted with green, black, brown, and pink putrescence, colors that should not be consumed. Solids had become gelatinous jellies or worse yet, soups. Ian was horrified to see some bugs backstroking in these spoiled pools. Food sludge oozed and dripped through the shelf racks.

Ian didn't have to see a single expiration date to know that none of the food inside the refrigerator was safe. Eating it could not even be a consideration, he thought. Missy must get all of her meals to go or delivered. She must. Nothing inside was remotely edible, except to the cockroaches.

Despite his brother's disobedience, Keith had his camera held out to record the refrigerator's interior. He hadn't counted on seeing this, but he wasn't going to let such obscene conditions inside Missy's house go undocumented. Will and Dani moved behind Keith and filmed the foul food storage over his shoulders.

Keith saw something inside the refrigerator that brought back a memory from elementary school, one that he had successfully suppressed for many years. On the middle shelf was a large, yellowish block of cheese, although he suspected that it had started out as another kind of food of a different color. There were countless little bugs, baby roaches he thought, crawling in lines that burrowed into the soft block.

These bugs were so small they reminded Keith of ants, in particular the ants in a glass case that had been temporarily displayed in his fifth grade classroom. The reason it had been temporary was because one afternoon, when the teacher had stepped out of the room, Keith had the not-so-bright idea of picking up the ant farm and shaking it, giving the little workers inside an earthquake. It seemed funny at the time, until he accidentally dropped it. Glass, soil, and ants exploded everywhere, and in his panic to sweep it up, dozens of the liberated little creatures had swarmed onto his hands, arms, and legs and bitten him repeatedly. He didn't even realize he was cutting his fingers and palms on the broken glass in his alarm.

While Keith's original intent had been to show off, he had ended up crying in front of everyone: the students, the returning teacher, and dour-faced Principal Haggerty, who had suspended him for two days and made him pay for it, which amounted to a month of lost allowance.

Keith tried to banish the memory as he zoomed in on the block of non-cheese and its minions. He was horrified to discover that the baby roaches really were ants, and his whole body shuddered. He was no friend of rats or roaches, but ants were the only bugs that profoundly disturbed him. Keith turned his eyes and camera away from the crawly critters and took a step back. He didn't want to be too close, since he was convinced the ants carried a grudge and would want to bite him for killing so many of their ancestors.

The stench of the decomposition overwhelmed the furthest of them. Nearest the noxious box, Ian dry heaved.

"Close that thing!" Dani demanded as she turned her head away.

Ian grabbed the door handle and did just that. What a great idea that was of Dani's, why hadn't he thought of that? He was once again faced with the multi-colored phrase YUMMY YUM BOX. Ian understood its purpose. It was encouragement for Missy's delusion.

Dani looked back, her eyes watering. "That made my eyes burn."

"I may never eat meat again," Will joked, and then thought he might not be joking, after all. He was not surprised that nobody was laughing.

Ian was relieved to have the refrigerator closed, and he noticed that he was shaking from his exposure to its interior. Now he knew just how bad it could get inside Missy's refrigerator, worse than his wildest gross imaginings, but his curiosity was still not satisfied. He had not looked in her freezer. He remembered what had been found in Jeffrey Dahmer's freezer. They weren't heads of lettuce.

Keith saw his brother's hesitation before the refrigerator and predicted what would happen next. He only had time to get out one word.

"No!"

Ian yanked open the top freezer door. He was wrong about this being Jeffrey Dahmer's freezer. This was much closer to that ridiculous *Blob* sequel he had seen as a kid, where the monstrous slime was released from a similar suburban icebox. That film seemed not so ridiculous now.

The packed, no longer frozen freezer was one big cube of wobbling putrescence. The spilled vanilla ice cream had the same consistency as the liquefied brown meat beside it. White and brown slime oozed toward the opening, seeking freedom along with the little roaches that were in a skittering panic upon exposure to light for the first time. A blob really was on the loose.

Now that Ian's curiosity had been satisfied, he regretted it. The fridge had been bad, but this was so much worse. That probably had to do with the fact that the freezer stored most of the meat, like Dahmer's. He let out a lurching retch and slammed the freezer door.

"What'd you do that for?" Keith asked with exasperation.

"I had to see if she had severed heads in her freezer."

"I'd prefer heads to that thawed diarrhea loaf," Will admitted in all honesty.

"Damn her!" Dani cried. All of the guys turned to her urgently. "How could she!?"

The guys knew from her tone that Dani wasn't reacting to the contents of Missy's icebox.

7

Dani had her handheld camera aimed toward the object of her outrage, and that's where the guys turned.

Back on one of the garbage mounds, beneath the raised cupboards, was a small cage. Locked in the tilted cage with little room to move was an emaciated cat. There were no water or food bowls in the cage, not that one bowl could fit inside with the poor creature.

Dani was consumed with a rage so pure, it scared her. Her worst suspicions about Missy had been confirmed, and she could not recall ever being so angry in her life. Seeing the cat skeleton in the basement had been bad enough. Seeing a live cat imprisoned in a cage too small for it, wasted away to a barely survivable weight, sparked an unexpected violent urge in her. She was not normally a violent person, and had never started a physical fight in her life, but she wanted to hurt Missy for hurting the cats. And if Fiddlesticks was found prisoner in this cat Hell, how could she possibly be expected to control herself? Torture would be too kind. The hungry cats could feed on Missy's face after Dani was done with her.

Dani knew one thing for certain; Missy was going to end up behind bars for what she was doing to these cats. Hopefully the cell would be too small for her to turn around in and the bars would be covered in her shit. Dani would make it her own personal crusade to end Missy's reign of feline terror.

Dani stopped filming, stuck the camera in her front pocket, and climbed onto the tall mound of dishes. Plates broke beneath her, and the mound shifted. Dani's arms pin wheeled and she started to slide back. Will was there to catch her and aid her climb.

"Careful."

Dani not so carefully scaled the mound, and more glass broke beneath her. She kept climbing, knocking loose utensils on the taller mound beside her.

Keith zoomed his camera in on the skin and bones cat within the cage. He focused first on the crap-splattered bars, and then on the trapped animal behind them. He had to get detailed footage of this cruelty before Dani set the cat free.

When Dani made it within reach of the cat's cage, the hoard collapsed nearly a foot beneath her. Dani pitched to the left, just out of Will's reach. Her empty left hand shot out and punched into a rotten, collapsed pumpkin. It felt disgusting, but it braced her fall.

Dani pulled her hand out of the rot. Her fingers were draped with withered pumpkin guts writhing with maggots. Dani didn't care, and she didn't hesitate to reach forward and open the cage. The cat was weak but hungry enough to escape its confines and slink off over the hoard, eager to find its next meal.

Ian was impressed with Dani. She had shown she had bigger balls than him. When his hand had been caked with wet wall rot and roaches, he had danced in disgust and flung his hand around like it was covered in cooties. He'd probably have done the same if he were in Dani's shoes right now (*maggots, ewww!*). Tough girl.

Dani was relieved to see the cat freed of its cage, but the whole house was a poison prison to any animal stuck within its warped walls. She knew it wouldn't take long for the hungry cat to find a meal, but it would not be a healthy one. Her anger had dissolved into a grim understanding that their mission into Missy's house had changed. This wasn't just about finding her cat anymore; it was about the liberation of Fiddlesticks' entire species.

"We have to open some windows and doors, to let the cats out," Dani said.

Dani no longer wanted to find Fiddlesticks here, better that her cat had just run away than become a malnourished prisoner inside Missy's house. The pound was more humane and hopeful than this. Still, every sad and diseased cat in the house needed to be released, and together they could get it done before Missy returned home from shopping.

Dani realized that with all of the cats and food containers she had seen, she could not recall seeing any cat food, or cat dishes, or kitty litter. These cats had to eat and shit wherever they could. A fresh surge of rage strengthened her conviction of what had to be done.

Ian heard something shift above him, and he turned to the open cupboards. Crammed between garbage on the top shelf was another dirty cage with a starving cat stuffed inside. No food, no water.

"Up there," Ian alerted the others.

Will's height made him the natural go-to guy for the cage, and he stepped as close to the cupboard as the mounds would allow. He reached for the cage but came up a few feet short.

"I can grab it," Ian offered.

"I got you."

Will grabbed Ian around the hips and lifted him up. Had this been the high school hall, this could never happen without joking around or name-calling. But inside Missy's house, they worked as an efficient team, and Ian's added height above Will put the cage within reach. Ian unlocked the door and pulled it open. The cat sprang out of the cage to freedom.

Will lowered Ian back down onto the lop-sided ground.

Dani had to put her outrage into words. "That bitch hoards cats. And she wastes all this food on herself while she starves them."

"I don't think I've ever seen her buy cat food," Will added.

Will was getting some disturbing insights into his least favorite customer. "She's probably lonely and these cats are her only friends. And she doesn't want them strong enough to escape." Will further imagined the cruelty of Missy's companionship. Crippled kids weren't likely to run away. The cages were the chains for the ones that tried.

"If she did this to my cat, I'll put her in a cage and starve her."

Coming from Dani, Will took that as a guarantee.

Keith understood Dani's rage, but he wasn't overwhelmed by it like she was. He saw her seething (*and damn if she wasn't still pretty even when she's seething!*), with pumpkin guts and maggots dripping from her hand. She didn't seem to notice, but he did.

Keith found a not-so-clean towel atop the hoard beside him, but there didn't appear to be any bugs on it, which made it nearly clean for Missy's house. He handed the towel to Dani.

"Here."

"Thanks."

Keith saw another towel that had been under the first, and he saw blood from his busted nose drip onto it. This towel wasn't as clean as the one he gave to Dani, but there were no bugs, so it would do. Keith picked up the towel, and it came up stiff with whatever liquid it had sopped up last. He gave the towel a cautionary shake, and used it to wipe the blood leaking from his nose. The towel stunk of mold. The myriad bad smells inside Missy's house were so potent, not even a broken, blood clogged nose could lessen them.

Dani was grateful for Keith's offering. As she wiped off the squirming spoilage on her hand, she marveled that she hadn't even noticed it. She hated any kind of worm or wet, slithery thing on her. She was alarmed at how many changes this dreary situation was bringing about in her, and how fast they were coming.

"We're not leaving until every cat is free," Dani stated.

There was not one dissenting voice among the guys. They all looked at each other and saw they shared Dani's conviction.

Keith understood this change to their original mission increased the danger that they could be caught, but he knew that his well laid plan no longer fit their situation. Denying Dani was simply not an option. Plus, he had seen the squalor and cruelty firsthand. Denying these sad and hurting cats their freedom was not something his heart could condone, or live with.

"Let's do it," Keith encouraged them all.

"It's the great escape, for cats," Ian joked, although he wasn't really joking. He expected Will was right about the cats being Missy's only friends, and he couldn't wait to see Missy friendless.

Dani led Keith, Will, and Ian through the culvert that served as their path. They passed from the kitchen into the dining room, although there was little to differentiate one room from the next. They were all hoard rooms, receptacles for every kind of junk imaginable, and unimaginable.

Dani was the first to reach the dining room table, which was stacked nearly to the ceiling and over its edges with everything from food and plates to boxes, appliances, books, and decorations, everything but the kitchen sink it seemed. Then Dani reconsidered; the sink could be hidden under the mountain of junk, since she hadn't seen it in the kitchen. There was some space left underneath, and Dani marveled that the table could stand with a ton of overbalanced weight on top. Gravity was a fragile and extremely threatening force within these walls.

Underneath the table, which was never used for dining, Dani spotted an askew cage with a lethargic cat inside. She stopped to get under the table, and the others had to stop, unable to pass around her. When Dani's hand landed on the cage door, she saw the reason for the cat's lethargy. The lazy cat's hair was a squirming fur of maggots. The maggots had a lot of life while the cat had none.

Dani rose without a word. She was past the stage of shock, but every new case of cat abuse she encountered added another notch to the belt of fury that was tightening around her. She knew there were more cages with living cargo to be found. Dani couldn't let her rage slow her down.

The guys followed Dani past the towering table, and then they stopped behind her when she reached the next blockade. The next room was raised a couple of feet higher than the one they were in. The floor was not elevated; it was the hoard that was higher. There were no paths through anymore. The hoard was a rocky landscape, and they were about to traverse Planet Detritus.

Now that they were right upon the room, the sound of a television reached them.

"Think anyone's watching the TV?" Dani asked.

"No, they would have heard us by now," Keith replied. Ian felt uncertainty at Keith's answer. Ian knew that the hoard absorbed heat. Perhaps it did the same with sound. He considered voicing his doubt, but he was too late.

Dani stepped up nearly three feet onto the next unstable surface. Will stood behind her, ready to help if she needed it. She didn't, and Will wasn't surprised. Ian thought he would go last, which was his permanent place, but Keith stepped aside and let Ian go third. Keith's reason for standing back was the same as Will's. He wanted to be in a more helpful spot in case his brother needed assistance, which of course he didn't.

Keith followed Ian up, and thought it was ironic that he had started this mission with the intent to always lead, and here he was bringing up the rear. Keith didn't mind, so long as his changed position brought added safety to the crew.

Had any of them known what was in store for them in the room they had entered, they would have aborted their noble cause and backtracked out of the house. They would have crawled back the way they had come if that's what it took.

The good thing about living with regret was at least you were still alive to enjoy it.

8

The four invaders in Missy's house needed a minute to study the living room before they could cross it. Keith's head tilted up and he noticed this room had an unnaturally high ceiling, which made for a more majestic mess. The higher the walls, the higher the hoard.

Since Ian had first stuck his head inside Missy's house, he knew that she was what the experts called a level five hoarder. Apparently, five was the highest level that hoarders could be graded. Ian didn't think that was right. Even Hell had seven levels. With what Ian was now faced with, he considered Missy a level fifty hoarder.

How does one become an expert on hoarders anyway, Ian wondered. The high-risk journey so far through Missy's house was hands-on education, he reasoned. He hadn't earned a merit badge here; he'd earned a degree. His diagnosis of Missy's exceedingly high hoarder level stood. His remedy would be a lit match, but only after all of the cats were cleared from the premises.

Ian realized that the stink in this room was the worst yet, and had been worsening with every room they passed through. The basement was noxious with dust, decay, and mold, while the kitchen was a smothering sea of food rot. The smell that dominated the living room was shit, and not just from vermin and cats. This was worse than the leaky sewer pipe in the basement, this was much more pungent. The solids were worse than the soups.

Ian couldn't see any shit from where he stood, which meant that the irregular ground ahead would be full of stinky surprises. He felt his eyes starting to burn, and he recognized a growing scent of ammonia, the likely culprit. He was right, but he didn't know that the source was the exceedingly high concentration of cat urine. It was so bad that he feared if he stayed in this room long enough, the ammonia would burn his trachea and lungs.

The label *living room* hadn't occurred to Keith as he observed their latest lair. He saw this as the entertainment center of Missy's house. He would have thought entertainment hub, but hub implied some degree of technology, and this was strictly a low-fi affair.

Among the modern media, the kind that required electricity, were innumerable VHS tapes and vinyl records, in piles and towers. Keith was amazed by one leaning stack of VHS cassettes that had to be over fifteen feet high. Upon closer inspection, they looked held together by a sticky combination of rat splat and spider webs. Missy's music included mounds of cassette and eight track tapes, piled by the hundreds, maybe by the thousands. He noticed a lot of crooners, like Johnny Mathis, Rod Stewart, and Elvis. *The kind of guys that get horny old broads wet*, he crassly thought. Some of the audio and videocassettes had all of the tape from the inside coiled in tangled blobs on the outside. Missy was not willing to let a good song or movie go, whether it was playable or not.

Keith also took notice of the modern gadgets that were missing. Missy had not yet reached the DVD or computer age. If she ever got on the Internet, Keith thought she would hoard Likes and become addicted to online shopping. And her house would fill up even faster.

Haphazardly mixed in with the media were the broken media players. Dead televisions numbered in the dozens, a few which had their screens shattered. More than a few TVs had their broken antennae replaced with crooked foil facsimiles. Keith was amused to see one hollowed out TV filled with emptied out TV dinner trays. It was an anti-commercial, the ugly waste of modern convenience.

The foil dinner trays also raised the question of where she cooked them. There certainly hadn't been an oven accessible or even visible in the kitchen. She must have a microwave or toaster oven hidden somewhere. He expected every instant meal she cooked was a house fire waiting to happen. And he certainly hadn't seen any fire extinguishers.

Keith spotted dozens of record players, radios, boom boxes, VCRs, and random speakers, never a pair. Keith didn't know what an eight-track player looked like, but he knew they were numbered in this low-tech graveyard. Rabbit ears rose out of the hoard like metallic weeds.

Dani saw enough reading material to fill a whole new wing at the public library. There were countless collapsed stacks of newspapers and magazines, many of the stacks covered in a white, crystallized substance. It almost looked like a sugar glaze, but there was nothing sweet about it. Dani knew it was the corrosive residue left by dried cat piss. A stubborn tabby she'd had three years ago had frequently left a similar glaze on her bedposts, her shoes, and her cherished hardcover Harry Potter collection. Dani thought that cat had been a pissy critic, and no tears were shed when he ran away. Fiddlesticks hadn't liked him anyway.

Missy might be cruel and dumb, Dani thought, but at least she was a reader. The towering bookcases that lined the walls were spilling books into mounds before them, the majority paperbacks. Predominate genres were romance and youth, and it was obvious Missy had a soft spot for big cartoon books with happy animals on their covers. There were a great many grins on display. She saw toys and board games spread out for playing, but they looked never played with. The cockroaches crawling over a checkerboard were playing an altogether different game.

What struck Will as he studied the living room was the familiarity of the garbage, because he sold so much of it at work. This was Missy's Mega-Mart. He knew the covers of the tabloids from the news racks he stocked, the brand names of the clothing they sold, and the food and drink containers like those Freshie's Fruit Punch bottles that were exclusive to his chain. Will was familiar with these products when they were new and prettied for purchase. Seeing the mass trashing of it all, being stomped on and reduced to piles of waste, was offensive to him, and depressing that his hard work led to this.

Will's attention was drawn to the shouting and fighting. Audience cheering and laughter greeted the fighting, and seemed to encourage it.

The verbal sparring came from high atop the tallest, forward leaning bookcase, from a nineteen-inch television with a round knob for turning the channels. Considering how high the television sat, he figured the channel was never changed. The television could not be easy to reach, and it appeared pre-remote control. The TV seemed to be held in place on the tilted shelf by cobwebs alone.

Will was not surprised that the television was tuned to a Springer-like show featuring feuds between families and lovers. The kind of program where the audience screamed in bloodlust at trailer park hussies and baby daddies in denial. Will now understood where Missy got her bossiness and bitchiness. He could imagine Missy's power shopping accompanied by an audience chanting her name in unison, in encouragement. Only with Missy there would be no baby daddies.

Will had another question about the television's curious placement atop the bookcase. There were no chairs to sit and watch it, nowhere to sit in this room at all. He thought the programming was annoying, but at least it wasn't a channel of sermons. He did not know Missy to be a God-fearing woman, which was a minor relief. Missy might be crazy, but she wasn't crazy for Christ. She seemed to worship the almighty dollar, the same dollars it was his job to count. Hers was a dirty God.

Dani did not see the living room as the next level of a Hell hoard, or as Missy's entertainment center, or a department store dumpster. Dani only saw the cages, dozens of them. This was a temple of suffering, a concentration camp for cats. She felt she was in a hungry lion's mouth.

Will was the first to voice an observation about the room. "Have you noticed, she has every light in the house on."

"All the better to see her lovely stuff," Keith said. Keith was partly correct in figuring that it wasn't enough for Missy to just buy or steal her possessions, she had to have them on constant display, in the light for her delight. This room was lit with many high-set frosted white light sconces that had turned yellow, with brown splotches that looked like bulb burns. Each light sconce was filled with over an inch of dead flies. Now that he'd seen them, he thought he could smell them, long roasted flies.

Ian offered his own theory. "Maybe she's afraid of the dark." Will always talked about how Missy acted, like a little kid, and a lot of little kids were afraid of the dark. He had been, until he reached the mature age of seven.

Dani aimed her camera at a far off cage. Keith saw Dani getting to business and he followed her lead.

"Every cat," Dani said.

"That's the plan," Keith confirmed.

The four fanned out through the hoard on their search and rescue mission. In their eagerness to film and open the cages, none of them bothered to open a door or window. All of the windows were blocked from view by dressers or other obstructions, and the front door was out of sight, in a foyer that held its own high hoard.

None of them actually walked through the room, it was just not possible. They had to brace at least one hand against objects for balance and frequently needed to be on all fours to climb over the constantly shifting surface.

As she worked toward a cage, Dani came upon a stack of newspapers that was entirely shredded. She knew that a machine was not responsible for the shredding, rats were. Dani gave the rats' nest a wide berth, since she knew its occupants wouldn't hesitate to protect their home by long tooth and contaminated claw.

Keith was the first to reach a cage in the living room, perched on a pile of garbage bags. He got down on one knee on the slope of bags to reach it. His knee immediately became wet, his pants saturated by some stagnant soup leaking from the sack. Marked by the muck, the pungent smell of the mystery liquid would follow his every step, just as the stink of sewer pipe water (*water, right*) on his hoodie followed him still.

The cat inside the cage had a lame ear and a gummy eye. Keith opened the cage door and the cat cowered inside. He didn't wait for it, leaving for the next rescue. Only after the horrible human had moved away did the scared cat venture out of its inhumane enclosure.

Ian reached a cage atop a pile of busted TVs. Inside was a restless white cat with black paws, excited by new company. The latch to the door of this cage was coated in cat feces, but Ian didn't hesitate to grab it. He did hesitate when he discovered the feces were fresh. Ian pulled the cage door open and turned to wipe his fingers off on top of a TV shell as the cat took leave of its prison. Not all of the rescues were scaredy cats, some were eager to greet their liberators.

As Ian cleaned off his fingers, he spotted movement beside him in the dark, hollow shell of a television that had its screen busted out. He saw a flash of brown fur.

"Come out, cat," Ian encouraged the animal.

A well-fed rat leapt out of the broken television with a defiant squeak. At least Ian figured it was a rat from the sound it made, since it was more the size of a Dachshund. Ian fell back against a towering stack of newspapers, causing its collapse, which in turn released a swarm of silverfish. Ian righted himself as the black pawed cat darted past him in pursuit of the juicy rat. The chase disappeared into the room's rubble.

"Don't pet the kitties," Keith advised.

Ian looked at his brother, trying to come up with a comeback to his quip. He could see the sly grin threatening to break on his brother's face, and he wanted to encourage it. They all needed a laugh to ease the heavy atmosphere over their heads caused by the heavier hoard under their feet.

Keith saw the rat reappear out of the garbage, coming his way. He took an instinctive step back, but there was no ground behind him to step onto.

Ian saw the sudden shock on Keith's face as he fell straight down out of view.

"Keith!"

Ian was the only one who saw his brother disappear, and he crawled over the hoard toward him. Dani and Will followed in Ian's direction, alarmed that their leader had so quickly vanished.

Keith's voice rose from the sea of garbage. "I fell in her nest!"

Ian found the hole that his brother had fallen into, and he got down on his hands and knees to look over the edge. Keith had called it a nest, but the size made Ian think it was more of a crater. The hole was mostly circular, and at least a dozen feet wide and over seven feet deep.

Keith turned in a circle to get footage of what was held in the hole of this human packrat. The bottom was piled with blankets and clothing and circled with cushions. Littered over the soft surfaces were discarded soda cups and food wrappers. Interspersed with the food waste were plastic grocery bags, many filled with a brown substance and tied in knots at the top. Keith also spotted countless water bottles filled to varying degrees with various shades of lemonade. He saw one bottle without a cap beside him and got a good whiff. He was wrong about the bottles' contents. They were filled with Missy's Lady Lemonade, bottled at the source, and they were long past the expiration (expulsion) date.

Keith looked up and saw that the tilted television on the bookcase across the room was in the perfect spot for viewing inside Missy's nest. The many human poo-bags and pee-bottles around him now made sense. Missy might miss the results of a particularly scandalous paternity test if she had to climb out of her nest to make waste, and it didn't look like her television had a pause or rewind function.

Ian extended a hand down to his brother, who took it, helping to haul him out. Will and Dani arrived at the edge and looked down in amazement.

"The Vulture's nest," Will announced. Only there were no eggs inside this nest, just bird turds. He was nauseous to notice that most of the tied off waste bags were emblazoned with the Mega-Mart logo. He had probably packed some of those bags with her groceries. The bags were partially transparent and light brown, recently packed with dark brown. Despite being tied off, Will could smell their contents, and he had to fight an urge to hurl. He also knew that the Mega-Mart bags were notoriously thin and prone to rip easily.

"Did you have a snack while you were down there?" Ian asked Keith.

"She has bags of her shit down there, right next to her dinner plates. You want some crap on a cracker?"

"No thanks, I'm cutting back."

Missy's nest didn't hold any cages or cats, so it was abandoned. They crawled toward separate cages.

Dani reached the next imprisoned cat. What she saw through the bars was heartbreaking, but it wasn't a surprise. The cat shivered in fear at the sight of her. Its fur was missing in patches, the exposed skin covered in sores. Whatever diseases afflicted these cats Dani hoped would spread to their caretaker, not that Missy took any care of her pets. She realized those sores could be bug bites, and that was somehow even worse, that these hungry cats provided the food for the overfed pests that could pass through the bars of the cages.

Dani opened the cage and extended a hand to the sick animal inside. Claws swiped at her. Dani was prepared for that reaction and had her hand out of the cage quickly.

"I'd hate humans, too."

Dani went in search of the next cage. She heard the unobserved animal escape its confines behind her, and she was relieved to know it had claimed its liberation.

Will spotted another cat trapped in a cage high above his head. This cage was on the top shelf of the teetering bookcase, right below the television. With his height, he figured he was the one responsible for the high level rescues. How the television, with its warring families, or the cage, with its restless feline, could remain where they were while everything else had fallen off of the shelves was a mystery to him. Perhaps they had extra adhesive holding them up, as in an extra layer of rat and cat turds.

Will stepped up onto the pile of garbage bags against the base of the leaning bookcase. He failed to consider that those bags were the only things keeping the bookcase from collapsing. Will didn't see the subtle shifts in the one hundred eighty-five pounds of stained oak towering over him.

Will didn't need to hoist Ian to reach the door and open this cage. He let the cage door fall open and turned away as the cat leaped out to the hoard below. Hearing a scraping sound beside him, Will looked up as dust drifted down into his eyes. He could hear but not see a studio audience laughing above him.

The cage had shifted from the feline's speedy exit, cracking the ancient crap that had kept the metal pen glued in place (Will had been correct on that count). With the seal broken, the cage let gravity have its way, and it slid off of the high shelf.

Ian, Keith, and Dani all heard the noise and spun toward it, eager to avoid the next potential avalanche.

Will flinched back while trying to keep his feet solid on the slope of slippery garbage sacks. The sliding cage caught on a hanging black power cord. The cord pulled taut and gave a jerk to the antique television on top. The cobwebs that had held it in place for years burst into dust. The studio audience pitched off of the top ledge.

Will looked up, and he registered that the audience on the screen coming down at him were actually jeering, probably at him to move out…

The television screen, which was flesh blistering hot due to its constant use, smashed into Will's upturned face. The jeering stopped the moment the screen shattered with a resounding pop. He heard a crunch of bones all too loudly, since they were inside his head, likely his nose or teeth, if he was lucky.

Will pitched to the left and the broken television rolled off of his head, stripping him of his camera cap. The smoking television landed shattered screen up in the garbage. Will's camera cap landed upright atop a cardboard box, unharmed.

Will stood hunched over with his head hanging navel level, yet miraculously he stood. As he slowly pulled himself up, the falling cage hit him in the right shoulder. The cage bounced off but did not spill him. He wavered with his back to his friends.

"Will!" Dani cried.

Will's friends worked toward him, from the sides and behind. Keith and Dani slipped their handheld cameras into their front pockets as they made their way, wanting their hands free to help him. Dani worried that the teetering bookcase might collapse next and flatten Will. If they moved fast enough, they could catch it if it fell.

Ian saw a burst of sparks from the shattered TV tube, and he hoped that none of them hit the brittle newspaper stacks. They were lucky the television had landed screen up. This room could light up like flash paper in an incinerator. Getting out of a fast moving conflagration in here would be a challenge to the quickest of them. Ian thought it would be wise to unplug the shattered television, but the end of the power cord disappeared into the deep hoard. It could take minutes, maybe hours to clear the hoard away and find the hidden plug.

Will remained with his head down, his back to his friends.

"Will, are you okay?" Keith asked with little hope that he was. From the impact of television to head that he'd seen, Keith was convinced that the least damage Will had sustained was a severe concussion and lacerations. A hospital visit would definitely be required.

Will finally pulled his head up and stood rigidly upright. His friends couldn't see his face but they heard his warning to them. It was a lot easier to hear in the room now that the commotion from the television had been silenced.

"Careful."

Will turned to his friends. His nose was bleeding and split, and his teeth were bloody and chipped. Those injuries went practically unnoticed, as everyone was looking at the one-inch shard of thick glass sticking out to the left of his nose. Blood dripped from the hooked end of the sliver.

Dani gasped and looked into Will's eyes. She realized that he had not yet seen, was not even aware of, the shard sticking out of his face.

It was the fear in Dani's eyes that made Will finally worry that he might be seriously injured. His eyes looked down and focused on the dripping tip of the glass.

Will pinched the end of the sliver with the thumb and index finger of his left hand. He pulled the splinter an inch out, then two, three, four inches, and more. The glass had a curve to it, widening the injury as it slid out. A white-hot feeling grew inside his head as the wound was emptied of the foreign object. On the seventh inch, the splinter pulled free from Will's face.

Will stood with his eyes locked on the shard in his fingers, colored with his blood. Only *shard* seemed too minor a term for a piece this size. This was a bloody glass knife, maybe more of a scythe. The glass dropped when his fingers opened.

Blood finally erupted from the wound beside Will's nose in a fan. Dani had to stop her advance to keep out of the spray.

"No!" Dani cried.

Will's last complete thought was an ironic one - *I've been served one of Missy's Omelets.* Then he dropped into deep dark unconsciousness, which was fine because the burning agony inside his head was too much to cope with. Sleep would ease the pain, only this was the kind of sleep he wouldn't wake from. Will slumped down onto the hoard.

Dani moved in on Will's side, no longer caring to avoid the spray of blood. The drops that landed on her hoodie could not be seen against the dark fabric, they were discernable only by their wetness. Keith and Ian arrived on Will's other side. The shattered TV sparked again beside Ian. He no longer cared about the sparks, which landed on the arm of his hoodie.

The fan of blood exiting Will's face slowed to a steady pulse. Dani put a hand over Will's wound, but his blood escaped between her fingers. Dani knew her action was not helping Will, but she had to do something. At the same time, she knew there was probably nothing they could do to prolong his life. They weren't professional lifesavers, and they lacked first aid supplies. Dani didn't think the CPR certification she had earned at camp a few years ago would make a bit of difference. Will was not

Resuscitation Annie. There were no second chances if she didn't get it right the first time. Besides, she couldn't breathe life back into a victim of blood loss. She also didn't think she could tie a tourniquet around his face.

"We have to call for help!" Dani pleaded to her friends.

"We didn't bring our phones! That was Will's idea!" Keith reminded them with a voice high-pitched in distress. Will's suggestion about their phones had seemed logical earlier. No phones or wallets, no identification to name them if lost or seized, no tracking chips to reveal their coordinates. Keith considered their safety for this expedition entirely his responsibility. He didn't know how he could live under the weight of Will's death. It would probably break his back, and his spirit.

Dani wasn't willing to accept the inevitability of Will's death yet. Not while his blood was still pumping through... *Oh God, oh shit!* Dani no longer felt a pulse of blood on her palm from Will's wound, although blood trickled through her fingers.

"Well she has to have a phone!" Dani shouted with anger, not at her friends, but at their vulnerability. Will began full body convulsions beneath her. Dani reluctantly removed her hand from Will's face, her palm dripping generously with his blood.

Keith looked around helplessly and shouted with exasperation. "Where do we even begin looking for a phone?" His hands gestured to encompass the whole hoard.

Ian knew his brother was right to doubt finding a line out. He remembered seeing a phone on the dining room table, only the hand piece had been removed, the rotary dial had been ripped off, and the cord had been cut. Finding another phone in this hoard could take hours or days, and if they were so lucky to find one, it probably wouldn't work anyway. Ian thought they could summon help faster if they ran down the middle of the street screaming for it. Except maybe not on this dark street, where the populace hid with their lights off and left screams for help unanswered.

They were on their own.

Will's eyes rolled up as his convulsing abated. Dani's head tilted tearfully beside Will. She made no move to wipe her eyes. Dani had never felt so helpless in her life, as she watched her friend's life bleed out before her.

"We're losing him, guys."

The guys could do nothing about it. They all watched silently as

Will's body became still. The brothers looked at each other. Neither tried to hide their tears, nor mock the other for being a crybaby. When they looked back at Will, they knew he was dead.

"We can't leave him," Ian said.

"We'll carry him out the front door, lay him by the bushes, and go for help." Keith accepted that his plan had been fatally flawed, and he had to adapt to its unraveling. The cats would have to wait as they dealt with their fallen friend.

Dani's sorrow evaporated, and she flared with anger. She welcomed it. Her outrage gave her focus, purpose, and motion. It was also preferable to the grief, which she found paralyzing. Dani did not damn Keith or their mission. The house and the hoarder were the recipients of her rage. She had wanted Missy to feel pain for the agony she had inflicted on the cats, but now with one of her best friends dead, she wanted Missy in a grave.

"She's gonna pay. This place is a death trap."

They froze as they heard the front door open.

9

The front door pushed open one foot, four inches before it butted up against the hoard inside and came to a solid stop. Missy's grocery bag draped arm reached in and wiggled the front door key out of the lock, since there was no way to gain passage through the limited opening with the key in the way.

Missy entered the only way she could, sliding in sideways, holding three plastic grocery bags in her hand. When her body passed through, her considerable breasts and muscular thighs pressed against the doorframe, which had been worn smooth and without paint from years of her curves' tight passage.

Missy looked in as she entered so she could greet her friends.

"Hello sweeties! Mama's home early!" Missy cooed in the voice she used with everyone, like they were children and she was on their level. She acted five instead of fifty. She spoke to her pets, dolls, and people the same way.

Missy's sweeties were the many cats that came out of hiding upon her arrival. Missy loved how her cats came running out to greet her when she came home from shopping. The meow-meows sure loved their mom-mom. Sometimes though she suspected her cats were greedy fat cats that were only coming to her for the yum-yums in her shopping bags.

The front door was the only working door for passage in and out of the house. There was a door to the garage in the dining room and a back door in the kitchen, but they had for years been abandoned of their purpose and covered completely by the hoard. The hidden kids in the house had passed the back doors without noticing they were there.

The real reason the cats came running when Missy arrived never occurred to her; the animals were trying to escape the house. Missy never opened the windows, and she had never considered installing a cat door. The front door was the only exit, and some weeks her Tuesday Mega-Mart outing was the only reason her door opened at all. The cats knew how slim their chances for escape were, and as a result the foyer was the most populated room for loose cats in the house. At least one cat a week would slip out around Missy's ankles when she was squeezing through the door. Meanwhile, Missy brought in new cats all the time, so their numbers never thinned within her walls despite the frequent escapees. Plus, they bred like bunnies.

As for why a great number of cats were imprisoned in uncomfortable steel cages instead of comfortable crates, Missy's reason was callous. Most crates that held pets kept them concealed from view. Missy wanted her locked up cats on full display for her constant amusement, even if the cats behind bars did not appear amused.

While the cats entered Missy's house domesticated, they became part of the feral pack in no time. Life was always a desperate fight for survival amid the squalor. The survival rate among the kittens was the lowest.

"Hello Calicoco! Cookies-N-Cream! Tiddilee Winks! Mr. Fittle Fattle."

Whether Calicoco, Cookies-N-Cream, Tiddilee Winks, and Mr. Fittle Fattle were among the cats coming to Missy, she didn't know. They were simply the pet names she liked to say the most, what Missy called *happy-happy* names.

Missy's other arm slipped in through the doorway, holding three more plastic bags of chips and punch. She let the bags hang off of her wrist as she engaged the door lock and deadbolt. Missy was always careful to make sure her fortress was locked and fortified. With all of her collections and cool stuff, she was convinced that everyone wanted to rob her of her riches. Who wouldn't find, in bulk, what their heart most desired inside Missy's house? She obviously lived in the lap of luxury.

Directly next to the front door was the only spot where she could stand on the floor. The next step was a step up onto garbage, the beginning of a three-foot climb onto the foyer hoard. The foyer was not much different from most; it was only obscene in its excesses. Shoes, sandals, and boots numbered in the high hundreds. A pile of coats rose over chest high. The garbage bags by the door needing to be taken out were stacked to the ceiling. Crawling over everything were the cats, over fifteen circling around their keeper. Everything was seasoned with cat turds and shellacked with cat piss. This being the room the cats nested in the most, every surface was covered in a layer of fur. Some hairballs were bigger than the cats they came from.

When Missy was not coming and going in the foyer, the cats avoided loitering against the closed door. The bottom foot was caked in dried blood and fur, where others of their kind had been killed during failed escape attempts. Every cat that hadn't made it out remained in Missy's house still, alive or dead.

Missy climbed up onto her hoard with a graceless ease and odd athleticism. When she had to put a hand out for balance, she used a fist. Calloused patches on her knuckles were a result of this. Her thick, muscular legs were well earned. She came to a stop so she could enjoy the welcoming committee circling her. She knew that they were surprised to see her back so early on shopping night.

From where Missy stood, over her shoulder, there was a sliver of the living room visible. The hoard in the next room was over four feet higher, and from her vantage point, if she turned around, she would see none of the invaders in her house.

"My meow-meows miss their mom-mom? You want some of Mommy's milk?"

Missy giggled at her generosity. The cats that circled her were not content. They meowed for mercy. They had not been fed or given water or milk for many weeks. She did not know that a few of their number were near the point of turning traitor and making a meal-meal of their mom-mom as she slept. A few felines had already turned cannibal. The babies were easiest to eat, and the juiciest.

As Missy enjoyed the ritualistic mewling of the cats, she noticed that something was very wrong inside her house. It was *Tuesday Night at the Fights* on Channel 5. She should have heard fighting, cheering, or a commercial, but instead she heard only meows and her own breathing. It was never this silent inside Missy's house. She found silence too loud and lonely.

"Why can't Mommy hear her TV?"

10

The three surviving kids looked toward the foyer and thought they were fucked. This had been their original worse case scenario, only things had changed.

When Missy's voice first reached them, their alarm increased. It wasn't the proximity of her voice, but her booming delivery that startled them. It sounded so directed and personal. For Missy, even the smallest statement had to be announced at the top of her lungs. She spoke as though she were addressing the back seats of a theater.

Would Missy greet them with a "*Hello sweeties!*"? Keith thought not.

Will was right, Ian thought, Missy did speak in an annoying kiddie voice. How could Will handle that annoying voice week after week at work? Then, like a punch to the soul, Ian realized Will didn't work at the Mega-Mart anymore. Will wouldn't have to hear Missy's ridiculously voiced demands, now that her hoard had issued him his pink slip and death certificate.

Keith pulled Ian and urged Dani to the bottom of Will's corpse, so they could huddle and talk in whispers. They heard the front door slam, but they were too far to hear the locks engage. Their freedom and possibly their lives depended on the next few seconds. Keith had to think clearly and avoid panic, while his bladder threatened to betray him and unleash a flash flood in his pants.

"We hide Will and go back out below." It was the first plan Keith thought of, and thus the only one he had time to formulate.

Dani and Ian offered no alternatives. Ian nodded in lieu of verbal confirmation. Dani heard Missy say the name Fittle Fattle and she silently mouthed "*Fittle?*" in outrage. Was Missy referring to her Fiddlesticks? Her cat's name was on the tags.

"If we get split up, we meet at our bikes," Keith added to the plan.

Dani saw a cat clawed and rat gnawed fuzzy blanket nearby, and she pulled it toward her, careful that its passage didn't cause any collapses. Once it was fully in her hands, she threw the hole riddled covering over Will's upper half, leaving only his legs below the knees exposed.

Ian saw what was left of Will to hide, located his own fabric, and pulled on it. The sheet pulled taut and upset a tower of VHS tapes, stacked an unstable forty-two tapes high. As the tower of tapes tipped toward him, he noticed that all forty-two collapsing stories were romantic comedies. He hated romantic comedies.

Ian lunged over and leaned his whole body against the tipping stack, barely preventing their noisy collapse. Keith moved in to help Ian straighten the tapes back into position.

Would Missy notice if some of the side titles were turned the other way? Keith hoped Missy wasn't that anal retentive, but considering her whole life revolved around product worship, he was pretty sure she was. It didn't matter, since there was no time to turn any tapes around.

Dani looked back at the foyer. Missy was still talking to her cats and out of sight.

Keith located a dress in the mess and used it to cover Will's lower half. Ian thought that Will's camouflage didn't work. It looked just like a shrouded body.

Ian grabbed an open pizza box and placed it over the head of Will's death shroud. Now he looked a little more like garbage. What a disgrace this was to Will. Ian had looked up to him almost as much as his brother. He could feel the shock of losing Will starting to numb his thoughts and slow his actions, and he had to push it away. *Move. Now!*

"Why can't Mommy hear her TV?"

Rustling began in the foyer, which meant Missy was on the

move. Ian, Keith, and Dani maneuvered as quickly and quietly as they could over the hoard, and they were neither quick nor quiet.

"Okay, follow Mommy now!"

The lightest and most lithe of the group, Ian pulled a distance ahead of the others without realizing it. Keith was glad to see Ian moving so far ahead. He hoped his brother would get out first.

Keith and Dani had a difficult time navigating over cushions littered with empty glass soda bottles. One bottle falling or knocking against another was enough to give away their presence. They had to grab rolling bottles as they traversed the hoard. Keith couldn't help thinking that Missy could become a millionaire if she only turned in her cash back recyclables.

Ian paused to look back and was surprised to see Keith and Dani far behind him. He waved at them to hurry.

Keith waved at Ian to hurry on without them, then that hand grabbed a rolling bottle. They made it off of the cushions and had to crawl over a landscape of constantly shifting boxes. At least these boxes were full and didn't collapse. It felt to Keith like they were filled with books. He looked nervously back.

Missy's high hair rose into view over the mountain of junk at the living room entrance. She was seconds from seeing them, and they had some distance to go to get out of the living room.

Keith spotted Will's fallen backpack, lying uncovered near the shrouded body. There was nothing they could do about it now, and he hoped it would go unnoticed by Missy, or be accepted as more garbage or treasure in her house.

Ian had nearly reached the edge of the slope down to the dining room when he risked another glance back.

Keith and Dani were completely out of sight. Meanwhile, Missy rose across the room, carrying multiple shopping bags. She was looking down at her feet as she climbed, so she hadn't seen him yet.

Ian dropped down behind stacks of newspapers and tall speakers with torn covers. He could not risk moving through her field of vision now. He hoped she wasn't making a beeline to the kitchen, but since she was carrying so many groceries, he knew it was a fool's hope. He was glad Keith and Dani had made it into hiding, but he was stuck in a seriously screwed position. Escape down the slope into the dining room was so close it was within spitting distance. Only so close was still too far.

Ian saw the twitching, beady snout of a rat protruding from a tear in the speaker next to his nose. He could deal with it. Having Missy's snout in his face would be a lot worse.

Keith and Dani were not out of the living room. They were deep in it, down inside Missy's nest. They were hidden for the moment, but they couldn't risk being out in the open in case she came their way.

Keith grabbed onto a tall wall mirror and tilted it over him, crouched down between the reflective side and mangy cushions. Glancing into the mirror, he was startled at the wild-eyed teen staring back at him and he quickly averted his eyes.

Seven feet away and facing Keith's hiding place, Dani crouched against the side cushions and pulled up a food and fecal stained sheet as a smelly shroud.

Missy did not head for the dining room or her nest. She headed for her fallen television. There was no rush. The television was obviously past the point of rescue.

"Poor, poor TV! Why'd you jump?"

Missy crouched over the busted television with some sadness. She had lost a great many TVs over the years, which wasn't a surprise considering once they went on they never went off. It always made her sad-sad. Every TV she had ever lost remained in the house, most in this room within the layers beneath her feet.

Hearing that Missy was distracted with the television's demise, Ian risked a peek. His eyes rose over the stack of newspapers yellowed by time and urine.

Ian's risk was rewarded with a view of Missy's backside. She was across the living room, turned away as she observed the television that was suicidal to her and lethal to his friend. He saw with alarm that Missy was positioned directly against the mound that hid Will. Missy bumped the empty pizza box that sat over Will's head, jostling it. Little did she know that she was pressed up against a not yet room temperature teenager who was less than three minutes dead and still bleeding out. Ian hoped that the blood from Will's fatal wound would not saturate through the shroud and reveal his whereabouts.

Ian could do nothing more to hide Will. He knew this was his chance, and he used the moment of Missy's distraction to crawl down into the dining room.

"You're no Humpty Dumpty. I can't put you back together

again," Missy told her TV. "R.I.P. TV!" She guffawed. Missy was full of funnies like that, and she always cracked herself up.

There were no more sparks from the broken television, but wisps of white and black smoke continued to rise in thin corkscrews. It never occurred to Missy to unplug the busted appliance. Little insignificant things like safety precautions rarely entered Missy's mind. Those things were boring, and Missy only had room for fun things in her life.

Missy turned away from the fallen TV, and her eyes fell on Will's camera cap, sitting on a nearby box. Will's backpack was also in her field of vision, but went unnoticed.

"Well look at that funny hat! I don't think I've worn you before!"

Truth be told, Missy could not remember buying this particular hat, which had a device on the bill that looked like a camera. How cool was that? While she couldn't remember the purchase, it gave her *the giddies* and was something she would purchase if the sale price was right. She didn't question its placement in her house.

Missy picked up Will's cap. The adjustable band on the back was set on the furthest snap, and the cap just fit onto Missy's big head, flattening her high hair. She was unaware that the camera on the bill was on. Missy's POV was being recorded onto a drive inside Will's backpack.

Missy looked at the brown and white cat that had taken a seat on top of the box where the cap was found.

"You like it, Cookies-N-Cream?"

Cookies-N-Cream meowed, demanding food. Missy squealed in response, taking the meow as a vote of approval.

"I like it, too!"

Missy turned around, the dining room entrance passing her view. Ian was no longer visible as he made his way through the kitchen.

Missy stopped turning when her nest was directly ahead. It was a good thing that Ian was gone and Keith and Dani couldn't see her, for they would have screamed if they'd seen what happened next. Grocery bags in hand, Missy climbed over the pizza box and blanket covering Will's head and upper body, knocking the pizza box askew. There was a moist crunch underneath the cardboard, but Missy was used to such sounds coming from the lower levels of her hoard, and she took no notice.

When Missy climbed off of the body, the pizza box remained dented. The corpse was left behind as Missy climbed forward. The shroud saturated with blood where she had crawled over it. The bloodstain took the shape of a face.

Hiding in the nest, Keith and Dani could hear the rustling of the hoard as Missy headed their way. They looked at each other, frozen in fear. Three plastic bags full of snacks and soft drinks dropped near the center of the nest, startling them.

Dani's eyes opened wide, afraid to even blink. More junk food bombs landed in the trench. A shadow fell over the nest momentarily, and Missy followed, climbing down backward, with her ass to the center. Dani closed her eyes, not wanting to see her approaching doom's descending backside.

Keith gulped and hoped that Missy couldn't hear it. It sounded as loud as a toilet flush to his ears. The tall mirror shielding Keith bowed toward him as pressure was applied on the other side. He pressed himself into the skanky cushions he was leaning against. The mirror pushed in further until it pressed against the side of Keith's face. He closed his eyes, hoping he wasn't about to suffer the same fate as Will and get a shard shoved into his skull.

When the mirror broke against Keith's left cheek, the sound in his ear was sharp and like a lance to his brain. Over a dozen cracks in the mirror extended like a web around his head. Despite cracking, the mirror did not shatter or reveal Keith's whereabouts to the hoardowner leaning against the other side.

Keith and Dani silenced their breathing while they heard Missy's breathing loud and clear, heavy from the exertion of climbing her hoard. Then they heard rustling from a plastic shopping bag, followed by the crinkling of foil or cellophane packaging. There was a moment where Missy and her movements went completely silent. Even her horse-heavy breathing seemed to stop.

POP! The sound of the potato chip bag being slapped open was unmistakable, and severely startling to the hidden kids.

Keith flinched hard from the sudden sound. His head hit the cracked mirror next to his face, making it bounce out an inch. The sheet shrouding Dani jerked, but made no sound.

Missy was surprised at the sudden movement beside her.

Keith's eyes opened wide in fear and locked with one of Dani's, as she peeked out from the side of her sheet.

The cracked mirror was pulled away and Keith was revealed, cowering in Missy's nest. He didn't move from his spot, instead he cringed back against the cushions, in the hope he might be absorbed into them like a stain. Missy set the mirror aside with the broken side facing the center of the pit. She did not notice the cracks in the mirror. All of her attention, and surprise, was on her strange guest.

As Missy leaned down over Keith, he noticed her face was spotted with bright red sores, at least a dozen, and many of them were seeping. These were the kind of sores that he would expect on a crack head, or somebody living a seriously toxic and unhealthy lifestyle. Will had been right about her horrid complexion, and its possible source. Crack had nothing to do with it. Cockroach shit did.

Keith could not mask the fear that flushed his face. He did not know whether to reason with her, run from her, or attack her. He did know it was imperative to keep the attention on himself, and away from Dani, at all costs.

Keith wasn't prepared for Missy's reaction. As her face hovered down over him, he was repulsed to recognize the camera cap on her head, and he felt a stab of pain in his heart that Will would never wear it again. He also saw that Missy wasn't just smiling, she was ecstatic.

11

The first thing Missy thought when she saw the boy behind her mirror was *What a cutie-patootie!* And it was a patootie she was familiar with, she just wasn't sure where from. But she would remember soon. She never forgot a face, or a patootie! She didn't see faces very often, unless she was shopping (her porch stealing she saw as nothing more than shopping outside of a store), so every face left an impression. And his was the kind of face you just wanted to eat up, if you had a taste for sweets.

"Oooo! A playmate! Who are you?"

"I… I'm Steve," Keith lied on the spot.

"What are you doing in my hidey-hole?"

In ordinary circumstances, Missy's phrase *hidey-hole* would have brought Keith to laughter. He wasn't laughing now. He was trying to formulate a plan that would save his sweating skin.

"I… my cat got loose. I chased him in here through a window. I have to find him."

Dani peeked carefully around her shrouding sheet, watching the exchange between delighted Missy and desperate Keith with one eye. Dani took the shallowest breaths she could, unable to move the tiniest bit or risk Missy's detection. Dani was impressed with Keith's improvised explanation for his entry into Missy's house. Not only might he save himself a criminal charge, his fiction made finding her cat Fiddlesticks a priority.

Missy's joyful features twisted with suspicion, and she leaned in closer to Keith. The bills of their matching camera caps were nearly touching.

"I don't know. I think you might be fibbing me."

Keith looked up wide-eyed at Missy like an animal snared in a trap. His voice that replied was soft and vulnerable.

"No, I don't fib."

Missy's suspicious face remained. "Are you sure you didn't come here just to see me?"

After an endless pause where all three occupants in the nest held their breath, Missy snorted laughter in Keith's face. It was a wet chortle, spraying saliva.

Keith released his breath in relief. He smiled back to indicate he was on her side. It took some effort. Even worse than her sores was her rotten breath, and his nose reflexively wrinkled in disgust. He made a mental note to ask Will if Missy ever bought toothpaste at the Mega-Mart, and then he tore up that note as he realized he'd never get to ask Will anything ever again.

"I'm fibbing you!" she squealed.

Missy reached down and tickled Keith's midsection, startling him and forcing a laugh of tickle panic. His arms pulled in to block his sides from her wiggly sausage fingers. He suddenly felt like a small, weak child confronted by a dog that was bigger and stronger. It was going to slobber on him, and if it wanted to bite, it would bite hard while taking him down.

Keith's laugh became a cough as he choked on blood from his broken nose. He turned his head and spit out an alarming clot of blood onto one of the crusty side cushions, Missy's cushions.

"I'm sorry about that," he apologized.

Missy's mirth was replaced with concern for Keith's nose. Somehow she hadn't noticed it until now, but it was easy for her to overlook when the boy behind the blood was so cute. "Oh, you poor thing."

Missy reached down and gave Keith's nose a hard pinch. Keith yelped in pain and surprise. *Why in the hell did she do that!?*

"Oh, that's a smarty. How did that happen?"

"I slipped, and a box hit me," Keith replied. It was partially true. Missy's hoard was responsible in Keith's fact and fiction.

"Well you have to be more careful, Mister Slip-N-Slide. Now hold still."

Missy grabbed Keith's shoulders, holding him in place. Keith's every instinct told him to fight against her and get loose, and then he thought of Ian getting out. It was better to keep her occupied, and stay on her good side for now.

Missy leaned into Keith and took a big lick of the blood beneath his nose. Keith squealed in revulsion and recoiled.

Missy grabbed the squirming boy harder. He was playing hard to get, as all young boys did in Missy's experience. But boys were just like her cats; there wasn't one she couldn't control. This wild boy needed her to help him heal. Plus, this boy was so salty and delicious she had to have more!

"Don't worry, I'm not going to eat you. Now let me clean you up. Saliva's sterile, you know."

Keith did know. He knew Missy was full of shit about that. He closed his eyes and tensed up as Missy leaned into him. Her hot tongue, which Keith unfortunately saw had a large yellowish patch in the center and was spotted with its own sores, slapped onto his chin and licked upward, following the blood trail up onto his lips. He clamped his lips closed to deny Missy's forceful tongue entry into his mouth. Her tongue nearly made it inside, until Keith bit into the inside of his lips to hold them closed. Apparently, his tangy blood wasn't enough; now she wanted a different juice.

Denied oral entry, Missy's tongue continued over his upper lip and up to his nose. Keith cringed, but he could not close those orifices. The tip of Missy's tongue probed up both of Keith's bloody nostrils, digging for any tasty treats. Keith could not help but squeal from the violation. The pain he didn't so much care about. It was the smell of Missy's tongue that overwhelmed him. It was like a sewer slug trying to bore up into his brain.

Keith thought of the big dog analogy again, but instead of a dog that wanted to bite, he thought of a dog that wanted to hump his leg. If the dog weighed over twice as much as him and stood a foot taller (on its hind legs), that dog could take him down and have its way with him. He feared Cuj-ette here was really after his bone.

Missy pulled back from Keith with bloody lips of her own. "There! All better!"

Keith's face was cleaned of some of the blood, but was messy with Missy's saliva. He would have preferred the former, and he was nauseated to see his blood on Missy's lips. He did not believe her claim that she would not bite. Keith expected Missy could go cannibal on him at any moment. She was all impulse and appetite. He needed to figure his next move with this mad, happy, and hungry woman very carefully.

Fighting past his fear and revulsion, Keith summoned his best manners and delivered a polite "Thank you."

Missy's eyes lit up. The boy's red sauce made her want more. Filling her belly was suddenly a priority, and she was happy to share. How often did she get to have a dinner guest? Not often enough. She was as hungry for company as she was for a meal.

"Oh, I'm hungry! Are you hungry?"

"No, I have to find…"

Missy interrupted Keith. "We'll find your kitty-kitty. But my tummy is rumbly, and we can't do all that searching until we eat!"

Missy stood and offered Keith a hand. Keith was overwhelmed with relief to gain a bit of space from her. She had been suffocating him with her close proximity. He took note that he could lure Missy away with a carrot, or chips, or the promise of a yummy-yum. That was good to know. He also suspected that while she really was hungry, she was more famished for friendship.

Keith took Missy's hand, and she pulled him effortlessly up onto his feet. Keith's right shoe stepped onto one of Missy's plastic potty bags and sank down. He looked away from it, masking his disgust. He did not want Missy to see his bad reaction to her horrible habits.

"You climb first," Missy instructed.

Keith did as he was told, turning toward the side of the nest. He gave one last glance down at Dani, which Missy missed. Dani's wide, peeking eyeball watched his every move.

Keith's hands tried to find a hold on the side of the nest, testing it to find a safe spot. Missy grabbed Keith's ass and gave him a shove upward. With such hot ham hocks in her hands, she couldn't help herself, and she squeezed and fondled them excitedly.

"Coochie-coo!"

Keith hated that he had to laugh, hated to give her the satisfaction. He scurried up to the top edge of the nest, eager to get his ass out of Missy's grabby hands. Missy the experienced climber, and groper, followed behind him.

Keith felt relief once he was out of the hole. He figured Ian was long out by now, and he was leading Missy away and giving Dani a chance to escape the hole unnoticed. He took his first step away and was jerked to a stop by Missy's hand around his wrist. It felt like an overly tight handcuff made of toughened flesh and bone.

"The kitchen's this way," Missy informed him.

Missy jerked Keith into motion, pulling him beside her. He would have easily followed her on his own, but she wouldn't give him the chance. Keith knew this was what a puppy getting jerked along on a chain must feel like.

Missy's familiarity with the hoard made it easier for her to cross over it; she knew just where to step. Keith did not and he kept slipping and getting knocked roughly into things. He couldn't follow in her footsteps because she kept yanking him off of his feet.

Keith considered himself lucky on one count. Missy had failed to notice the camera jutting out of his front hoodie pocket. It continued to record, and Keith thought that was good. Nobody would believe what Missy's behavior was like unless they saw it for themselves.

Keith kept his eyes mostly on his shoes, afraid of taking a tumble that would hurt or impale him like Will. He didn't see the slope down into the dining room coming and wasn't prepared when Missy dropped down over the edge. Keith gasped as his arm was pulled hard, almost enough to wrench it out of its socket. He was yanked down over the lip of the hoard.

Left alone in the living room was Dani, out of sight inside Missy's nest. She pulled off the sheet shrouding her, took a deep breath of air, and didn't like the stink of it. Having limited air was bad, but in this hole, more air was worse.

Dani looked to her left and was startled by her reflection in the cracked mirror that Missy had set aside. She didn't like the fear plastered on her face. The plaster broke as resolve took fear's place. Fear made her just as ineffectual as grief had. Having a goal helped her focus, and her goal was getting out of this hoardy-hole and Missy's house. Freedom for the remaining cats would have to wait. Hopefully, Fiddlesticks would survive long enough for her to get an armada of animal control trucks here later tonight.

Dani began a careful climb out of the nest, peeking over the edge before hoisting herself out. Having heard Missy's mission for munchies, she looked in the direction of the dining room. Missy and Keith were out of her sight.

A cat darted directly before Dani, running over her right hand, which had the furthermost grip over the nest's edge. Dani pulled her hand back from the cat's piercing claws, and realized too late that her right hand had been all that was holding her up. She immediately scolded herself for once again letting an animal startle her into letting go, just like in the basement.

Dani fell backward off of the nest's edge, dropping backward and landing on her back on the soft cushions and squishy caca bags. Dani's sight went straight up, and she saw the dark Rorschach patterns of the mold-saturated ceiling. There was no sound to warn her about the standing, cracked mirror, which had been disturbed by the bounce of her landing.

Dani had only a fraction of a second to register the broken mirror falling toward her head. The mirror met her face, and the number of cracks in the glass doubled.

12

Missy led her guest through the dining room with delight. She pulled him hard since he was being such a slow poke. If he only knew what tasty treats she had in store, he'd be clawing over her head to get the first serving. But in Missy's house, the chef got served first. It was only fair.

"You want one of my special chocolate syrup and peanut butter sandwiches?"

Keith thought Missy's special sounded positively unappetizing. "No, I couldn't."

"Oh, I got something better!"

Missy figured her boy friend would get hungry once he set foot in her kitchen, and with one final heave, that's where they arrived. Missy let Keith's wrist go so she could get down to some home style cooking.

Keith didn't attempt to run, since running was not possible inside Missy's house. Running required a floor or semi-flat surface. He looked at the sore, red ring Missy had left around his wrist. She didn't know her own strength, or worse yet, didn't care.

Keith had to keep Missy's company until Ian and Dani were out of the house. He'd give them five minutes, and then he'd find a way to follow, hopefully with Missy's blessing. He had to get out before the rabid, horny bull in this made-in-China shop trampled him.

Missy knew what she was looking for, but couldn't locate it. She always knew where everything was, which was why she was so bewildered she couldn't find her loaf of white bread. It was almost as if somebody else had been in her house and moved things around. She'd have to ask her boyfriend if he'd seen anyone strange inside today.

Keith glanced toward the basement door where Ian had fled and was shocked to see his brother peeking in at him. He was instantly furious at Ian for sticking around when he had directly told him to go. There could not be a worse time for his brother to defy him, when their freedom depended on it.

Missy gave up on finding the bread. If she gave herself a minute, she'd remember its placement. Instead, she reached behind the pile of plates and pulled out a half empty jar of peanut butter, setting it on a nearby box top, a mini makeshift counter. Next, she reached into the packed garbage on the counter to the right of the sink (which only Missy knew was there) and pulled out a bottle of chocolate syrup missing its cap, a raised trail of dried chocolate running down the side.

Keith looked at Missy to make sure she hadn't seen Ian. Missy's back was to the boys as she gathered her menu. When Keith turned back to the basement, Ian waved him on his way. Keith shook his head subtly, but sternly, and shooed him away.

Missy reached into the utensils pile and pulled out a butter knife caked with butter. Butter happened to be Missy's favorite condiment, the one thing she could add to anything. Sometimes she'd get the knife heaping with soft, room temperature butter and spread it on her tongue, often followed with a dash of salt. She thought butter was the one condiment you could eat as a meal. Missy turned to Keith to see if he'd agree, and saw him looking to the right. Missy looked to the right at the basement door, which appeared empty.

"What is it?" Missy inquired, making Keith jump.

"I think I saw my cat."

"What's his name?"

"Fiddlesticks."

Missy's giddiness was so sudden and severe, Keith realized that making Missy happy carried as much risk as making her mad. Not that he'd been trying to please her with his answer. Anything he said could produce an unexpected, maniacal overreaction from her.

"Fiddlesticks! I love that! I have a Mister Fittle Fattle! Wait here."

Missy pushed past Keith, nearly knocking him over, as she moved to the basement door. She didn't see the alarm that seized Keith's face, and didn't recognize it in his voice either.

"No, wait, I'll call him!"

"I'm already there."

Missy reached the half blocked basement doorway and stuck her head through the opening. Down below, she did not see any cats, or Ian. She also didn't see Keith standing behind her holding his breath.

It occurred to Keith that he could run forward and push Missy down the stairs, but she might not budge, and if she did, Ian could be in her path below. Plus, he could neither run nor sneak up quietly behind her. Any attempted murder of Missy would be complicated thanks to her hoard.

"Fiddlesticks! Your papa wants to see you!"

Ian watched Missy leaning into the basement. He was unseen above her, balanced on the high wooden ceiling beam, which was newly cleared after the storage avalanche. He had never been more focused and still in his life, afraid that one move would reveal him. This was more heart pounding than the time he had hidden behind the far side of Keith's bed, interrupted in his search for his brother's porno magazines (a suspenseful ordeal that had ended with the disappointing discovery of Keith's *Playboys*; he preferred the far raunchier *Hustler*).

Missy kept looking directly below Ian. "Come out! Don't be a Fiddle-Stick-In-The-Mud!"

The wait seemed endless to Ian. What was occupying her attention for so long? He feared that Missy might be considering the aftermath of the storage collapse, which would turn her attention up to his hiding spot soon after.

What Missy said was a relief to Ian before her and Keith behind her. "Poor light, you went out! I'll have to change you soon. Very, very soon."

Ian realized one important fact about Missy. She did not know the details of her hoard as much as she probably thought she did, not if the storage collapse with its relocated radiator and Frosty the Snowman failed to register with her.

Missy turned away from the door, and for Ian it was just in

time. Holding his breath for so long had made him feel faint.

Ian let out his long held air and wiped the sweat that had sprung out on his brow. That was too much movement to keep balanced, and he rolled off the beam to the left. Both of Ian's hands caught the side of the beam, and his body dangled over the steep slope. If Missy turned back now, he'd be swinging before her like a slab of meat on the butcher's hook.

Missy's tummy growled as she marched back toward Keith. Her priorities had changed. She mistook the relief on Keith's face for hunger. "Don't worry, your cat will come running when he smells our yummy-yums," Missy reassured him.

Keith saw Missy stomping directly at him and he shifted aside. She stormed past without slowing down, and he knew if he hadn't moved, she would have plowed right over him. When Missy was on a mission, it was wise to get out of her way, and quickly.

Missy stopped at her dishes pile and pulled out two filthy plates, caked in what looked like mashed potatoes, curdled gravy, and roach droppings. Her elbow brushed against a towel covered in rotten pumpkin guts, causing it to slide off of a loaf of bread.

"There it is! My whitey-white bread!" Missy cried out. Keith winced at the high screech of her perpetually projected voice. It was as sharp and annoying as a dog's yelp or a baby's wail. Why in the hell did she have to scream everything she said, especially when the distance between her mouth and his ears was only a few feet? It was no wonder that Missy didn't have any friends.

"I hope you like white bread, it's my favorite," Missy said.

Keith not only liked white bread, it was his favorite, too. However, the bread that Missy pulled out of the package was anything but white. The slices were gray and fuzzy around the crust, the sides a swirl of darker blues and lighter greens. Missy couldn't possibly think that non-white bread was good to eat, could she? Keith didn't know that what he called poisonous mold, she called flavor crystals.

Missy made her sandwich in a jiffy. All of Missy's meals were jiffy meals, their preparation from start to finish the length of a commercial break. She unscrewed the cap on the jar of peanut butter and stuck the butter caked knife inside. It took her only three heaping swipes to cover the blue/green bread with peanut butter. Keith noticed that the jar said the contents were of the creamy variety, but the product coming out of the jar was most definitely chunky.

Next, Missy grabbed the bottle of chocolate syrup and squirted the goop on top of the peanut butter, and squirted, and squirted. Missy never skimped on the good stuff. More was always better. She applied the chocolate syrup until it was dripping off the edges of the bread onto her fingers. That was just enough. She slapped the other moldy slice of bread on top.

Missy turned to Keith with her sloppy sandwich. He looked at the mess in her hand, which was held out toward him. He realized that the plates she had retrieved had been forgotten about, which was good because those plates had been filthy. Problem was, that sandwich was filthier. Plus, she hadn't washed her hands before handling the ingredients.

Keith had been compliant and falsely friendly with Missy since meeting her; he and his friends' hides depended on it. But if Missy insisted that he consume that sick sandwich, there was only one reply he could imagine. *No... fucking... way.* The brown syrup had white chunks in it, and what could possibly be white in chocolate syrup? Keith saw the white specks were squirming. They were maggots. No fucking way!

Missy held the sandwich for an extended moment, looking at her guest as he looked at her jiffy meal. She knew her steady Steve was hungry for it. Missy lifted the sandwich and took a big, messy bite. She was the chef, after all, so firsties were hers.

Keith was simultaneously relieved that he didn't have to eat that crap sandwich and nauseated that Missy could. He had seen more than enough of her house and living conditions to know that she must eat this way regularly, but as his stomach did cartwheels, he wondered how it was humanly possible. Had she become immune to salmonella and e-coli? Perhaps she was what she ate; Missy was foodborne illness made flesh. And her contaminated tongue had licked his face and probed up his nose. He certainly wasn't immune to salmonella and e-coli, as evidenced by an unfortunate trip to the emergency room after eating an undercooked rotisserie chicken three years ago. Keith shuddered, and then he noticed that Missy had consumed nearly half of her sandwich. Was she even chewing it, or was she swallowing the squirming bites whole? She probably liked the tickling in her tummy. That's what made it so rumbly.

Missy set her sandwich down on the towel covered in pumpkin guts and licked the syrup off of her fingers. She looked at Keith with chocolaty lips and giggled. At least the chocolate covered his blood that had been her former lipstick. Keith grinned back, and Missy couldn't tell it was forced.

Missy bet that her honey-bunny was just as delicious as her chocolate and peanut butter sandwich, and she knew he was going to just love what she had in store for him. She had saved the best sandwich of all, just for him!

Missy took two more moldy slices of bread from the loaf.

Keith took in a sudden intake of air. If Missy heard his gasp, she didn't acknowledge it.

"No, thank you. I'm good," Keith insisted.

"You're a growing boy, and growing boys need to eat," Missy lectured him. Missy moved to the refrigerator and grabbed the sticky handle.

"Don't!" Keith shouted, and was ignored.

Missy opened the refrigerator and reached into its noxious interior. Keith covered his nose, knowing a blast of stink was coming, and his hand did little to lessen it. She didn't appear to notice the smell as she pulled out a wad of well-worn tin foil, followed by a crusty bottle of mustard. Missy closed the refrigerator door, and there was a peeling sound as her hand separated from the sticky handle.

"Who doesn't love ham?" Missy called out excitedly.

"I don't!"

Missy heard Keith's shout but didn't comprehend his words, his exclamation mistaken for affirmation. She peeled open the tin foil. The ham slices inside were glistening with green slime and crawling with cockroaches. Missy unpeeled two slices (like her hand on the fridge handle, Keith could hear them separate) and placed them on the bread, green on green. Dr. Seuss didn't seem so funny to Keith anymore. He knew the green eggs were still in the refrigerator.

"No, that's not good ham. There're roaches on it," Keith reasoned in a gentler voice.

"Those are protein pellets, they're good for you," Missy said. Geez, he sure was being a silly-silly. She didn't have roaches. How could she, when she kept such a clean and orderly house? She should have been offended, but how could she hate a lie when it came from such a pretty mouth? She was about to make his mouth and tummy so happy!

Missy picked up the mustard bottle and squeezed it over the

ham. Coming out of the bottle first was a watery squirt, followed by curdled yellow chunks, applied until it was running off the sides of the bread like the chocolate syrup. Missy slapped on the top slice of bread and held out the dripping, crawling sandwich to Keith.

"Made with love!" Missy exclaimed, and her sentiment gave Keith more cause for concern. He recognized that Missy's behavior was unpredictable and frequently inappropriate, and her gauge for self-control was long broken. She grabbed whatever she liked, whether to tickle or eat. She was rude and bossy to strangers (the Mega-Mart staff) and friends (himself) alike, but he feared most for those that Missy took an attraction to. She was a mentally stunted woman-child without boundaries or relationship experience, and he knew that issues like age and consent never crossed her mind. Keith didn't fear death at Missy's hands; he feared rape.

Keith was reluctant to accept the food/love offering. It wasn't just disgusting, it would solidify her bond to him to have her *love* inside his belly.

"No, really, I can't."

"Take it!"

Missy's outburst was so extreme, Keith knew he had better take what she offered. She might bite his head off otherwise, in a few big chomps like her sloppy sandwich. He reached out and took hold of the ham sandwich. Immediately, his hand was spotted with cockroaches seeking escape from their breaded prison. Keith shook his hand, some of the roaches falling off. It took all of his effort not to drop the sandwich.

Missy picked up her half eaten sandwich. She didn't see the pumpkin guts hanging off the bottom slice, but Keith did. He wasn't about to say anything about it, though. "What do you say?"

"Thank you?"

"You're welcome," Missy replied in a soft voice Keith found uncharacteristic of her, dare he call her tone seductive. Of course it was followed by the expected shout. "Yummy-yum for your tummy-tum!"

Missy took another big bite of her sandwich, now with an added hint of pumpkin. Her eyelids fluttered in sweet food bliss. "Mmm-mmmm!"

Keith looked at Missy's hoard-made sandwich in his hand, and it wasn't *mmm-mmmm* he thought. It was *barf-barf.*

As Keith was contemplating what to do with the ham sandwich in the kitchen, an escape attempt was in progress in the living room.

Dani's head peeked over the edge of the nest, in the same spot she had fallen from. There were two beads of blood on her cheek, a one-inch gash on her forehead that wasn't deep enough to bleed, and a nick on her chin that was the deepest new injury.

She considered herself lucky that only a mirror had landed on her face. Will had not been so lucky across this same room.

Dani saw that the rocky coast was clear in the living room. She could hear the occasional squeals from Missy as Keith kept her occupied in the kitchen, but she couldn't follow their conversation. This was her chance.

Dani climbed out of Missy's nest. There were no charging cats to trigger a fall this time. When Dani stood atop the living room hoard, she looked around for an escape.

The dining room and basement beyond were out of the question. She turned around, and looking across the room she saw the foyer that Missy had entered from. The front door and escape were just beyond her sight, but looking back over her shoulder, Dani saw that the foyer was in line with the dining room. If she climbed her way toward the foyer, she risked being seen from where she knew Missy was. It wasn't a risk she wanted to take.

Dani continued to circle as she looked for another way out. Between two towering bookcases across the room, Dani saw a stack of furniture that stood nearly ten feet tall, much of it sideways and upside down. She focused harder on the furniture pile, and noticed light was shining between the interlocked legs and wood panels.

The furniture was jammed together in a hallway. The entrance was heavily blocked, but it was still a hallway, and a possible way out of the living room.

Dani had her destination, and she started for it, heading around the edge of the nest. She nearly passed another cat in a cage that was obscured by old speakers leaning against two sides and a sheet of webs over the front bars. Dani stopped for it, tearing through the webs with no hesitation to open the cage, furious that this cat had to keep the constant company of spiders and other pests.

On further consideration, spiders might make for better company than Missy. What Dani had witnessed of Missy's behavior while being trapped in the nest with her for a few minutes had been shocking. You only had to look around Missy's house and at the neglected cats to know she wasn't right in the head. To see Missy's psychoses in action - her boisterous bullying, her delusional fantasies, her molesting fingers and tongue – painted a far more terrifying picture of her. The kind of painting done by John Wayne Gacy. It might look like a happy clown, but it was hiding something far more sinister under its smiling surface.

Dani sought her escape as the cat did the same.

Missy swallowed a big mouthful of chewy goodness, in a state of ecstasy. Her head was tilted up, her eyes were closed, and she let out a low moan. Her pleasure was so great, it was becoming an erotic moment. She always ate for gratification, never for nutrition. Missy knew her pleasure eating gave her great curves. All them nutritionist nuts looked like sickly string beans. What was so healthy about that?

Missy lowered her head and noticed that Keith had not taken a bite of his sandwich, the most delicious sandwich in the world that she had put so much love, not to mention hard work and lots of money, into making for him.

"Eat up!" Missy encouraged him.

"No thanks, I…"

Missy seized Keith's right wrist in a vice grip. All he had to do was take one bite and he'd see how yummy it was, and then he'd gobble the rest and give her a kiss smack on the lips for it. His breath might smell like ham, but that was okay. She loved ham, too!

Missy pushed Keith's hand and sandwich toward his mouth. His arm resisted her, but she was fourteen inches taller and one hundred forty-two pounds heavier than him. She had no problem guiding his hand exactly where she wanted it to go.

"We don't waste food here. Eat it, it's good for you."

"Not good!" Keith cried.

Keith pursed his lips closed when the ham sandwich came upon them. Missy knew a way to open his lips. She stomped on Keith's left foot as hard as she could. He opened his mouth to yell and Missy stuck the sandwich where it was meant to go. She shoved it in as much as she could so he could get the most flavorful bite possible. A protein pellet climbed out from between the bread and ran up Keith's face.

"Bite before you choke on it."

Keith bit through the bread and meat, yellowish mustard juice running down his chin. Missy freed Keith's wrist. He'd finish the sandwich now for sure. And he better. This was turning out to be far more work than she intended. This was like teaching a baby how to eat.

"There you go! Chew it good."

Keith chewed, and chewed, and chewed, and Missy got irritated with his squished up face. He was trying to pretend he didn't enjoy it!

"Swallow."

Keith gulped the big bite down. Bigger than Keith's grimace was Missy's grin.

"See? Wasn't that yummy yummy yummy yummy yummy?"

Missy closed her eyes and took another joyous bite of her syrupy sandwich. She was so excited that they were eating together, her bosoms tickled. She didn't notice Keith's reply, which was a retch.

Keith dropped his ham sandwich, shivering with nausea. Missy was watching.

Oh, that ungrateful little punk, Missy thought as her mirthful eyes took on a hard glare. She spoke with her mouth full, which was allowed because she had something important to say. She sprayed little bits of her sandwich into his face, and she hoped a chunk would land in his mouth so he could eat that, too.

"You will eat my sandwich."

Keith made a yuck face as he spit out two words. "Can't. Poison."

"We don't waste here. Pick it up."

This boy was turning into a sniveling scallywag, and he did what all scallywags do, he tried to slither away from her. He hadn't finished a full turn before she got her hand around his left wrist. He was forcing her to hold him tighter.

"Pick! It! Up!"

Missy increased her grip and liked the feel of grinding tendons and bones. She heard and felt a satisfying crack in Keith's wrist.

"Okay!" the scallywag cried.

Missy relaxed her grip but didn't release her hold on him. He wasn't going to wiggle his way away from her. She allowed him to squat and retrieve the ham sandwich off of the floor. The sandwich had stayed together during its fall. That was because Missy made her sandwiches with love and magic.

Missy saw Keith looking at his rescued ham sandwich, and then she saw that sandwich flying right at her. She felt the cold, wet slap of her jiffy meal right in her face. In her surprise, he got out of her grip.

Keith spun away from his captor. Missy delivered a right hook to Keith's face from behind, and she watched him drop onto his back. Her left hand never lost hold of her sandwich.

Missy knew she could knock some sense into this one. She held out hope that they could be friends, special friends. She just had to calm him down and show him how things worked in her house. Plus, she wanted to rub it in a bit and show him what a treat he was missing.

"If you won't eat with me, you can just sit there until I'm finished."

Missy stepped over Keith's head and sat down. Keith instinctively lifted his injured left hand in protest and she sat on that, too. Whatever had cracked in his wrist before now broke. She felt the break, between her legs, and that was also satisfying. He squirmed for freedom and breath between her muscular thighs.

Missy squirmed too as she consumed the rest of her chocolate syrup and peanut butter special. She moaned from the sensations. Her tingles were getting lower. She was *rubbing… it… in!*

Missy licked the dark brown syrup off of her fingers with a satisfied smirk.

"So good," Missy moaned. Now that she was finished with her jiffy meal, it was time to entertain her playmate again. She stood up and looked down at his sweet face.

Keith remained on his back, gasping for air and gurgling blood. His already busted nose was further flattened. His left hand rested by his head, cocked at an awkward angle at the wrist. Missy figured he was just playing possum with her, which wasn't nice. He should be showing appreciation for her hospitality and home cooked meal.

"I told you I don't waste," Missy reiterated.

Missy picked up the fallen ham sandwich, which was glued together with its special sauce. She sat back down on the same seat. Keith's head shook in protest until the weight of Missy's ass settled on it.

Missy took a bite of Keith's forfeited sandwich. It was so good she wondered why she had offered it away in the first place.

"That's delicious! Your loss," Missy directed down between her legs.

Missy continued to consume the second sandwich, stopping to giggle when the tickling down below got too great. He wasn't going to get any of her yummy-yummy sandwich, but he just might get gravy on his face! Missy wiggled, and then disappointment set in when he slowed down beneath her. She thought a young whippersnapper like him shouldn't tire out so easily. Must be all those video games kids played today, that was what they always said on those catty TV shows she watched and swore by.

It never occurred to Missy that he might be suffocating.

Missy took the final two bites together, wiping her messy hands on her clothes. She never forgot to wipe her hands off after she ate. She prided herself on being a clean person.

Missy stood up from her meal, fully gratified, and looked down at her guest. He was no longer squirming. In fact, he didn't appear to be moving at all. She thought he looked adorable all sleepy like that, like a baby kitten. That was good because she was planning on seeing him sleeping every night now, right next to her in her majestic bed.

"You can nap now, Keith. We'll find your Fiddlesticks later. I need a drinkie-poo."

Missy looked around and found an overturned fountain drink with the lid and straw intact. She grabbed the cup and slurped the mystery liquid until she reached the hateful bubbling at the bottom. It was never enough.

Missy tossed the empty cup to the side, where all garbage went, its proper place, and looked down at Keith. She realized that she had just called him Keith even though he had told her his name was Steve.

Now she knew exactly who this silly goose was, and she could hardly wait until after his naptime to ask him why he had fibbed to her.

13

Dani's climb toward the hidden hallway was slowed by her need to be quiet. There was silence coming from the kitchen, and that worried her more than hearing Missy's grating, shouting voice. She knew one wrong step could set off another collapse of potential death dealing dominoes or reveal her whereabouts to the heinous homeowner. She could not let that happen. The cats needed to be saved, and Will's death needed to be avenged.

As Dani came upon the hallway, her hopes were soured, and all she could say was what she smelled. "Shit."

The hallway looked long, at least thirty feet, and every foot was packed tight with furniture. Dani saw sofas, bookcases, tables, chairs, a walker, and a grade school desk, and that's just what she could see up front. She did see light coming from the other side, so the hallway led somewhere, and there were a few crawlspaces visible.

Dani thought somebody as thin and slight as her or Ian might possibly get through this stuffed tunnel, but Missy could never follow through. She had to give it a try.

Dani grabbed onto the nearest chair leg and gave it a tug. As the chair shifted out of place, a table fell down behind it to fill the void, and suddenly every piece of furniture up front was shifting, one crawlspace collapsing. Worse yet was the sound of wood banging on wood. She hoped it wasn't heard in the kitchen, but there was little hope of that.

"No way."

Dani turned back to the living room, defeated. She heard banging from the kitchen. It sounded like Missy was on the move.

Dani's defeat became panic, which was better because it urged her into motion. She looked around the living room with intense concentration. Perhaps she had missed something, or maybe she could find a better hiding spot as Missy passed through.

Dani thought of the basement, which had also seemed without an exit at first. They had found a hidden staircase, and she realized that's what was missing. From outside, Missy's house stood two towering stories or more, so where were the stairs to the second floor? The staircase in most houses was located in the living room.

Dani's eyes picked out levels in the hoard ahead and a path clarified before her eyes, like a blurry image coming into focus. Her way out of this room would be a way further into the house.

Across the room from Dani was a mountain of clothing that appeared to reach the ceiling, and the peak disappeared into a dark hole. Similar to the basement, the stairs to the second floor had been swallowed by the hoard, which in this room was the hamper of the house.

Dani was immediately on the move toward the slope. Perhaps upstairs would lead to some other staircase or exit, even a second floor window that she could jump out of.

Dani heard more noise from the kitchen, what sounded like pots and pans banging together, closer than before. Dani stopped her advance to take a look back. She knew one bad step forward without her eyes on her path could trigger a fatal collision.

Missy was not yet in sight. The next noise sounded like the kicking of a cage, coming from the dining room. Missy was definitely heading in Dani's direction.

Dani continued to climb toward the slope of clothing. She hurried as fast as she could over the shifting hoard, no longer caring about making noise. She came upon another cat in a cage, the prisoner moving to the front bars and meowing for release. Dani could not spare the few seconds to open the cage door and free it, and it broke her heart.

"Sorry," Dani said as she passed the cage. She promised herself she would come back later and make sure this cat received its release. She just had to get out of Missy's sight to make that happen. She had to free herself from Missy's cage first.

When Dani reached the bottom of the hidden staircase, she looked to the top and saw this slope was just as steep as the basement stairs, only more slippery with its carpet of loose clothing. She momentarily wondered whether Missy's habit of burying her staircases was a symptom of her hoarding, or something more nefarious, like hiding escape routes from trapped people. Dani looked back again.

A box tumbled from the dining room into the living room, presaging Missy's arrival. Considering the living room was a few feet higher than the dining room, the box must have been propelled by Missy's fist.

Dani began her crawl up the clothing slope. The surface was just as unstable as she feared, causing her to slip repeatedly. Missy's voice boomed behind her in the living room.

"I'm so thirsty!"

Every few steps Dani climbed she slid back one, not that any steps were visible beneath her. Her speed made her sloppy, but she gained elevation, the top lip of the clothing slide closing in distance. Dani risked a glance down to the side, and she could see Missy's lower half climbing over the living room hoard, likely heading for her nest. Dani looked back up at her destination and did not slow until she crawled over the top edge.

Dani stood and observed the corridor before her. The long hallway had two doors on the left, one door on the right, and an open door at the end. Dani was not the least bit surprised to find this corridor as packed with junk as every room beneath her.

Missy climbed down into her nest. She fished through the plastic bags from tonight's aborted shopping excursion (due to that horrible Mrs. Cunt-ter, she thought with a giggle but would never dare say aloud, because she was a classy lady) until she found what she was looking for, a two-liter bottle of Freshie's Fruit Punch.

"I love my Red!" Missy exclaimed as she took a seat.

Missy broke the seal and unscrewed the cap, tossing it aside. There would be no need to recap this bottle; she was thirsty. Missy chugged, and chugged, and chugged some more. A thin line of fruit punch ran down her chin, and her tongue followed in an attempt to catch every escaping drop. The drops that got away did a suicide plunge off of her chin and splattered on the jutting rocks of her breasts, staining the fabric of her shirt in bright red splotches. Her shirt bore the evidence of many prior food and drink suicides.

Missy let loose a juicy (and fruity) belch as she tossed the bottle aside into her ever filling nest. She looked instinctively up at the spot where her TV was supposed to be, and she was disappointed that she'd have to wait until the next Late Bird Sale to get the lowest television purchase price. That was a long wait, so maybe she'd have to borrow the one currently in use upstairs. It was so quiet and boring downstairs without one.

Luckily, she wouldn't be bored for long. Once her boyfriend was finished with his nap, he'd come find her and they would play. But she wouldn't be surprised if he asked her for something to eat first.

Once Ian could no longer hear any conversation from the kitchen, followed by Missy's bulldozer style departure back into the house, he dropped down off the basement high beam onto a slippery slope.

The recently disturbed slide of garbage shifted beneath his feet, as he'd feared it might. His decision to land facing the basement doorway proved to be a bad one as he fell backwards, landing hard on his back. He started to slide down head first, unable to see what was in his path.

The top of Ian's head hit the edge of a cardboard box, and his right shoulder clipped the sharp edge of the fallen radiator that was delicately balanced on the cracked table edge. Ian's hands could not stop his slide, so he cupped them over the back of his head to prevent any more cranial damage. It also kept his camera cap on as he slid. He knew this would make some awesome footage.

Unbalanced by Ian's passage, the radiator began to roll down the remainder of the slope.

Ian reached the bottom of the slide headfirst. He sat up and saw he had seconds to live. The cartwheeling radiator was coming down right on top of him. The metal box hit a fallen hat rack that was sticking out over the path. Miraculously, the hat rack stopped the radiator's descent. It looked like a toothpick holding up a boulder.

Ian looked stunned at the radiator balancing above him, and then he noticed the hat rack was starting to bow downward.

Ian rolled his body to the left as the hat rack snapped. The radiator finished its fall and landed where Ian had stopped moments before.

Ian looked at the radiator and the plume of dust that was rising around it. He counted his blessings, since this radiator was a lot heavier than the television that had killed Will. He and his friends had been inside Missy's house for less than an hour, and death by hoard had been nipping at their heels the entire time. How was Missy able to survive in this death trap, year after year, decade after decade? Her luck was disgusting.

Ian hoped that the rolling radiator would not draw Missy's attention and bring her back, but he had a feeling Missy heard only what she wanted to hear. Fortunately for him, house disrepair didn't seem very high on her list of concerns.

Ian was faced with a critical decision. Exit the basement window as Keith had ordered him, by word and later by the waving of his hand, or venture back up the unsafe slide into the house to help him out, should he need it. He really didn't need to think about it. They were brothers, after all.

14

Dani journeyed through the upstairs hallway. There was a thin channel that snaked like a creek from side to side that Dani twisted her way through. She thought her best bet for getting out of this house was to find an upstairs window and climb out. She could manage a second story drop. She was not afraid of heights, and she was good at climbing and gymnastics. A landing roll on the lawn would not hurt her, at least not much.

Dani hoped she could find a window. She remembered seeing many when they first approached the house, and they had all been covered. During her downstairs journey from the kitchen to dining room to living room, she could not recall seeing one window. Dani realized that Missy didn't just cover her windows; she kept them hidden from view on the inside.

Dani came upon the first doorway on the left. As she looked into the room, she noticed that the door was stuck in the open position by the hoard on each side. Privacy did not appear to be an issue inside Missy's house.

Dani figured that the room she was looking into was Missy's bedroom. It held the most sparkling and colorful hoard in the house. It was an even split between the room of an adolescent girl and a landfill. There were unicorns and rainbows and everything was sprinkled in colored glitter and confetti, including the trash. There were no windows visible inside, even though Dani was sure the room had to have one. The hoard climbed so high against every wall, a window could be anywhere. She'd come back and search for a window only if she came upon no other options.

Dani continued through the corridor, coming upon the second door on the left, which was also wedged open. She knew what room it was before she looked inside, cupping a hand over her nose to lessen the stench. When she did stop in the doorway, she was appalled to a new level. This made the most heinous Honey Bucket she had ever been in (at a skateboarding competition, which made sense – *boys*) look like a model of cleanliness in comparison.

This was perhaps the darkest room of the house, cast in a dim, brown shade, and looking up, Dani saw that the light bulb was covered in crap. The whole ceiling looked like it had been on the receiving end of explosive diarrhea. She didn't know how that could be possible, but obviously it was. The sink held a stagnant soup, filled to overflowing. Bugs backstroked in the chunky stew. The floor was covered with a carpet of used toilet paper and maxi-pads. The shower curtain was thankfully closed, concealing who knew what horrors behind it. The water stained and mold streaked shower curtain had more than a few brown handprints on it. Even the mirror on the wall had shit stains in the center, right where the looker's face should be. Mirror, mirror on the wall, who's the most shit-faced of them all?

Dani tried to ignore the room's most sickening centerpiece, the toilet. Her eyes kept passing over it without really seeing it. And then her eyes fell on a cage sitting atop the toilet tank. There was a cat inside of it, its white fur slathered in brown, just like every other surface of the bathroom.

Dani knew she couldn't save every cat at the moment, her own immediate escape was mandatory, but there was no way she could live with herself if she didn't free this cat covered in its keeper's feces. Dani turned her head back, took a deep breath of the hallway air, which wasn't very fresh either, and then she entered the bathroom.

Dani slipped more than stepped toward the toilet. The gruesome details of her destination could no longer be avoided. The toilet had a mountain of shit rising out of it, the top over four feet above the bowl. It was almost like a hard brown volcano with runny brown lava going down the sides. A Styrofoam hamburger container stuck out of the middle, indicating where much of the mountain originated.

When the cage was close enough, Dani carefully reached over the toilet bowl to unlatch the door. The latch was crusty and harder to open than the others. She had to jiggle the latch to get the crap to crack, and that sent a flurry of cockroaches scurrying over the toilet tank and up the wall. How long could this cat have been in this cage, that the lock could corrode this much? Dani didn't really need an answer to that question, she was mad enough already.

The lock on the cage finally disengaged, and with the crumbling of crap, Dani pulled the cage door open. The cat was desperate for freedom and leapt out. Its back legs hit the top of the toilet bowl lid, knocking it toward the mound of shit.

Dani took a quick step back and slipped, eager to get far enough away in case shit mountain avalanched toward her.

The toilet lid hit the waste and stopped. The mound was solidified and could not be easily moved from the bowl it rose from. Dozens more cockroaches scattered from the back of the lid around the front and down the shitty slope.

Dani was revolted but relieved. At least she hadn't been hit with waste. She looked at the cat as it ran out of the bathroom, trailing toilet paper from both of its back paws. She intended to follow it, but her eyes turned to the bathtub. She looked above the shower curtain and saw the top edge of a thin window. She had to investigate it. This could be her escape hatch.

Dani slid over the TP and maxi-pads toward the bathtub. She now knew altogether too much about Missy's feminine hygiene, such as the severity of her flow (excessive). Dani stopped before the tub and grabbed a non-soiled edge of the shower curtain, which hung outside instead of inside the basin. Her fingers broke the cobwebs that connected the curtain to the wall, proof that the tub had long been off limits. She yanked the stiff curtain open and found out why.

The bathtub was filled to the brim with excrement. It appeared that once the toilet had overfilled, the tub had taken over as the crapper. The turds had clogged the drain, and no amount of Draino was going to open up the pipe. This waste remained wet in the center, while dry and cracked on the edges. A mummified, screeching cat was half submerged in the waste like a fossil stuck in the tar pits.

Dani wrenched her disbelieving eyes away from the cat carcass as she remembered her reason for pulling open the shower curtain. She looked up at the thin window, only about a foot and a half wide and two feet tall. Now that the whole window was revealed, she was disappointed to discover boards nailed over it. The window looked just big enough to squeeze through, if she could remove the boards. In order to reach and pry them off, she would have to stand in fifty plus gallons of Missy's waste. There was no way around it, and there was no way she was going to do it. There had to be other windows upstairs that weren't situated over a sewer.

Dani looked at the cat corpse and wondered how horrible it must have been to die in this fecal sludge. She began to retch. She was surprised she hadn't started retching earlier.

Dani yanked the shower curtain closed, but she knew the image of what lay beyond it would be seared into her mind for life. She turned away and hurried out of the bathroom with an arm over her lower face.

Dani stopped in the hallway and gulped in the stale but considerably less putrid air. She couldn't stop thinking of the cat's frozen scream, and she wished it was Missy stuck in her shit pit for eternity. It was what she deserved. "Fucking cat killer," she seethed.

Dani's rage and desire to bring Missy to justice got her moving again. She squeezed through the path, which took her to the one door on the right side of the hallway. This door was not wide open like all the others; it was cracked open only a few inches. Dani could not see what lay inside, although if she had to bet, she'd put her money on more hoard.

Dani pushed on the door and it started to open without resistance, which made it unlike any other door in the house. Maybe there was something special about this room that required concealment and easy entrance. The door opened half a foot, and that's when the smell hit her. This was worse than the moldy basement, worse than the rancid refrigerator, and worse than the sea of shit in the bathroom. What the smell was, Dani couldn't say and didn't want to guess, but it disturbed her so deeply she chickened out.

Dani was normally not one to turn down a dare or get frightened off. Her hanging around with boys all the time had thickened her skin. It wasn't the absence of the guys that made

Dani lose her bravery. It was something deeper, a survival instinct that made her shut the door. If she had to describe the smell, the only words that might fit would be *graveyard gas*. She knew for a fact that there was death behind the door, and she was not willing to face it.

"No way." Dani realized that she had spoken without thought to her volume, and she looked back down the hallway to make sure she wasn't being followed. Missy wasn't there, and that wasn't a surprise. Noise would have announced her arrival. It was time to get moving again.

Dani continued her trek through the corridor toward the open door at the end. She glanced down to watch her footing and saw a chunk of soiled toilet paper stuck to her ankle, much like the cat that had escaped the bathroom before her. She had to stop and get rid of this bathroom tagalong. Dani stepped up to a dresser, and she ran her ankle against an edge until the crappy wad found another surface to stick to.

An extended, wheezing cough came out of the open door at the end of the hall, making Dani yelp in surprise. She didn't think it could be Missy, unless Missy had a hidden, alternate route upstairs she hadn't discovered yet. The voice that followed the cough made her gasp.

"Who's there?!"

The voice that came from the back room was definitely not Missy's. The tone had a genderless quality to it. She could also hear the low voices from a familiar television program, possibly the same one that had been broadcasting downstairs when the TV fell and…

Dani broke the thought. She knew the questioning voice was not from the television; it was louder than that. The voice also shared the quality of those coughs, sickly. Despite Will and Keith's assurances, Missy's house did have a second occupant, a hidden hoarder.

Dani quickly weighed her options. She could retreat the way she came, but that would take her back to where, and who, she had escaped from. She could retreat to the bathroom window, but there was no guarantee that she could get the boards off, assuming she didn't drown in the La Missy Shit Pits first. There was also that mystery room she hadn't entered, but that was not among the options she was willing to consider.

The voice ahead called out again, and made Dani's decision for her.

"I need help!"

Dani pegged the voice as that of an invalid. She'd had enough experience to learn their tonal quality during the years her grandmother had been in a nursing home before she died. Grammy's originally lilting voice had grown deeper as she had deteriorated, becoming genderless as well. There was also an innate weakness she recognized in invalids' voices, and she heard it in the mystery speaker ahead of her.

A distressing thought occurred to Dani. What if the speaker, the invalid, needed help because he or she was being kept prisoner inside Missy's house, just like the cats? Could there be a huge cage ahead with a person locked inside, underfed, dehydrated, and soiled in his/her own waste? Dani's mission so far had been all about avoiding detection. Now here she was, about to reveal herself to offer help to someone who might need it.

Dani didn't want to call out in response, since she still had to avoid Missy. She walked forward, and the closer she got to the room, the worse the smell became. She waved away the odor and some accompanying flies, but neither could be shooed. She could pinpoint some of the stench as feces, but it wasn't the same smell as the bathroom, or any of the previous rooms. Every room inside Missy's house seemed to have its own distinct stink. Vomitus variety was the rank spice of Missy's life.

"Help me!" the hidden person called.

Dani stopped before entering the room. She pulled the handheld camera out of her pocket. She had a feeling that whatever lied ahead would require documentation.

Dani stepped into the room at the end of the hallway. First she saw the television atop a food waste packed stand. Sure enough, it was tuned to the same trash talk show that had been playing downstairs. Missy's mysterious housemate appeared to share the same taste in entertainment. Unless this person couldn't change the channel and was forced to watch what Missy wanted them to.

When Dani saw the occupant across the room, facing the TV, she immediately regretted her decision. She should have decided on another plan of escape. Even the scary graveyard room that had turned her feet around at the threshold would have been a better choice than this. She closed her eyes for a few seconds, and opened them fresh to verify her vision, and what she saw didn't change.

Dani thought *Oh my God I'm so stupid! What is it? WHAT IS IT!?*

15

Dani was a strong girl. She was used to the rough realities of life, and while she might not like the bad things, she could deal with them. Reality wasn't always nice or fair, but it was reliable. The person that she saw in the bedroom stretched her idea of reality past the acceptance point. That uncertainty made her feel like she was walking through a nightmare, where reality was lost and monsters lurked. That's what Dani thought she was looking at. A monster.

Panic flooded Dani's system fast, and she had to fight it off in order to keep control and not do something she might regret. Like scream. She was a tough girl in life, but in her nightmares she ran and screamed from the scaries, like any young girl would.

The trashy talk show that provided a constant stream of shouting broke through Dani's panic, and she seized on it. This monster was a person, like she often saw on a different kind of reality show that she watched on other, more educational channels (or so they purported of their sensational programming). Shows like *The Guy With the 125 Pound Scrotum.* Or *The Man Who Lost His Face To A Monkey.* Or *The Woman With Six Uteruses On the Outside,* that had been a particularly memorable episode. If she could just remember that this monst… this *person* in front of her was just like the unfortunates on those shock ailment shows, she could deal with it.

Sitting on a giant sofa with an abnormally wide seat (perhaps it was a sofa bed, she couldn't tell) against a mold-covered wall was the second hoarder, who appeared as genderless as its voice. Dani safely assumed this person was a hoarder, since this room was as much of a garbage dump as the rest of the house. This hoarder's thin and stringy brown hair was long, unkempt, and gummed together with food. There was some squiggly chin and mole hair on its face, but not enough to signify gender.

What made this hoarder so grotesque was its sheer size. Dani wondered if there was a size category beyond morbidly obese. This hoarder had to be one thousand pounds, and then Dani thought that might be a gross underestimate. Too large for clothes, this hoarder had only a torn, food and human waste stained sheet covering its lap. The exposed legs ended in thick trunks, the toes and feet likely long lost to diabetic amputation.

What disturbed Dani the most was the hoarder's face, mainly because it was so hard to locate. The head blended into the body in a way that was more slug than human. The hoarder's tiny, beady eyes were barely visible in the folds of facial flesh, and they were looking right at Dani. The nose was just not visible from across the room. The hoarder's mouth was nearly indiscernible among the many folds, but one of those folds was turned up at each end. Dani thought this hoarder just might be grinning.

Dani grinned back and had to suppress a mad laugh. She felt like she was looking at a close relative of Jabba the Hut. What she felt was no longer fear, it was disgust. She also felt disgust at herself, in the event this person could not help its obese condition. She thought it possible that she was interacting with a thousand pound tumor. She should feel pity for it.

"I thought I heard voices! Is Missy throwing another party?" the hoarder asked excitedly. Dani knew this hoarder liked a party, she could tell by the way it was wiggling its wide fingers. Even the fingers had folds of fat, which wiggled as well.

"Yes," Dani replied. So be it, let this be a party. A party was better than a crisis.

Dani stepped closer to the hoarder, closing the proximity primarily so they could lower their voices. This hoarder's booming voice might draw Missy, whose party Dani had not been formally invited to.

"What's your name, pretty girl?" it blubbered in lieu of

language.

"Sally," Dani lied, "What's yours?"

"Tickles! My name is Tickles Honey Boo-Boo!"

Dani could not tell if the hoarder was being genuine or not with the name, but it didn't matter. Tickles Honey Boo-Boo it was, or Tickles for short. Dani found it appropriate that Tickles' name in no way tipped her off to its gender.

Tickles lived up to its name, tickling its exposed, jiggling breasts, another non-gender signifier due to Tickles' size. The nipples were not the size of pepperonis; they were more the size of mini-pizzas.

"You got a video camera?" Tickles asked.

In her initial shock, Dani had forgotten that she was filming with her handheld camera. She thought that her footage might make for a great freak of the week reality show, the kind she was guilty of enjoying. She might have to change the title, though. *Tickles Honey Boo-Boo* might incur a lawsuit.

"Yeah," Dani admitted. It was too late to hide the camera now.

"Oh goodie-goodie! I always told Missy I'm gonna be on TV! I could have my own show! Am I TV material or what?"

Or what! Dani thought but did not say. Dani looked at the tawdry television program and back at Tickles, who was posing and puckering like a spoiled beauty queen. Tickles had its own unique version of a duck face, but it looked less like a duck and more like a seal. Dani considered a title for their show. *The Person Swallowed By Their Skin* might be a good one.

"You sure are," Dani agreed, to Tickles' delight.

Tickles picked a peeled cube of butter out of a metal bucket on the sofa. Dani saw about a dozen more peeled cubes inside the pail. Tickles' cube was dipped into a bag of sugar leaning against the bucket. The confection made curly-cues through the air on its way into Tickles' mouth. Half of the cube was devoured in one drooling bite.

Dani tried to hide her revulsion at Tickles' messy eating, but it wasn't really possible. The image of a blob of flesh eating a cube of butter almost slipped her back into nightmare territory. She focused on her camera and folded out the flip screen. Somehow it was easier to accept the image through a digital filter, and it gave her a job to focus on. She was a documentarian.

As Dani advanced closer, she zoomed in on Tickles' eating. The flip screen was filled with the image of fleshy folds opening wide with butter stretching between them, and butter coating considerably rotten teeth.

Dani no longer felt pity for this person. This was not the victim of a runaway tumor or ailment. Its overgrown state was the result of its insatiable appetites, gluttony with extra butter on top. Dani felt justified in her disgust.

Tickles dipped the second half of the butter cube into the bag of sugar, swirling it around to get all sides covered. The cube spilled sugar as it was pulled out of the bag. Tickles looked at the cube, drooling butter, and in a surprising display of generosity, held the confection out to Dani.

"Want some of my sweet stick?"

"No, thanks."

Tickles squealed and appeared overjoyed that she had declined, and the remaining sweet stick did a flying corkscrew into its maw.

As Tickles ate, oblivious to Dani, she moved the zoom over its massive body, at folds of flesh messy with food, fuzz, and even – *Oh God!* – cobwebs. The sea of skin was spotted with sores and crawling with cockroaches. Tickles didn't appear to notice the roaches, or just didn't care. Perhaps Tickles didn't even feel them. Circulation and numbness had to be part of Tickles' many problems. She also noticed that where Tickles' trunk legs ended, the skin was course and peeling in dry patches, another symptom of bad circulation and neglect.

Seeing Tickles in such bliss, Dani wondered why she had been called into the room, and risked revealing herself, in the first place.

"You were calling for help."

"I need help! I dropped my remote, and I can't find it!"

Dani could not believe she had been so easily deceived into this trivial rescue. Her disgust toward this hoarder was growing. Tickles seemed like the perfect roommate for Missy. They were equally greedy and gross.

Dani looked below Tickles' trunk legs, and lying on top of a carpet of fast food refuse was the missing remote control. It was the oversize kind with big buttons usually used by the elderly or the sight impaired.

"It's right at your…" *don't say feet!* "It's right below you," Dani corrected herself.

"I can't reach it," Tickles said in the most annoying, whiny voice Dani had ever heard, where the final two letter word was drawn out like it was a dozen letters long.

Tickles, to its credit, did try to reach forward, but only its arms and stub legs had any real movement. Tickles' massive blob of a body could not move forward off of the rotted sofa fabric.

Dani was having a dark realization concerning Tickles' immobility, and she zoomed in closer with her camera to investigate her suspicion. She cringed as she viewed the details through her flip screen.

Tickles was not just sitting on the sofa; Tickles had absorbed the sofa. Wherever Tickles' skin met the upholstery, they were fused together by a natural glue of hair and excrement, pressed into each other by so much weight and time. Only Tickles' arms and trunk legs remained mobile. Even its neck and the back of its head were fused to its seat. Tickles could barely move its head out of the forward position, which explained why the television was directly opposite the sofa on an even sight line.

As Tickles tried to lean forward, flesh and fabric pulled together as one. The bond looked strong, and it wasn't clear to Dani whether the skin or sofa would tear first.

Dani found herself past the point of fearing Tickles. This person was not going to chase or harm her. Revolting, for sure, but Dani felt that Tickles was more pathetic than anything else. What kind of life was living in one room, in one spot, immobilized in a cocoon of your own waste? A pathetic life was what it was. What bewildered her most was that this being seemed to live in a state of constant elation and delusional TV land make-believe. Tickles' mind mimicked the rest of it; it was a useless pile of dumb jelly.

As uniquely grotesque as the sight was, Dani knew that Tickles was not alone in its condition. She remembered a similar story on one of those freaky reality shows she enjoyed so much, one titled *The Man Who Grew Into His Bed.* A massive man had melded with his mattress, through a new skin of hair and shit, and they had to break down a wall to get him out, and when they tried to pull the man off of the bed, he had… Dani banished the shock ending of that episode. What she was dealing with now was bad enough.

The ruined sheet covering Tickles' lap was jostled loose by its reaching hands, and it slid over its left trunk and piled beside the remote. Fully exposed, Tickles' gender remained elusive. The folds of flesh hid any genitals. It giggled at its nakedness, but Dani did not giggle back. Tickles was actually flirting, making goo-goo eyes and wiggling to accentuate its countless curves. "Oo, oo," Tickles cooed.

Tickles gave up the struggle to reach the remote. The effort had exhausted and pained it. Sweat ran down its grimacing... *face?* It was all grimace.

"I can't. Can you get it for me please, sweetie-pie? I need to turn this up."

Dani scanned the walls for windows. The only visible window was directly above the sofa that Tickles was fused to. She couldn't believe that she hadn't noticed it before. The window was completely covered, as they all were, this one with newspapers that appeared to be glued over each other.

A disturbing detail above the window caught Dani's attention. Over the black mold were wide streaks of a viscous brown and gray substance, running down from the ceiling all the way to the window. Dani knew it wasn't a fungus. It was bat guano, and evidence that those winged pests held high residence inside Missy's house. The attic above them could no longer hold the weight of the waste. She could even smell the guano, an all-new offensive reek. The word *RABIES!* flashed in her mind, and she worried for Keith and the hand injury he had received yesterday. Rabies could conceivably be rampant within the house. It might explain Missy's sores and insanity. Could a human survive with rabies long term? The rabies issue brought up another anxiety. If the disease were rampant within the house, how many of the rescues would have to be put down?

Dani knew what she had to do. So what if she got a bit of rabid bat guano in her hair? Dani looked down from the window and into Tickles' deep-set eyes. "Sure, I'll get it for you," she replied.

Tickles excitedly looked from the TV to Dani to the TV again. Dani slowly approached Tickles, surprised that she had lost its attention already to the tawdry rerun. She needed to use that to her advantage.

"They gonna reveal the baby daddy!" Tickles announced. Dani shared none of Tickles' enthusiasm, not that Tickles noticed.

Dani squatted to grab the remote, which was covered in food and boogers. She did not hesitate to touch it. Her plan required it, and she'd touched worse things in this house already. One of Tickles' trunk legs darted at her, brushing against her face. The cracked skin felt like sandpaper against her cheek, and she hoped it didn't contain a fungus that would make her face corrode in the same manner. Dani pushed away with the remote, Tickles' trunks waving at her. Tickles laughed (at least Dani assumed that the sputtering wheeze it made was a laugh) until it saw the remote in her hands.

"Here! Give it to me!" Tickles demanded.

Dani not only denied Tickles the object it desired, she used the remote against it. Dani turned, stuck the remote out toward the TV, and hit the volume button down until the television was silent.

"No! What are you doing?" it squealed in outrage. Tickles might be weak under its flabby flesh, but it was strong in emotion and vocal projection, enough to make Dani wince.

Oh, the horror! Dani thought. *Now we might never find out the results of the paternity test!*

"Answer one question first, then you can have it," Dani said. It was the one and only question she had for Tickles, and like Missy, it would be the thing upon which it would be judged. "The cats in this house, are they yours or Missy's?"

"They're both of ours! The happy cats of Wormwood manor! Now gimme!"

Tickles' outstretched fingers wiggled and jiggled for the remote.

Dani seethed, and could only get one word out with her venom. "Happy."

Dani thought of every cat she had seen in this house. Not one of them was happy. Cats living and dying in squalor, prone to disease and bad breeding, imprisoned in cruel cages, and worst of all, starving. All of them starving. All while this *person* ate butter by the bucketful. She found herself surprised that the cats had not turned mutinous to their captor and eaten Tickles alive. The cats could have feasted for a month before they got to the bones.

Dani used the remote to taunt Tickles, waving it just out of its reach. Tickles whined with the exertion of reaching and more from the disappointment of the spoiled program. Dani tossed the remote onto the far right end of the sofa, out of Tickles' reach.

"No! This is my favorite part!"

As Tickles reached over for the remote, the flesh and fabric stretched again, far more than before. It appeared to Dani that something might rip if Tickles reached any further. She looked up at the window again, her way out.

"Gimme it! The baby daddy!" Tickles squealed, and then

something did rip. Dani was distracted from her destination by the sound. She looked over as the situation, and Tickles, unfolded.

The far right corner of Tickles' shoulder had opened up at the seam where sofa met skin. The wound gaped open, a foot long. The blood was not immediate; it had a lot of fat to travel through first.

Having gained a few inches toward the remote, Tickles heaved to the side even harder. Tickles' only pain was in missing the program. The wound tore in two directions, down the right edge of its back, and across the top, on its way to Tickles' left shoulder (there was no shoulder blade visible). Tickles gained nearly a foot toward the remote from the peeling. All of its hard work was going to pay off.

Dani gaped as she saw Tickles' back peeling open before her, the wound appearing like a slice of cheese peeled off the block from the corner. Tickles' skinned back was a mass of quivering adipose with blood slowly seeping through. There were no muscles or bone visible, just jiggling jelly. The peeled skin was the new upholstery on the sofa. The hair and shit had finally become stronger than flesh.

This is what Dani had remembered and forcefully forgotten earlier, only it could never really be forgotten. This was *The Man Who Grew Into His Bed* all over again, where the rescuers had skinned the guy alive in their disastrous attempt at removing the man from his mattress. The difference this time was, the skinner was also the skinned.

Dani tore her eyes away from the distraction, that's all it was. She had to forget this live reality horror show and get moving. Dani stepped up onto the left side of the sofa as Tickles was distracted right beside her. She kicked the bucket of butter cubes out of her way. The cubes did not spill out; they stuck together in one greasy clump inside the pail.

"Gimme!" Tickles cried. The loosening of Tickles' flesh got it within inches of the remote control. Tickles had probably not moved so far in months, if not years. Despite the growing injury, which appeared to bring it no pain, Tickles leaned further. The left seam down Tickles' back opened up, tearing down as far as the right. Tickles gained more inches over the couch as its ass began to rip off with the skin of its back. Now that the flesh was torn, the wounds were all too easy to widen, like perforated paper. Tickles didn't seem to notice.

Dani glanced down at the wet, ripping sounds. She was repulsed to see the wide sheet of bloody meat that was the new upholstery already crawling with bugs eager for a taste.

Dani tore her eyes away from the shed skin as she tried to get a good step up. The top edge of the sofa was so stuffed with garbage, she couldn't find a foothold, and she had to scoot trash away with her shoe to find a spot. Among the vermin that went scattering, she was most surprised by the centipedes, which were crawling over her shoe.

Dani grabbed onto the window frame, which had its own stash of garbage. She knocked empty soda cans and cups out of her way. She got splashed by a few of the falling drinks, and barely noticed. Dani's tolerance for exposure to yucky stuff had risen exponentially in the last hour, and getting a splash of stale soda with fuzz on top was really the least of her worries.

With both of her shoes planted atop the back of the sofa, Dani reached further for the window latch, disengaging it and lifting the handle. The window would not budge. Dani noticed that Tickles' wailing had stopped.

Dani pushed harder, and then severe disappointment made her stop. She spotted over one dozen long, rusty nails pounded into the window frame, much like the basement window they had broken through.

Dani noted Tickles' silence and was not surprised. *The Man Who Grew Into His Bed* had featured a grim denouement; the subject had not survived his painful predicament. Nor was she saddened at this. There would be no tears from her for this living, soon to be non-living, human Sloth.

Dani had nothing on her hard enough to bust out the window, except for her camera. She needed the camera to work, and the footage inside to sink Missy, so it was not a useful option. She'd have to get down and find something else, perhaps the pail of butter cubes. She knew it was metal and would make a good battering ram. That was when Dani heard the rising applause and commotion, followed by a proclamation.

"You are NOT the father!"

Dani realized she hadn't thrown the remote control far enough. Two hands the size of hams seized Dani around the waist. Dani was pulled off the back of the sofa down onto Tickles' massive, naked lap. Dani recognized that Tickles was sitting back in its peeled backside, and she thought with horror of the bugs that must be trapped and burrowing inside its skin.

"Coochie-coochie the coochie!" Tickles squealed in delight.

Dani gasped as Tickles tickled her body in overdrive with bloated, Bratwurst-sized fingers. Once the gasp was out, she could not get air back in, and hysteria set in. Dani hated getting tickled, absolutely hated it, and she had always set fear into anyone that tried to get his or her wiggly fingers on her. Except for Ian, she had let him get away with it, if only because she had started it by tickling him.

What Tickles was doing went far beyond its name, what it was doing to Dani was a violation. Its assaulting fingers kept wrapping around her breasts, yanking on them. Dani had never experienced a sexual assault like this before, and the shock made her ability to take a much-needed breath even harder. If she had enough air, she would have certainly been screaming, regardless that it might draw Missy's attention. A painful cramp seized her stomach as she tried to fold in on herself.

Tickles' assault on Dani got worse once its hands spread, one clamping over her crotch, the other over her face. Tickles' fingers were trying to probe into every orifice they could find. Dani crossed her legs and tried to twist her crotch away. One of Tickles' fingers probed into her left ear, and then another finger slipped into her mouth. Dani chomped on the fleshy digit hard, and this injury Tickles did feel. The hand pulled back from her face and returned to her chest, since her breasts weren't likely to bite back.

As Dani struggled on Tickles' lap, she realized she had grossly underestimated this hoarder's danger and desires. How often did Tickles have company besides Missy? She thought probably never, despite Tickles' talk of Missy's parties. To have such a pretty young thing as herself in its vicinity, it didn't really matter if Tickles was a man or woman; to it she was a juicy plaything to be seized and fondled. Only Tickles seemed like the type to break all of its toys. She feared she would be eaten alive, smothered, tickled to death, or worst of all, locked in a cage she couldn't get out of.

Tickles giggled and drooled madly as it played its favorite game, coochie-coochie the coochie. The handheld camera smashed into what Dani approximated was Tickles' face, but that didn't stop its laughing. Dani hit Tickles' face again and again with her camera, and Tickles just kept jiggling and giggling. Tickles didn't even bleed from the new lacerations it received. She had to wonder whether Tickles could even bruise under all that fat.

Dani's free hand grabbed for another weapon and came upon the open bag of sugar. She flung the bag at Tickles' face. Tickles cried out in surprise, and it was a cry of delight. The sugar barely reached Tickles' deep-set eyes, and it stuck generously to the drool around its mouth. Tickles' tongue poked out between its non-lips but was not long enough to lick the sugar off.

"Yummy!" Tickles cried as it relentlessly tickled its prey.

Tortured by the tickling, Dani realized that she had neither the size nor strength to harm this half-ton hoarder. It had been partially skinned and still posed a mortal threat. Her flailing left hand hit the overturned bucket, and she changed her plan.

Dani pocketed her camera as she thrashed, remembering she had to keep it protected. Dani's hand dove into the bucket and closed around a cube of butter. She shoved the cube at Tickles, smearing some of it over its face before sticking the cube into its mouth.

Tickles was all too happy to be fed by its guest. It let Dani go so it could finish shoving the cube into its hungry hole, and then it sucked on its buttery fingers.

Dani rolled off of Tickles' lap and landed before its trunk legs, which waved above her. She pushed up and stepped forward, but she was jerked right back. Dani twisted to look over her shoulder.

No longer a complete prisoner to the sofa or its skin, Tickles leaned far forward in order to keep a hold on Dani's hoodie.

Tickles pleaded with a desperation that topped its cries for the remote. "Don't leave!"

Dani pulled away from Tickles as hard as she could, hoping that its buttery fingers would fail to keep hold of her. She considered slipping out of her hoodie, but Tickles' grip included her shirt underneath. She could slip out of both (*a peeling for a peeling*, she regrettably thought), but she would not give it the satisfaction of seeing her in a state of undress. Tickles could jiggle its titties out in the open; she would not.

Tickles' strength was not increased in relation to its size; it was severely decreased. Tickles was not big boned, but big fat. What muscles remained had withered from years of non-use. Muscular atrophy was most pronounced in Tickles' legs, which had not stood due to a lack of feet in over five years.

No longer fused to the sofa, except by the peeled flesh of its backside (which Tickles had no idea had even happened due to a lack of working pain receptors), Tickles was tugged forward as it held onto Dani's hoodie. Tickles leaned over the front cushions of its wide seat and realized too late the serious error of its actions.

Tickles hovered momentarily unbalanced, and then over one half ton of fat pitched forward. Tickles didn't fall so much as roll off of the sofa. The flesh on the back of Tickles' upper thighs ripped down to the knees, and remained connected there. When Tickles hit the ground face first, Dani felt the room shake. She also heard cracking, not from bones, but from the floor, which was straining from the relocated weight. Tickles released Dani's hoodie, and she lunged away.

Dani turned to see the damage done. The fast food refuse beneath Tickles was crushed flat. Tickles blubbered and wailed, arms and half-legs thrashing in its completely impossible effort to get back up. Blood was beginning to pool in the fatty, skinless landscape of Tickles' backside, from the shoulders down past its thighs. From the back of the knees up over the sofa was the red, wet blanket of Tickles' flesh, forever fused in a sitting position.

"Ahhh, help! Missy! Help me up!" Tickles cried out.

Dani got the distinct impression that Tickles was not crying over a mortal injury, but from its newly obstructed view of the television. Dani found the squirming body and its bloody backside repulsive, and she knew her walking into this room had led to this gory and tragic scene. She would feel no guilt, though. Tickles' own unquenched appetites had brought on its demise. Gluttony was Tickles' real killer, not her.

Dani hoped that Tickles didn't feel too much pain, and then she thought of the cruelties inflicted upon the cats in this house, which were the admitted happy pets of both occupants, and she hoped Tickles suffered greatly. Now was the time for the cats to come out of hiding and feast. Their co-tormentor had been opened up like a human food can, leaving the juicy, meaty contents ready for devouring. She hoped the cats would come quickly, while their dinner was warm.

Despite what looked like a mortal injury, Tickles continued to squeal for Missy, pounding its fists against a floor that might not hold much longer beneath it.

Dani knew she didn't have much time or many options left. Tickles' blubbering would certainly have Missy on the move this way. She considered finding some fabric and stuffing it into Tickles' mouth to silence it, and then she changed her mind. She wanted no more contact with this molesting mass. She didn't even want to be within fondling distance.

Dani looked up at the nailed window she had attempted to reach earlier. She could search for something heavy to shatter the glass, but it wasn't wise to remain in the room that Missy was being summoned to. She also wanted to avoid climbing up onto the sofa right above the XXXL human skin suit. She didn't fancy the idea of falling and trying it on for size.

Decided, Dani hurried over the garbage on her way back to the hallway door. As she departed, the last thing she heard was not Tickles' cries, or any further paternity test results. The final sounds to reach her were the meows from a cat food commercial, and the pitch from the announcer.

"Your kitty will come running back for more!"

16

Dani plowed her way back through the hallway hoard. The number of choices she had before her equaled the number of doors. As she came upon the nearly closed door of the mystery room, which she thought of as the indoor graveyard, she didn't give it any real consideration. Despite the deepening crisis, she would exhaust the other options first.

Dani had never had such a strong intuition to avoid a bad place before, but she trusted it. If some primordial, self-preservation instinct was ringing alarm bells in her head, she would be wise to listen and act accordingly. Stop and retreat. The bathroom window was not a desired escape route either, was in fact rife for disaster and disease, but she had a third choice to consider. Dani had passed Missy's bedroom earlier without going inside. Every bedroom had to have a window; she just had to find it.

From the bedroom doorway behind Dani came Tickles' shout. "I hurt! My back burns!"

From the buried staircase ahead of Dani rose Missy's reply, "I'm coming, honey-bunny!"

Dani increased her speed through the channel that wound through the hall. Rising up the slope ahead, Dani saw another baseball camera cap, like the ones she and her friends were wearing. She suspected Missy was wearing Will's hat, but she couldn't wait around to find out. Nor could she get to the bedroom door in time.

Dani slipped into the bathroom doorway and slid across the foul floor. She needed to find a hiding spot fast, at least until Missy made it to Tickles' room, at which time she could duck out of the bathroom. With Missy out of her way, she could take the slide back downstairs and get out through the front door. That beat looking for a window in Missy's room, an escape that would probably be nailed shut anyway.

But where could she hide in this exploded Honey Bucket? She saw the shower curtain, and thinking of the tub of turds with the fossilized cat behind it, she shook her head. That was not an option. The space between the toilet and the door was packed with dirty tissues and wipes, heaped higher than the toilet. On the other side of the toilet was the overflowing sink, which had a limited amount of dark space beneath it. It could hide her, if she cowered back far enough and Missy passed in the hallway fast enough without looking in. Good thing this old-fashioned sink didn't have any cupboards beneath it, like all bathroom sinks she'd ever had.

Dani crouched down before the sink and saw it was dripping in several spots over the rim. Knowing that what was overfilling the sink was meant for the toilet, Dani pulled the hood over her head before she maneuvered underneath the basin.

As Dani turned her crouched body to face the door, she noticed that every shift of her feet caused a squelch from the wet floor beneath her. The tile didn't only sound wet; it felt soft. The toes of her right foot began to feel wet, which wasn't a surprise considering the hole-riddled, secondhand shoes she was wearing. They were her best athletic shoes, but they would be going into the garbage after tonight's excursion. Only fire might be better for her shoes and clothing. From this point on, she would be reluctant to throw anything personal away in a dumpster, in the event a hoarder like Missy might dig through it and keep her no longer personals as their own.

Missy stomped in and out of view in the hallway as she responded to Tickles' cries. "Quit your hollering! I'm almost there!" Missy yelled as she went by. She didn't look into the bathroom.

Dani was relieved to see Missy pass by so quickly, but her relief was very short lived.

There was a wet snapping sound beneath her. She looked down

and saw only the brown, soggy ground. Whatever she heard had to be under, or inside, the floor. She didn't like the sound of it, because it was a sound she could also feel.

Dani forgot the floor as the conversation outside started. She looked desperately at the door, not even seeing the dripping brown sink water an inch in front of her face.

"What happened?!" Missy yelled at her housemate with annoyance. Dani wondered what relation Missy had with Tickles. Her tone was more befitting of a roommate or family member than a spouse, unless their relationship had gone as sour as everything in their refrigerator. Any family resemblance would be beyond her notice; Tickles didn't even resemble its own species.

"I fell! That girl pulled me!" Tickles blubbered, in tears. To Dani they sounded like faux tears, for manipulation and not from pain. She was also personally offended that it was blaming her for its self-inflicted injury.

"What girl?!" Missy shouted back. Dani thought Missy sounded like she was in the hallway outside Tickles' room. She didn't dare move from her moist hiding spot yet.

"The girl filming my reality show!" Tickles shouted back. Dani realized that Missy and Tickles mirrored each other in another way. They shouted everything they said. That was to be expected considering they had to talk over noisy television shows that were nothing but shouting.

There was a wet crack that reverberated through the floor beneath Dani. She looked down and saw herself sinking into the sponge-like, water damaged boards. They were dissolving beneath her.

Dani decided to risk a face to face with Missy over staying under the slushy sink, but she wouldn't get the chance. She gasped as she plunged straight down through the soaked ceiling to the first floor. Chunks of wet brown floor dropped with her. She also, regrettably, unleashed a scream.

17

Dani landed on her back on a wet pile of garbage. The fall wasn't too far, since over half of the room was filled with more hoard. She was stunned and momentarily disoriented, but she considered herself lucky that she hadn't been knocked unconscious. Somehow her camera cap had stayed on during the fall, and her handheld camera still jutted out of her front hoodie pocket. She really should consider a future as a combat photographer or documentarian in crisis situations.

The first thing Dani saw above was the black hole in the ceiling that she had dropped through, dripping brown water and darker brown mush which could either be floor or feces, they had the same smell and consistency. She turned her head to the side to avoid a foul facial from the draining bathroom above her. That simple head turn revealed her ultimate horror, the worst sight she had hoped to never see. A scream might have offered her a modicum of relief, but she couldn't get enough air in to voice it after having it all knocked out of her.

Upon landing, Dani's left hand had ripped through something that felt like a wet paper bag. That bag was actually a dead cat bloated with rot. Her hand had punched through the stomach, which was a slush of rotten innards and maggots. Despite its spoilage, the cat was instantly recognizable to her. It was Fiddlesticks. She even recognized the collar she had personally chosen for her cat, with his name engraved in the paw shaped tag.

"Fiddlesticks!" Dani cried out in horror.

Dani didn't give a thought to Missy or the volume of her voice. Everything had become a spiraling nightmare down into a hoard of death. Dani pulled her hand out of her cat's stomach. She saw more movement than just maggots; the intestines hanging from her hand were squirming. Whatever worms these were, Dani didn't care to know, and she flung the ghoulish guts off of her hand with a shriek. Dani was finally like all of the other girls her age, and she realized she didn't care. Sometimes you just had to give voice to your vulnerability. If it helped her cope, she saw no shame in it.

Dani had to turn her head away from her cat in order to get a grip on herself. She sat up on the bed of garbage to take in her surroundings.

No longer looking up at the ceiling, Dani didn't see Missy looking down through the new hole in the bathroom floor. Missy did not look angrily at her surprise guest or the damage done to her house. She was curious, and surprised to see that Tickles was right. Missy's head departed from the hole above Dani.

The room was nothing more than a massive garbage bin; there was no other visible theme or purpose to it. A mound of broken furniture blocked the door out, the last bulky additions to this room's waste. Getting out meant moving a lot of furniture out of the way. At least there weren't as many furnishings as the hallway that had been clogged end to end.

Dani looked to the other side and saw a large square of aluminum foil on the discolored outer wall. She thought if she were to peel the foil off, she would find a window underneath. Dani clambered quickly over the garbage, foil-bound, no longer hiding her noise. Missy wasn't hiding her noise either, and Dani looked up as she heard Missy stomping overhead, likely through the second floor corridor.

Dani reached the foil patch on the wall, which was over three square feet in size. She peeled the foil in layers, ripping off long strips. It was like a present with never-ending gift-wrapping. Dani counted over a half dozen layers before she found what was beneath, a splintery board which sent one long sliver of wood deep into her right middle finger. The splinter gave no delay as Dani continued ripping foil. The splinter broke off in her finger, but that was okay because now it was out of the way. She could tweeze the rest out later.

Dani discovered the wood belonged to a 2x4 board, nailed horizontally. More tearing revealed more boards secured over the window with rusty nails on the ends. The window they covered was not visible.

"Fuck!" Dani cried out.

Dani grabbed the end of the board that was sticking out the most, and found it loose. She wiggled the board and pulled the rusty nails on one side, and then the other. She wrenched the 2x4 off of the window frame and threw it to the side the same way Missy discarded her garbage, with no thought to where it would land.

Behind the board, the window appeared to be painted black. Dani grabbed the next board down and was frustrated to find it gave no wiggle at all. The 2x4 was nailed down solid. Dani grabbed the bottom of the next board up, her fingers breaking webs in the dark space. A bloated black widow ran off a web and over Dani's hand, and she didn't bother to flick it off. Missy was the bigger black widow she was trying to escape.

The board above was nailed as solidly as the one beneath it. As she struggled to budge a board, Dani could hear the thumps of Missy coming down the staircase. Considering the stairs were so deeply buried beneath clothing, the bangs might have been coming from Missy's hand slamming against the wall to aid her descent.

Dani gave up on the remaining boards, there was no way she was going to pry them loose by hand. She shook her head in denial, and in desperation for another idea.

"Shit!" Dani exclaimed. She'd dealt with and smelled far too much of it tonight. Couldn't see get a break and a breath of fresh air?

Dani looked to the right of the window, where the wall was saturated with wet mold, running down from the ceiling beneath the leaking bathtub. A nearly two square foot section was sunken in with dark rot.

Dani remembered Ian's fall against the basement wall, and how easily his hand had punched through the spoiled structure. She also remembered Ian's claim that they should have dug through the wall instead of breaking the window to get in. What Ian had joked about, she now thought was her best chance at escape. She would dig her way out of Missy's two-story coffin. And to think of how eager she was to get into this house earlier. How naïve she had been.

Dani grabbed onto the board she had discarded. Holding it near one end, careful of the rusty nails, she swung it at the collapsed center of the wall. The nails and board sank into the wall that was the consistency of soft serve ice cream. Pulling the board out, a newly liberated colony of pests fled their toppled tower.

Dani swung the board repeatedly into the wall, using the nails to peel softened wood and knock wet chunks loose. She didn't have to remove the entire wall; she only had to make the hole big enough for her to crawl through, and small enough to prevent Missy's passage.

Dani heard the door open behind her and knew who had come calling. She looked back anyway and saw Missy behind the tall furniture hoard inside the door, which blocked her entry.

"There you are! What are you doing?" Missy questioned from outside the door. Dani found Missy's tone curiously soft, not at all the reaction she expected from a homeowner who had just found an intruder vandalizing her home. Dani didn't care to make friends or conversation with Missy, who she knew as a klepto and a cat killer and who knew what worse things. Escape was all she wanted, and she wailed at the wall with her board.

Missy grabbed the first chair blocking her entrance and threw it behind her. "Don't do that!" Missy yelled, "You're ruining my wall! You can use a door!"

Dani knew the wall was well ruined before she started widening the hole, but she wasn't going to argue the point with Missy. She punched her 2x4 forward and it broke through the rotten outer wall. When she pulled the board back, she could see a glimpse of the yard outside through a ragged hole. The outdoors had never looked more appealing in her life. She had to get on the other side of this wasted wall, into the outside.

"Stay! I can make you a sandwich!" Missy called out to her new playmate. She grabbed onto a card table and yanked it out of the door, its removal triggering an avalanche of TV trays behind it. She tossed the TV trays aside, getting close to having enough space to gain entry into the room, which Missy considered storage and which Dani considered an indoor dump.

As the wet wall was chipped away, a rat leaped out of the hole, in attack for having its home obliterated. Dani didn't know that this rat was also a protecting mother, with a nest of newborns within the wall.

Dani swung the board, impaling the rodent on the rusty nails at the end. Dani cringed at the rat's death shriek, but the sound of thrown furniture behind her distressed her even more. It almost sounded like Missy was on the move within the room, but she could not spare a second to look back and confirm her fear.

Dani beat at the wall in overdrive with the rat impaled board. Flying along with the black mush were little rat babies, juicy balls of pink flesh that burst like tiny blood balloons when the board smashed into them. Dani noticed the nest she was wrecking and became nauseous, and then she didn't care anymore because she could see a few square feet of the yard ahead of her. The hole in the wall was just big enough for her to fit through.

Dani tossed the board to the side with a shudder, revolted that the mother rat had been joined by a few of her babies on the impaling nails. She dove into the hole in the wall, pushing her upper half out of Missy's house.

When Dani's head was finally outside, she marveled at how delicious the outdoor air was. After being trapped in Missy's house and smelling so much shit, piss, mold, rot, and gasses that had to be harmful to a healthy human, her first deep breath of fresh air brought her renewed clarity and strength.

The sweet, life-giving breath was wrenched out of her and her vision became a backwards blur as she was pulled roughly back into the house. Missy had a hold on both of Dani's ankles, and she was pulling her in as she had moved the heavy furniture, very roughly.

Dani grabbed the side of the hole as she passed back through it, and the wet wall came apart in her hands. The hoard was then back in view beneath her. Missy exclaimed one word at her, and it was a plea.

"Wait!"

Dani had no intention of obeying Missy's command, and she kicked her legs wildly. Missy could not keep hold of her thrashing guest, and she lost her grip on Dani's left leg. That leg kicked back into Missy's stomach (the sudden *OOMPH!* she heard from her captor was gratifying), and Dani's right leg was freed.

Dani lunged toward the hole, not caring if her landing on the lawn was a hard one. Dani's head did not make it back outside.

Missy had a thick handful of the back of her hoodie.

"I said stay!" Missy ordered her disobedient guest.

Dani pulled away from Missy, but her shirt had been seized along with her hoodie in Missy's vice-like grip. She could see the hole to the outside world so close, but unreachable.

Dani's clothing was released for a fraction of a second, and then Missy's hands seized the sides of her head. Calloused fingers wrapped around Dani's face. Missy turned Dani's head to the right.

Dani resisted Missy's turning of her vision, but Missy's control was complete. Dani's head turned ninety degrees and then she heard a deep crack, kind of like the snap of wet wood earlier, but much louder since it came from inside of her. Still her eyes were turning, or being forcibly turned, and then Dani saw Missy face to face. That vision of Missy, looking satisfied at finally having control, froze in Dani's mind before the image faded into a blinding light. That brightness flashed off like a broken bulb, and Dani never saw anything ever again.

What Dani's eyes could no longer see, the camera on her cap continued to film in close-up. Missy's satisfaction had turned to glee.

Missy let go of Dani's head, and the dead teenager slumped down on the hoard before her. She thought the girl's glassy eyes looked like pretty doll eyes.

"There! I told you not to leave yet. I want you to film me for a show, too!"

Missy could not believe her luck. It was almost like a party, having so many young people in her house again. It was a party for her, with cameras, which meant the whole world was invited.

Missy knew that her love of parties was in large part due to her lack of them growing up. Parties were fun, and her parents had not one fun bone between them. Growing up in this house had been such a lonely and dreary affair for her. No parties, no friends allowed inside to contaminate the house with their germs, not even one television, which she thought might be criminal for parents to deny a growing child.

The whole huge house had been practically bare growing up, with few furnishings, no art on the walls, and no toys for Missy to leave out and cause a clutter. In her opinion, the house had looked as bare as a mausoleum, and was about as much fun.

Missy knew her parents had been crazy in their cleanliness, and she had justifiably revolted against their compulsions. They had not been poor, but they had been so cheap, the use of electricity inside the house had been severely limited. As a result, the house had been frightfully dark growing up, and Missy's skin had also been dark with the endless bruises she acquired bumping into things she couldn't see. Her bedroom never had one light bulb in it. If it was dark outside, it was dark inside, and time for boring bed.

Missy thought of the first third of her life as her Dark Ages.

Missy's first party had been for her eighteenth birthday, and it had initially been against her parents' wishes. But they had finally come around and allowed her. It was only a shame that they had not been able to attend, due to the accident they suffered just hours before it started.

Her parents had been mopping the upstairs landing together, giving it a pre-party shine, and it had been just so horrible how the mop water had spilled and they had taken a bad slip and tumbled down those treacherous wooden stairs and broken both of their scrawny necks and fragile skulls. She had even managed to shed some tears. Only the paramedics didn't know that they were tears of joy. She encouraged them to remove the bodies quickly. She had a party planned, after all.

Missy thought of the night of her eighteenth birthday as her Golden Dawn.

Missy had no friends to invite to her seminal birthday party, but less than one hour after her parents were removed on shrouded stretchers, the Sears delivery man had arrived with her first color television set. He even helped her set it up and showed her how to operate it, an added gift for the birthday girl. She could stay up all night now and watch shows she had only heard about, while discovering others that really tickled her fancy, like Donahue's, and Springer's, and that handsome Geraldo's.

The lights were turned on all over the house (after bulbs were screwed into all of the empty sockets), so she could appreciate its size and splendor for the first time. The house did look kind of bland, but she had all the time in the world to decorate it to her liking, and fill it with all of her favorite things. Missy the collector was born.

Missy's house had not been cleaned once since her Golden Dawn began. The crazy clean freaks had given birth and rise to a crazier filth freak.

In Missy's mind, the party that started that night had never ended. Only tonight was an all new kind of party, a surprise party!

Missy turned Dani's body around so it was facing her, although Dani's head was turned at an owlish angle. She figured that Keith and this girl were actually working, filming their reality shows. They were lucky though, because even working inside Missy's house was like a party.

Missy was eager to take control of this big Hollywood production. Tickles might be a camera whore, but she was the real star of the show. And it was her house. Unfortunately, this young girl with the camera tucked into her front pocket was a lazy sleepybones like Keith in the kitchen. Oh well, she'd use their break time to doll herself up for the cameras. She would have gussied herself up earlier if she had known they were coming. She might have even swept up a little. Or prepared them all dinner.

Missy grabbed onto Dani's hood and dragged her over the hoard toward the door. Now that she had her, she had to watch her. Missy didn't want this girl waking up and running back upstairs to film Tickles again.

Missy wanted the girl to come along for her beauty treatment. Maybe she'd even share some of her beauty secrets with her. The girl was looking a little peaked.

As Missy pulled the hood of the hoodie, Dani's body slid on her back toward the door with her head twisted to the side. Dani's nose passed within inches of Fiddlestick's ruptured remains. The camera on her cap got a good passing close-up of the cat's squirming insides.

Missy dragged her new playmate through the newly cleared doorway. The door they came out of was near the bottom of the staircase, and had previously gone unnoticed by Dani and her friends due to a large tapestry that hung over it.

Missy dragged Dani's body up the clothing packed stairs. She had no problem with the weight she was dragging, her grocery bags usually weighed more than this skinny little sweet. They needed to serve better meals in Hollywood. This girl weighed about as much as the leaves in the salads she probably ate for breakfast, lunch, and dinner. She'd have to make this girl a jiffy meal later, maybe something with ham, and hopefully she'd be more appreciative than Keith.

"If we're filming my reality show, I want to put on my good dress first!" Missy squealed to her new friend. Missy stopped for a moment to pick up a dirty, tattered red garment off of the stairs, and then she continued upward with her new friend in one hand and her good dress in the other.

18

Ian's disobedience brought him over the top lip of the basement staircase back into the kitchen. He heard more garbage roll down the steep slope behind him, but he didn't bother to look back. He only hoped the clamor wasn't loud enough to draw Missy. The fact that Missy had not been summoned to the rolling radiator was surprising. He guessed she was used to the sounds of her house crumbling. The structure's wrecked condition could not have come about quietly.

As Ian entered the kitchen, he saw the black clothing and hoodie of a body lying motionless on the garbage ahead, before the refrigerator. His soul sank as he crossed the kitchen in a hurry. When Ian saw his fallen comrade was Keith, his stomach headed in the opposite direction of his soul, and he struggled to keep its contents down. He had to keep everything inside and stay in control. Keith was depending on him now.

And Ian wasn't the type to leave a yucky mess or bad smell in somebody else's house, especially not in their kitchen. That would be rude.

Keith wasn't moving. He didn't even appear to be breathing. Ian's soul sank further, and he recognized what he was feeling wasn't panic. It was dread.

Ian crouched next to his brother. "Keith", he said, and shook him. Relief flooded him just to feel his brother was warm.

Ian got down on his hands and knees to lean closer to Keith, turning an ear to his brother's mouth. He definitely didn't like the look of Keith's busted, blood caked nose, which canted alarmingly to the left. Keith breathing was only noticeable up close, and Ian heard a wet, gurgling sound deep inside Keith's chest. He didn't like that gurgling and the internal injuries it alluded to, but at least there was some sound of life.

Ian tilted Keith's head to the side. Keith's nose and mouth leaked blood, but more air got in and Keith's breathing deepened. Only Keith's consciousness remained elusive.

"Come on," Ian goaded his brother. Perhaps he should be a bigger pest, as younger brothers do so well. He could call Keith a sissy or pansy and pester him back to consciousness. He was about to call him Rip Van Stinkle when Keith began coughing up blood. Ian patted Keith's back and helped him sit up; it was too soon for Keith to stand.

Keith's return to consciousness had him cataloguing his numerous hurts as he coughed on blood and what tasted like bile. His nose had felt broken by Dani's shoe plant in the basement. Now his nose felt shattered, like he had snorted thin shards of broken glass. Some of those glass needles felt like they'd made it down into his lungs.

Next on his injury list, Keith's right cheek throbbed and felt split on the inside, plus the molars beneath felt loose in their sockets. That must have been where Missy had knocked him out, although he couldn't remember how. He had been hurrying away from Missy and her shit sandwich and then *WHAM!* Perhaps she had smashed him in the face with a toaster, swinging the appliance by its cord, that's how bad the damage felt.

Keith's worst injury had thankfully gone nearly numb, and that was his broken left wrist. When he glanced at it lying beside him at such an unnatural angle, the numbness became a painful, cold pressure, and he had to look away. Better not to see or feel it.

When Keith turned his mind away from his numerous agonies, he thought of their inflictor. They had all underestimated Missy and her capacity for violence. Keith remembered how much quieter Missy's voice had been when she turned violent on him. Gone was the he-he ha-ha hollering that was her normal, playful, and ever annoying kiddy voice. When she got serious, her tone had turned soft and seething. Gone were all niceties when she got down to business, the business of delivering pain.

Worse yet, Keith had received all of his life threatening injuries when he was Missy's friend. What might she do if she saw him as her enemy, which is what he really was? Good thing she was too lonely and loony to see it.

As Keith spit out the blood that was choking him, he saw something green and slimy on the ground of garbage. It looked like a slice of Missy's ham, and then he could smell it, too. It didn't smell like ham anymore. It was enough to trigger the taste of what he had been force fed, Missy's Puke Plate Special. He quickly leaned over to regurgitate his last meal, bracing his right hand on the ground for balance.

Ian sat back from Keith to avoid getting any upchuck on him. Normally the sight of somebody vomiting disgusted him, but he only felt relief that Keith was conscious and able to void the bad stuff from his system. Then he saw the disturbing angle of Keith's left hand, and his relief disappeared. Keith's wrist was swelling and turning red. There also seemed to be a bone sitting entirely the wrong angle, stretching the skin taut as it pushed for release. It was the kind of injury that needed a doctor right away if there was going to be any hope of it healing correctly. He didn't want to see Keith gimped for life.

Following the blood and vomit, Keith got a mouthful of the burning bile again. He welcomed the fiery fluid; it neutralized the taste of the horrid ham.

"Water," Keith said in a raspy whisper. It was the only voice he could muster.

Ian snapped into action and instinctively grabbed the refrigerator door handle. Remembering what festered behind the door (not that he'd ever be able to forget it), he knew any liquid in that sea of spoilage would only poison his brother further. He let the door handle go with difficulty; the sticky handle did not want to let go of him.

Ian looked for the sink and remembered he hadn't been able to find it earlier. Every counter was buried by the hoard up to the cupboards. The sink could be anywhere. If he dug for it he knew he'd find the sink eventually, but it could be counted on not to work. That he also remembered from the hoarder shows he watched. *The sink broke* was an excuse a majority of hoarders used to justify the shameful state of their kitchens.

Keith was wracked with dry gagging, and Ian saw that the precious little spittle he was spraying was actually blood. Ian's worry worsened as he looked around the kitchen. Water was his brother's one request, and from the sounds he was making, he desperately needed it. Water was such a simple request and life supporting element, and it was obscene to him that something so necessary could be completely missing from Missy's house, or at least missing from the room where it should have been the most easily accessible.

If he couldn't find water, some other drink would have to suffice. The kitchen was generously filled with aluminum soda cans, but they were all empty, making a mockery of their dire situation.

Ian spotted a translucent soda cup with its lid and straw intact, two inches of stale liquid at the bottom. He grabbed it with relief and peeled off the lid. The cup's limited contents was neither liquid nor slush, it was a solid.

Ian tossed the cup aside with frustration and gave voice to his worry. "There's no water. There's nothing to drink, nothing safe."

Keith was finally getting his heaving under control, and he spit out one last bloody glob from his throat, which landed right before Ian's shoes.

"Sorry," Keith rasped out.

"That's okay, I'm used to your bad breath," Ian ribbed him.

Keith appreciated the jab and managed a minor smile. He sat up on his knees to test his balance. He looked down and saw his handheld camera was still sticking out of the hoodie pocket, recording. Keith couldn't believe his luck at that. The footage of Missy's attempted murder of him would be priceless when Missy finally went on trial. The whole world would, and should, get to see inside Missy's house and just how bat-shit crazy she was.

Keith had been relieved to find Ian at his side when he had come to, felt he needed it in fact, but the grim reality of their situation returned and disappointment at Ian's disobedience set in. Keith did not want Ian to cross paths with the impossibly strong madwoman of the house. Ian didn't know how violent she was, although he might make an educated guess based on the sorry state he'd found his brother in.

Keith had also suffered, and was still suffering a number of outrageous injuries in order for his younger brother to get to safety, yet here Ian was sitting at the scene of the crimes.

Keith could not be mad at Ian's decision. It wasn't meant as disobedience, he recognized it was an act of love, and love always made people do foolish things. And had their roles and ages been reversed, he would have done the same. They were in this nightmare house together, and they had to help each other get out.

"What are you still doing here? I told you to get out," Keith scolded Ian anyway.

"I'm not leaving you."

Keith might frequently be hard on his brother, but he knew he was smart. Hopefully, Ian's smarts would not falter in a terrifying, life threatening situation like this. Only Keith considered himself smart, and Will as well, and it hadn't helped them much. Remembering Will's fate, Keith's heart hurt.

"Where's Dani?" Keith asked with renewed worry. Dani was a strong girl, the toughest one he knew. Dani might even be stronger than his mother, who had recently shown a surprising amount of fortitude and strength following the abandonment of her husband and his father. So Dani was a tough cookie, but Missy was the butcher baker. He had barely survived his encounter with Missy; how would Dani fare in a grudge match with her? He hoped Dani had gotten out before she could find out.

"I don't know. I think I heard her scream. It sounded like the whole house was coming apart," Ian replied.

That was not at all what Keith wanted to hear, but he hoped the house was indeed coming apart, and even better if Dani had triggered its collapse.

"I hope it is. I hope this house sinks into the ground. Where is that bitch?"

"I heard stomping upstairs, just before you came to."

Keith and Ian looked up at the water stained ceiling. There was no sound of movement above them now. Keith hoped that Missy's stomping wouldn't send her through her rotten floor on top of them. He didn't want to be sat on again.

19

Missy stood before her dresser mirror so she could inspect her good dress. The reflective surface, along with every surface in her bedroom, was sprinkled in colorful glitter. There were also smudges of make-up, dried blood, and shit on the mirror she admired herself in. She didn't mind the mess on the mirror. It took a lot of hard work to get looking this good.

The red dress that had replaced her shopping outfit was extra tight and torn, with her sore spotted flesh bulging out of the tears. It hadn't been this tight when she had worn it last, a few months ago (actually eight years), but she was a more voluptuous woman now, so that was to be expected. She didn't mind the new tears in it either. So what if she showed off a little more skin? The viewing audience always wanted to see more flesh, and she hoped deep down inside her fallopian tubes that her new playmate Keith would, too.

The dress that could barely contain Missy was decorated with neglect, namely food, footprints, and skid marks. Missy didn't see these stains, all she saw was her favorite color red behind them. All this red made her feel hot, like a Red Hots candy, and she knew all the boys liked to suck on Red Hots!

Missy loved her outfit, but her favorite accouterment was her new one. Normally she would tease out her hair, high and wide, because big hair was like a turkey's display of pretty tail feathers; it was a way to attract a mate. But that cap she had found in the living room was so cool, with the deely bobber on the brim. She recognized it as the same cap that the crew kids in her house were wearing. If she wore on her show the same thing all the kids were wearing nowadays, maybe they'd think she was their age, too.

Missy appraised her outfit from head to toes (those were mostly covered in sneakers that had both big toes sticking out). She looked so good she turned herself on!

"Oh lookie-lookie-lee! America will love me!"

Missy gave her reflection a sultry wiggle and giggled. Her outfit was red hotsy-totsy, but she was far from done. She had to put on her face.

Missy looked at the make-up spread across her dresser. Uncapped lipstick, open rouge, empty eye shadow trays, and dripping tubes of foundation numbered in the hundreds, all generously sprinkled with glitter and rat scat. Much of the make-up was used up, but she found some of her reddest rouge, uncapped, and applied it to her cheeks to clown-like levels, using her fingers instead of an applicator or brush.

"I love to wear and eat red!" And she meant it, as she sucked the rouge off of her fingertips.

Missy picked up an uncapped lipstick she considered a beautiful (blood) red. She applied it to her lips, and much of her face around her lips. More red always looked better. The lipstick was dropped, bounced off an empty bottle of nail polish remover, and tipped over the edge of her make-up table, landing in an empty Styrofoam cup. Missy was too busy to notice little things like that, busy puckering at her reflection. She blew herself a kiss, caught it, and ate it back up messily, turning her fingertips red again.

Now that her face was all done, Missy wanted a second opinion. She looked to the side, where Dani's body was propped up on an askew folding chair. Dani sat to the side on the chair, but her twisted head was pointed toward Missy. Dani's head was tilted back, eyes open wide and rolled up in their sockets. A line of red ran from the lower left corner of her lips, starting to dry and draw flies, or *baby butterflies* as Missy called them.

"What do you think?" Missy asked her girlfriend. She puckered her lips with her arms over her head, posing like the old fashion pin-up model she knew she was. Dani's response was obvious from her wide-eyed stare; she was very impressed.

"You want some, too?" Missy asked the girl that Tickles had called Sally. The girl had a bit of make-up on, a line of red lipstick streaking down from her nose and the side of her mouth, what Missy thought of as a punk rock style. But besides that, Sally seemed too pale.

Since the girl didn't object, Missy went ahead and shared her make-up. She smeared rouge on Dani's cheeks with her fingers first. That certainly helped the girl look more cheerful. The best thing about sharing make-up was she got to suck on her red fingertips again.

Missy looked for the lipstick. She didn't see it on the table anywhere. That was weird, since she never misplaced anything.

A disturbing thought gnawed at the back of Missy's mind. What if this girl had swiped her lipstick? Maybe she'd have to search the film crew when they were finished. Kids were always stealing things these days, and they liked to stash their booty in their underpants. But Missy was wise to them, and there was nowhere a curious bird like her wouldn't peck. Including their underpants.

The girl needed some color on her lips, so Missy leaned over, took Dani's head in her hands, and planted a big kiss on her lips, rubbing them together to get a good transfer of color. Missy considered herself a very generous person to share like that.

Missy sat back and considered her girlfriend, whose head was cocked to the side. The girl looked a lot more colorful now. Missy noticed that some of the girl's red punk make-up had transferred to her lips, as well. Her tongue licked some of the new red to get a taste of the girl. She tasted kind of bitter.

Missy and her girlfriend were now both Red Hots, but their last piece was missing, hundreds of little pieces actually. Missy scooped up a handful of glitter from a plastic freezer bag and applied it to her face and hair. She did not shake it over her head like a soft rain; she threw it hard into her face like a snowball. A second handful of glitter was scooped up and thrown onto her girlfriend. Hopefully, Sally would thank her later for her sparkling generosity. Glitter wasn't cheap.

Dani didn't blink, despite getting glitter on her eyeballs.

Missy decided this special event, the filming of her premiere episode, was worth it. She grabbed a third handful of glitter and threw it at them both.

"We sparkle!"

20

The situation had changed. Keith conceded failure in his original mission, but he would triumph in a new endgame. While he appreciated Ian sticking around to help, his brother's part in this was done. Ian had to get out of Missy's house now. He would join Ian outside once his plan had been executed along with the homeowner.

"You need to go, Ian. Through the basement."

"No way. I'm not going back down there," Ian responded resolutely.

The more Keith's head cleared from his knockout in Missy's ring, the more it was clouded by rage at his opponent. He didn't care how much the delusional harridan harped about their lovey-dovey relationship. That crazy bitch had tried to kill him, had nearly succeeded, in fact. That made them closer than friends or lovers. Their dance with mortality would end with her death.

Keith was not selfish in his desire for murder. He was going to prevent what had happened to him, and Will, from happening to Dani and Ian. He and Will were the biggest and strongest of their group, and Missy and her hoard had bowled them over like they were nothing. He didn't think the weaker ones stood a chance at surviving an encounter with Missy. Missy - her name was deceiving, because it played her down. She was Monsoon.

On his feet, wobbly as they were, Keith lurched to the utensils pile. He looked the record size selection over and pulled out an eight-inch butcher knife with his right hand. His left hand wasn't grabbing anything, hanging limp at his side, the wrist swollen to twice its size and a few shades darker red.

Keith looked over the blade. It was dirty with grease, shredded meat, and rat droppings, but it was long and wide. It would do fine. The blade's cleanliness played no part here, but its dirtiness did. Should Missy somehow survive a deep stab of this blade, infection could be the follow-up killer.

Ian didn't like the look of the butcher knife in his brother's hand. He knew what Keith intended it for. Ian still had to ask and hear it for himself. "What's that for?"

"She tried to kill me. And she broke my fucking wrist."

Ian thought that wasn't an explanation, it was justification.

"You should protect yourself, too," Keith added.

Ian looked at Keith's gruesomely twisted wrist and understood they were up against a considerable foe. He also had complete confidence that should this big bully woman come after him, he would have the litheness and speed to get away from her. He didn't think he needed a knife for himself. Keith was seriously injured though, and might not have the ability to get out of her way. He recognized he was his older brother's protector now. A knife was a necessity and he grabbed one, although the blade he selected was smaller than his brother's and easier for him to handle.

Ian was not surprised to find his knife dirty. Finding a clean utensil in this kitchen would be near impossible. The blade was caked with what might have been stale refried beans, or refried shit. It smelled more like the latter.

Ian looked up and saw that Keith had maneuvered to the entrance to the dining room. He started after him and shouted just loud enough for him to hear. "Wait up!"

Keith did not wait up. Instead, he sped up. "Don't follow me."

Ian defied his brother again, but that had been their lifelong pattern. They both expected and accepted it; it was part of their bond. Keith wanted this to be a one-man mission, but Ian knew they were in it together. They both had Dani at the forefront of their minds.

Ian picked up his pace and made up some ground on his brother. He kept looking over Keith's shoulders, on the lookout for the beast in their midst, although that wasn't entirely true. They were in the beast's midst. They did not have home/hoard advantage, and that put them at a serious disadvantage. They did not intimately know the paths and corners of this hoard, nor had they built up the legs for it.

What worried Ian the most was that Keith was not trying to keep under cover. He was a walking target. Keith was already on the climb that would take them into the living room, and he might as well have a trumpet to announce his arrival. It appeared Keith intended to charge and stab on sight, and that seemed like a bad plan. This was escalating way too fast.

Ian followed at Keith's heels up into the living room. Had Ian been in the lead, he would have slithered up the slope like a snake and peeked over the edge first, preferring to strike unannounced.

Ian stopped beside Keith on the edge of the living room, the terrible room that had taken the life of one of their closest friends. They looked around, Ian with worry, Keith with frustration. There was no sign of Missy.

Ian's worry didn't dissipate just because Missy wasn't in the room. He couldn't let his brother go through with his deadly vendetta. Keith might think it was justified, and he did too for that matter, but Ian coldly suspected that whatever trial came of this horrible fiasco they found themselves in, Keith would be prosecuted for his actions. They were clearly the victims, but they were also trespassing and wearing hoodies. The world and the juries were too frequently unfair about that. Plus, Ian had already suffered the loss, through abandonment, of his father this year. He couldn't imagine how he or their mother could deal with Keith's removal from their lives through imprisonment, or his mother's grief if he were locked up as well. He was accompanying his brother on this criminal mission that was leading to a murder.

Keith located the clothing packed staircase and climbed that way. Traversing the immense and difficult room took a lot of careful maneuvering in order for Keith to not hit his broken wrist hanging uselessly at his side. He had to use the knuckles of his right hand for balance, as his fingers remained tightly clenched around the handle of the butcher knife.

Perhaps if Ian could get Keith to admit to his murder plan first, it might be harder for him to execute his plan and his target. "What are you planning to do?" Ian asked.

Keith didn't answer. His eyes had fallen on the shrouded body of Will, who was more family than friend. The covering and pizza box over Will were dented grotesquely. Ian's eyes saw the same thing and he shared in a moment of cruel silence. Keith could not control the fury in his voice, which bordered on breaking.

"Just head for the door and wait for me outside. I don't want you to be a part of this."

Ian wasn't surprised that Keith couldn't put his killing plan into words, and he deeply believed that Keith really wouldn't, and couldn't, go through with it. Keith was not the type to fight. The only two scrap matches he could remember Keith getting into were provoked by another party, and in both instances Keith had been defending others. And neither of them had ever been hunting, it had never even been a consideration for them, which was why the image of Keith the killer was such a disturbing thought. He couldn't take Keith's order to abandon him, since he had to stick around to protect him. The easiest way to do that would be to talk Keith out of his rage fueled revenge plot.

All of Ian's reasons for escape went out the window, assuming a window could be found, when he remembered Dani's scream, which had definitely been inside the house. And Keith knew it, too. So maybe they did have to search through this deadly maze for her, but they would be much safer if they proceeded in a creepy-crawl to avoid detection.

Keith got up from his grieving spot and continued his one armed climb toward the steep slope. He leaned toward a tall speaker and was about to put his knuckles against the top when he saw the entire surface was a dumping ground for cat shit. His knuckles caught the side of the speaker for support. As he moved past it, he realized his shattered nose did have one special benefit. He couldn't smell the cat shit, or any of the noxious smells inside Missy's house anymore. That or he was just getting used to the stench, which was a more unsettling thought.

Ian followed in his brother's path, which was the safest way to travel through a hoard like this. While Keith only looked ahead, Ian looked to the right, and his fear was immediate.

They had made a big mistake in forgetting Missy's nest. It was more than deep enough to conceal her from view. She could be sitting down there, listening to them revealing their plans. They had to be more careful than that.

Ian ventured seven uneven steps to the right in order to look down into the nest. Missy had thankfully flown the coup.

Ian quickly retraced his steps and followed his brother again. Since they were alone, he had something to say. "I am a part of this. I can't leave without Dani either."

Keith paused, braced his right knuckles against a box, and looked over his shoulder at Ian. "If she hurt Dani…" Keith began, and his single-minded purpose turned him back ahead. He spoke without looking back at Ian; he had to keep climbing. "I'm stopping her. Then we get Will out, and burn this hell house down."

Ian noticed that Keith had said *we* instead of *I*. That meant his brother had finally accepted him on this grim mission. They were at war together. At war inside a suburban house just a few miles from their apartment. How could they be so close to home and so far from safety? Enemy territory could be a few streets away, or right next door.

Ian liked Keith's idea of a fire. It would be a mercy for the land the house stood on. He was also beginning to think they might be wise to fuel the fire with their cameras. The footage could turn poisonous, and despite Missy's many cruelties on display, they were planning a murder on the same tapes. Footage could be the ultimate evidence used to convict them.

"And burn our cameras," Ian added. Keith didn't object, which Ian hoped meant he was considering his suggestion.

Keith arrived at the bottom of the second slope. The clothing slide was disorienting to look up, and he momentarily swooned. The living room, or any room, was hard enough to climb through. This loose fabric slide looked like it was going to be a new kind of bitch to climb. To add to the difficulty, this slope looked steeper and taller than the basement incline. Keith wasn't surprised, considering the living room ceiling was exceptionally high.

Keith started up on both knees and the knuckles of his right hand, keeping the butcher knife pointed to the outside. If he slipped, he didn't want the blade beneath him.

Ian followed Keith up the slope, giving himself a few feet of separation. In case Keith slipped, Ian didn't want a shoe planting on his face. His brother had already taught him that lesson through example.

Keith didn't crawl so much as scoot up the staircase. There was not one stable step or hold to be had, and every push upward threatened to send him sliding back down. He was trying to climb with one broken wrist, but had he the use of all four limbs, he figured the climb would still be extremely difficult.

Keith made it nearly halfway up the slope before his first major slip, as he crawled over a silky, flesh colored girdle. He fell flat on his belly, his left elbow hitting the slope but not his broken hand. Regardless, the vibration from his elbow's impact killed in his wrist, which was no longer numb. His slide back down started immediately.

Ian saw Keith's slip and slide, and he shifted to the side to get out of the way. He needn't have bothered.

With his right hand full and nothing solid to grab onto, Keith stabbed his knife down. The blade penetrated many layers of dirty clothes and held on the step buried beneath, stopping Keith's slide and giving him purchase on the buried stairs again.

Once his feet found spots to brace against and he was certain his position was secured, Keith pulled the knife out and stabbed higher with it. He used his right arm to pull himself up a foot. It was a slow and strenuous process, but it appeared the safest way to proceed. Keith continued using the butcher knife like a climbing pick to ascend the slope.

Seeing his brother resume his climb, Ian continued up behind him. He managed only a few feet before he stopped. There was something stuck to the bottom of his right hand, likely some small article of clothing. He feared it might be a soiled panty. Ian turned his hand palm and garment up. It wasn't a panty.

Ian tried to tell himself what was stuck to his hand was some kind of rag or handkerchief, and it had been used to clean up raspberry jam or spilled nail polish. Then he realized the garment was a doily. Ian suppressed a gag when he finally admitted to himself it wasn't jam or nail polish on the doily. It was blood.

Ian slowly peeled the blood-saturated doily off of his hand, and this time he did gag. It was as sticky as the refrigerator door handle, and left some of its residue on him. Ian had to wonder how Missy's doily had gotten bloody in the first place. Was it her blood, or cat's blood, or another unfortunate guest's? Considering its partial freshness, he knew the bloody doily had been dropped recently. The thought *feminine hygiene* occurred to him, and he immediately regretted it. The mystery of the bloody doily was the kind of queasy question that would nag at him till his last day.

Once the doily was freed, Ian flung it to the side with revulsion. The bloody doily stuck to the wall.

"Gross me out."

Ian took a moment to wipe the clotted palm of his hand on the clothing beside him. He didn't worry about leaving Missy's clothes a mess; they had been deposited that way. He saw that some of the blood remained in the lines and pores of his fingers and would need to be scrubbed off with soap and some very hot water. Boiling maybe. Followed by a splash of bleach.

Ian realized he had probably fallen far behind his brother. He couldn't even hear Keith's stab and slide anymore. Ian looked up.

Keith had not advanced a good distance above Ian. He had come down, very close. Too close. Keith wasn't sliding, but his right shoe came down fast. The shoe didn't land on Ian's face, it landed on his right shoulder. Keith wasn't kicking to hurt Ian, but he applied enough pressure to knock Ian off of his spot and send him sliding all the way down.

Keith didn't wait around to see where Ian landed. He hauled his sliding ass up the slope with renewed urgency.

At the bottom, Ian looked up incredulous. "Wait!" Ian cried up.

"Get out!" Keith called back just before he crawled over the top lip of the staircase.

Ian didn't want to argue, they had already shouted too much when they needed to be silent and not summon their foe. And that had been his stupid fault for shouting first, an emotional reaction. Ian didn't feel bossed around by his brother, he felt betrayed. This was no longer about sibling rivalry. This was about Dani, and she might need them both. Keith had only one hand to help, while Ian had two.

Ian started his climb up the clothing for a second time. He increased his speed, which only made him slip and slide back more.

21

Keith felt bad for forcing a separation with his brother, with a kick from above, but he didn't regret his decision. Confronting Missy was something he had to do alone, and he didn't want his brother to see their reunion play out. Keith did have a death wish, only the death he wished for was not his own.

Keith didn't just fear that Ian would be traumatized by what he saw if he stuck around, he also feared for Ian's safety. He saw stepping into this confrontation with Missy the same as if he were to jump the fence and trespass into the gorilla sanctuary at the zoo. They were already inside the gorillas' cage, and the mean mother ape was ahead, possibly around the corner. If forced to choose between a face to face with Missy or a large gorilla, he would undoubtedly pick the primate. Gorillas could be mean, but they were predictable in their behavior and survival instincts. Missy was completely off her rocker and more dangerous due to her delusions and unpredictability.

Keith momentarily thought of Missy as a baby giant that had no idea her strength could hurt people. Humans were the giant's playthings, and this giant broke her toys all the time. Her house was cluttered with the broken pieces.

Keith realized that Missy and the gorillas were startlingly alike in another way. They both liked to throw their shit all over the place, where they slept and where they ate. Marking their territory.

Once off the staircase, Keith was faced with the cluttered second floor corridor. He saw two open doors on the left, one closed door on the right, and an open door at the end, from which he could hear the sounds of another television cranked loud. Keith figured his best chance for finding Missy would be to follow the sounds of occupancy. Keith hurried ahead, giving only a quick, cursory glance into the two open doors on the left. He didn't look long enough into the bathroom to see the hole in the floor that Dani had fallen through.

Keith had to hurry with his plan if he didn't want Ian as a witness. He had shoed Ian away literally, with a shoe, but Keith expected the kid would scurry right back up the stairs in continued pursuit despite his order to get out. So he decided not to waste time checking the closed door on the right, and he passed it on his way to the open door at the end. Ian might only be a minute behind him, or less, and he wanted to get this ugly business over with before he lost his nerve. Once he removed Missy from the picture, from the land of the living, the worry would end, and they could work on freeing the cats and removing Will before torching the place.

The damage done to Keith's nose kept him from noticing the particularly ripe smell that emanated from the back bedroom, and it kept him from noticing the new scent that had joined it, the coppery smell of freshly spilled blood, the smell of a slaughterhouse. Keith didn't hesitate for a second in stomping over the threshold.

Keith came to a sudden stop in the back bedroom. He didn't see Missy; he saw something far worse. Keith thought he should have taken his own advice to Ian and hightailed it out of the house. He had never seen such a horrible sight in all his life, and it paralyzed him.

Ninety-eight seconds after his brother had done the same, Ian climbed over the top lip of the slope into the upstairs corridor. He stood on the lopsided surface and studied his surroundings.

Keith was nowhere in sight.

"Damn it," Ian said softly to himself.

Ian was correct in his earlier assessment of the upstairs climate.

It was like an oven. He guessed the temperature had jumped another ten degrees from the hotbox below, maybe more. He felt uncomfortably damp all over: his face, his neck, his shirt and underarms, his under shorts. Maybe that was a good thing, the sweat might clean the poisons out of his pores. At least he didn't smell his nervous sweat. The stench of Missy's house was the dominant perfume.

Ian needed to cool off a bit, but he didn't want to unzip his hoodie in here. He pushed his hoodie sleeves up over his elbows, and it provided a bit of relief. He accepted it and moved on.

There were four doors ahead of Ian. He'd check each one he passed until he found his brother. Keith had to be close. He just had to be quiet about it. Shouting for Keith was out.

Ian came upon the first open door on the left and looked inside. He figured the sparkling hoard within was a bedroom, one that looked like it belonged to a little girl. Which meant this was probably Missy's room. Missy was far from little or a girl, but her mental state had her locked in a perpetual state of giddy childhood. This colorful chaos fit her personality.

Ian studied the room from the doorway. He could see the make-up table and the mirror where Missy put on her face. The leaning chair remained beside the table, but Dani's corpse was no longer sitting on it. There was nobody visible inside.

Ian started to turn away from Missy's bedroom when he spotted movement to the far left of the room. He turned back to investigate.

To the left was a mound of multi-colored blankets, which might have covered a bed. It was a mass of sheets, comforters, a spring flower bedspread, a wool blanket, and an electric blanket with a frayed power cord sticking up like an antenna. Sitting on top was a shit and glitter covered cage, and inside the cage was a hairless, shit and glitter covered cat. This cat slunk around its limited confines with its head down. The sight was pathetic, and it made Ian's heart feel smothered with sharp edged, piercing glitter.

Ian wondered why there would be a cage on Missy's unmade bed, if it were a bed. He saw pillows to the left of the cage, so his assumption was probably right. Little girls often slept with their stuffed animals or pets, and Missy was a big little girl. In Missy's case, the pet had to be confined behind bars to prevent its escape.

"I hate cats," Ian tried to convince himself. And it was partly true. Ian was more of a dog person. He had never met a dog he didn't like. Cats, on the other hand, didn't care if you liked them or not, they were much more critical and cold to the humans that harbored them. In Missy's house, the kitty's hate was more than justified. Regardless that he would never keep a cat as a pet, he couldn't bear to see this sad creature, covered in celebratory glitter, suffer like this for one moment longer.

Putting his mission to find Keith and Dani on hold, just for a minute, Ian entered Missy's bedroom and climbed the hoard to save a small animal that might die without him.

22

Keith ventured slowly forward in the back bedroom, trying to comprehend what he was seeing, as well as how to react to it without losing his wits. His initial, honest reaction was a coward's response, to just spin where he stood and beat a fast retreat out of the room and Missy's house. Who cared if his buddies laughed or teased him? They hadn't seen what he was seeing. Only his buddies wouldn't laugh because Will was dead downstairs, Dani had been heard screaming and was missing, and Ian would be at his heels in no time and also be a witness to this mind-shattering scene.

Keith had to keep his plan in motion and keep control in the face of this unimaginable horror. Loved ones were depending on him.

The shouting from the television briefly took Keith's attention. The same host from the show downstairs was acting as a referee between two trailer park hussies in a hair pulling catfight over some skin and bones, toothless lothario who would make a prize to no woman. The warring ladies looked like mother and daughter, although both appeared prematurely aged due to the same diet as their crack head Casanova. It wasn't the drama of this unfortunate threesome that briefly pulled Keith's attention, it was the volume of their shrieking. The sound on this television had been cranked up, probably to its limit.

Keith looked back at the room's sole occupant, who probably needed the TV cranked since the viewer had no ears that he could see. "Good God," Keith mumbled under his breath. He could have shouted it and wouldn't have been heard under the caterwauling from the cable program.

Tickles was on the sofa, helped back up by Missy's assistance. It sat back into its previously peeled and still seeping upholstery of skin. On the left side that was most visible to Keith, there were around a dozen large Band-Aids taping Tickles back to its sofa-fused flesh.

Tickles was sitting au natural, although there was nothing natural about its body. The sheet that had covered Tickles' nakedness had been discarded on the floor and was wet with blood. It was the amount of blood that alarmed Keith. Most of the sofa and the garbage piled, and flattened, before it were saturated with blood from Tickles' peeling. It looked like a large pig had been skinned in this room, which Keith thought might not be very far from the truth. He just hoped that none of the spilled blood was Dani's.

Keith had entered the room with the intent to kill, but his target had been Missy, not this person, this *thing*. He could only proceed with morbid curiosity. He did not try to hide himself or his knife from the room's occupant.

This person was so preoccupied with the televised hussy tussle that it didn't even notice Keith was approaching. Tickles had a pained grimace on its face, which was understandable considering the size of its injury. Only when Keith changed his direction, stepping almost directly before the TV, did Tickles discover it had a guest. Its grimace became a goonish grin.

"Ooo! Are you part of the camera crew?" Tickles asked excitedly.

Keith, like Dani before him, could not make a decision on this hoarder's gender, even after it spoke. He took it a step further and didn't think this hoarder was even human. It spoke English, but so did other monsters like Dracula, Frankenstein, Freddy, and Pinhead. Those guys had started as humans, but become monsters through horrible circumstances. This thing in front of Keith was going to have to prove its humanity to him.

Keith recognized one similarity between Missy and her mysterious oversize houseguest. Neither occupant had shown anger or surprise at his intrusion. In fact, he would have preferred they react with suspicion instead of this excitable acceptance. Missy's house was the last place he wanted to feel welcomed.

Keith considered what Tickles had said, something about being part of a camera crew. Had Missy told it that? He looked down and saw his handheld camera sticking out of his front hoodie pocket, the red recording light on. Plus, he had the mini camera on his cap. Perhaps Tickles had recognized that, too. Keith figured he would proceed as he had with Missy, by validating this person's, or creature's crazy talk. The fact that this hoarder did not figure a stranger approaching with a knife was any kind of threat gave him an advantage. At least this thing had no intention of calling to Missy for help.

"Yeah. This is my camera." Keith raised the butcher knife in his hand. Tickles didn't appear to know the difference, and it tickled its massive titties in delight.

"Can you help me out, Hon?" Tickles asked.

Hon was a term that Keith had been called before, and attributed mostly to women. It was the standard from his nearly ninety-year-old grandma Margaret when he was a tenth her age, and he recognized that she called everyone Hon, young and old, because remembering names was long past her. Hon was endearingly used by Susan, the hot elementary school nurse who had tended to his scrapes and bruises all too often in his mother's opinion, and not often enough in his own. He was still called Hon by his silver haired neighbor and flaming homo Charlie, but he didn't mind him using that word since Charlie was the coolest tenant in their building. He was a former hippie, still was actually, and his stories of attending the 1968 Democratic National Convention were a source of inspiration to him. Charlie knew how to stick it to *The Man*, in more ways than one Keith often joked. Charlie always laughed at that and agreed.

Tickles' use of *Hon* was not enough of a signifier for Keith to guess its gender, assuming it even had one. Maybe it had two. Or three.

"Sure," Keith replied. It was easy enough to make friends with this creature. Keith could not get that moniker for this hoarder out of his head. The program playing was tabloid television, but Keith knew he had really stepped into a creature feature.

"Closer," Tickles hissed. Keith stepped forward. He was being drawn in, just like Dracula's hypnotized victims stepped toward their un-maker. The butcher knife remained upheld, or his camera in this hoarder's buried eyes.

Keith didn't like the way its trunk legs spread wider as he stepped closer, revealing no genitals to speak of, only flaps and folds. That didn't mean this creature couldn't be male. He remembered watching the Smallest Penis Contest on *The Howard Stern Show*, a program that was also an influence in his rebellious development. A few of the unfortunate top contenders of that hilarious contest had junk that measured in the negative. They had innies. Male did not always mean a protuberance.

"That bucket down there. Can you get a cube and rub it on Tickles' wound?" Tickles asked in a pleading voice.

Tickles! This thing calls itself Tickles! Keith thought. The name didn't carry the chill of Nosferatu or threat of Jigsaw, but the Blob and the Creeping Flesh were already taken. The name Tickles didn't fit, and he wouldn't entertain its usage. To him it would remain the *creature*, with an apology to the svelte Creature from the Black Lagoon.

Keith couldn't make sense of the creature's request, and then he saw where it was pointing. There was a tipped bucket before the sofa, filled with cubes of butter, speckled in blood.

"Butter," Keith said disbelievingly. Was this creature putting him on? This felt like some other kind of reality show, the kind with a celebrity around the corner playing an elaborate prank. Only these scare tactics were no prank, he had too many injuries to count to believe that.

"It's a salve, you know," Tickles said, like Keith was stupid for not knowing that home remedy. "My back burns."

Keith saw the seeping injury that circled Tickles' backside that no amount of Band-Aids and butter was going to heal, and he bet it burned like a bitch. He looked back into the bucket and wondered if he should butter his butcher knife before putting it to use. This creature would probably like that. And toss some salt on the wound after for some added zest.

Tickles lunged forward and grabbed Keith's broken wrist. Keith never thought that such a massive, immobile lump of flesh could move with such speed and force, which was why he was caught totally off guard. He pulled back instinctively and suffered the error of that move. He thought his wrist was going to completely shatter and his hand separate from his arm.

Tickles squealed, and damned if it wasn't in delight. Keith thought that it squealed like a pig, which was partly right. He was dealing with a Were-Pig.

The bandages that connected Tickles to the sofa snapped off in rapid procession and Tickles' back was once again separated from its skin. A few of the roaches that were trapped inside the skin ran for freedom onto the sofa. Other roaches remained on the open wound, their all-you-can-eat buffet unfinished.

The pain in Keith's left wrist was too much for him to bear. He reacted the only way he could, with a strong swing of his butcher knife. He wasn't surprised to discover that Tickles' skin cut like butter.

A seven-inch gash was opened from the right to the left in what approximated for a neck on this creature. Keith's guess was right, because the jugular was hit, releasing a jet spray of blood that Tickles began to gurgle on. It wouldn't be calling him Hon again.

Tickles' grip around Keith's wrist tightened with such force he thought he might pass out from the pain. Then the blubbery hand that held him released its grip. Keith pulled away as Tickles' hand kept clutching in spasms.

Keith struggled to step backward on the garbage packed floor, but he couldn't stop looking before him. He had committed bloody murder, and it was a messy, ongoing process on ugly display before him. He could not turn away from what he had done. He had to learn whatever horrible lessons it had to teach him. The neck wound no longer sprayed, but released pulsing gouts of blood. The god-awful gurgling became a wheeze that got continually weaker. This was the worst reality of war, the drawn out battlefield casualties.

The blood dripping, death dealing butcher knife remained held up in front of Keith in a shaking hand. His shock had to be manifested in some fashion. He kept backing up, not toward the door, but in a straight line, taking him past the television that had just lost its most loyal viewer.

Keith heard a powerful wet splatter and felt a resurgence of fear. He knew the voiding of bowels was a cruel part of the death process, and he was expecting it. Only this wet splatter had not come from before him. Once he had passed the television and its front speakers, he regained some of his hearing. He was certain that this splatter had come from behind him on his right.

Keith took a step backward. A sliver of light appeared between what had at first appeared to be bookcases. Only these cases didn't hold books. They held fast food bags, Styrofoam containers, drink cups, and dirty napkins, all emblazoned with familiar fast food logos.

Keith took a few more steps back and discovered a previously concealed passageway between the bookcases, leading into a room or corridor that remained just out of his view. He approached this secret corridor, his knife upheld.

Keith's anger increased with every step. Missy had clobbered and smothered him and broken his wrist, and then this hidden hoarder had further shattered his wrist, with squealing glee. It was highly possible he'd never have normal use of that hand again.

He was the long overdue exterminator who was tasked with removing the home's most destructive pests, the two hoarders that occupied it. He would feel no guilt for his actions tonight, he would only feel regret that he had brought his loved ones along.

There was a massive, floor shaking thump to Keith's left, and he stopped to look at its source. Tickles had collapsed off of its perch, skinned for the second time. Its bloody back fat had coagulated into a quivering red jelly, and that was the only movement it had left. For Keith, this was when the creature returned to its human state, only in death. The way the Wolfman became a naked man again after taking a silver bullet.

Another forceful splatter turned Keith to the passageway. As he navigated toward it, he saw the bookcase on the left stood four feet further out than the right, with the width of the passageway between them almost three feet wide. When Keith stepped between the bookcases, he saw the source of the noise ahead and knew he would never be able to forget it.

Missy's backside was turned toward him. Her over tight red dress was hitched up to her belly, and he recognized that she had changed since he'd seen her last. She was hunched over, looking like she was riding an invisible bike. Keith thought she should be riding the porcelain bus instead.

A plastic shopping bag was held open behind her, covering her ass. There came another noisome splatter, and the plastic bag ballooned out further.

Keith knew the reason for Missy's explosive elimination. He

had seen what she ate firsthand, and he himself had taken a big bite. He was even more revolted to think that this bowel blowing reaction to her diet probably occurred with regularity. He fully expected to have his own splattery session the next time he had to go.

Keith had to tear his eyes away from Missy's shit show. He looked at his butcher knife and remembered his purpose, the only thing that mattered. His business with the blade.

Keith probably wouldn't get a better chance to strike than now, while Missy was fully turned and occupied with her potty break off the pot. Keith thought he lucked out that Missy still had some modesty and found defecation a private matter, which was why she had moved into this passageway out of the other hoarder's view.

Keith stepped ahead as gently as he could, trying to avoid the crinkle of garbage underfoot. The crinkle from Missy's plastic bag was louder.

As Keith came closer to Missy, her surroundings widened. He recognized that she was standing on a landing before a second staircase going down to the first floor. He could hear her grunting, trying to force the last of her meal out, and then she ended with a sigh.

Missy stood up and removed the bag, fully exposing her dirty rump to Keith. He held in a retch. With one hand Missy pulled her dress down. Keith could not help but notice that she had not cleaned herself afterward, and she wasn't wearing panties. More fun facts to add to the Missy files.

Keith picked up his pace and inevitably increased the noise of his approach. Missy might turn around any second. Noisier steps that were faster were a risk he had to take. He needed the ability to strike first. A few more seconds and all this fear could be over.

And then the fire could start. Keith longed to smell Missy's house in cinders. When Keith was eight and his brother six, their parents had taken them on a precautionary tour of a neighborhood house that had been destroyed by a kitchen fire. Only the kitchen and part of the dining room had been charred, but it was enough to render the entire house a total loss. Keith had been confused when they had toured the kids' rooms upstairs, which looked relatively okay. He remembered most vividly the big teddy bear that had been abandoned. Its fur had a soft layer of soot on it, but that could be washed off, Keith emphatically told his parents. The soot could be cleaned, but the charred smell of the house that permeated the bear's every stitch could not, his father had explained. Keith had complete recall of that memory's smell and could not wait to be the cause of it here.

It was a bittersweet memory, but it had been a good lesson that his asshole, abandoning father had taught him with that tour. Keith would never be a firebug; he feared and respected the element. Its use would be required just this one time. Burning the village was a valid tactic when trying to win a war.

Missy was making noise of her own, tying the top of her piping hot poop bag into a knot. Her dirty fingers got a bit dirtier in the process. She did not hear the footsteps coming behind her.

Missy tossed the bag down the stairs. Instead of clothes, these stairs were carpeted in crap bags. As the front staircase was the hamper of the house, the back staircase was the open septic tank. Her number twos had to go somewhere since her toilet had long ago grown a stool volcano.

Keith rushed out of the passageway and onto the landing, the butcher knife held straight out before him. The blade stabbed five inches deep into Missy's back left side. This stab was nothing like the slash of Tickles' soft neck. The blade encountered much resistance and required far more force to get in. He could feel the puncture of tough flesh, the resistance of strong muscle, and the scraping against bones, which were probably her ribs.

Keith shuddered with revulsion and let the handle go. He stepped back from his horrible handiwork. In her tight red dress, Missy almost looked like a stabbed, hanging slab of beef.

Only this slab wasn't dead. Missy turned around and regarded Keith with annoyance.

"Oh, you. Let me guess, you'd like a sandwich now."

Keith stared at Missy with utter disbelief. He expected her to fall, he expected her to scream, he expected her to just fucking die already. He had not expected this, the threat of another sandwich.

"I stabbed you," Keith stated matter-of-factly.

Missy gave Keith a sly look, like he was pulling her leg. Keith looked down at her left side, indicating to her with his eyes the general location of her injury. Missy felt around her abdomen until her hand located the blade embedded in her back. Her fingers wrapped around the handle and slid the knife effortlessly out.

Keith stared at Missy with his mouth agape. How could she not feel that? She should have been screaming bloody murder, namely her own. Yet she didn't seem to know she had been mortally wounded. Did she not feel pain? Did her poisonous diet make her immune to mortality? Keith was starting to think of Missy like he thought of the other hoarder. She was a creature, too, since creatures were far harder to kill than humans.

"I thought I felt a poke. Thought it was my fibro flaring up again," Missy said. She held up the knife and looked at the bloody tip with disappointment. "You're all kinds of trouble, aren't you? It's almost not worth having you Hollywood types messing up my house."

Keith looked at the tip of the blade and was a bit reassured to see that her blood was red, not zombie black or alien green.

"You're bleeding," Keith said with a seriousness that he hoped would transfer to Missy. Keith looked down toward her wound, hoping she would tend to its severity with urgency.

Missy didn't care to address or dress her wound. She looked at Keith with irritation.

"We have a rule here in Wormwood Manor, no knives leave the kitchen. People get hurt that way, you know."

She has got to be fucking kidding! Keith thought. He'd seen knives throughout the hoard in practically every room of the house. Kitchen knives, butter knives, the back bedroom had literally hundreds of plastic knives. Did she seriously not see knives everywhere, because he sure as fuck did. Keith looked up at Missy to tell her and he saw a knife. His butcher knife. It was making a fast arc down toward him.

Missy plunged the knife into the center of Keith's chest, about four inches in. She didn't want to go too deep and hurt him.

Keith felt like he had just received the ultimate punch to his chest, and to his heart, worse than his worst wipeout ever, where he had landed on the top edge of his skateboard and broken two ribs near his sternum. Keith looked down at the handle of the blade sticking out of him and knew this was a lot more serious than any skateboard wipeout.

"Now you take that knife back down and put it in the kitchen where it belongs," Missy instructed him.

Keith turned around and followed Missy's order. That was awful nice of him. She'd forgive him his goof-up. She was really starting to like him again. Truth be told, she never really stopped.

They were an item, after all.

Keith kept his eyes on his stumbling feet as they took him back into the bedroom, the beginning of the long trek downstairs. Looking at his feet, he was also looking at the knife, and the blood that was making his hoodie glisten.

Keith had no intention of following Missy's order. He would defy her to the end. The kitchen was not where he was going, the front door was. He knew he needed serious help, and fast. Removing the blade the way Missy had would most likely lead to his bleeding out and death. Leaving it in didn't feel like such a good idea either, since the blade seemed to be increasing steadily in temperature inside of him. It could start burning so hot he might not be able to stop himself. His hand could revolt and pull the knife out in an attempt to put out the fire.

Keith retraced his steps through the television room, past the television, past the no longer moving bloody mass on the floor. The further Keith went, the harder his struggle with things like walking, equilibrium, breathing, and consciousness became. He was no longer thinking in coherent sentences, just random words and repetitive phrases. As Keith came upon the bedroom door, he thought *Wormwood Manor must escape Wormwood WormWOOD! Out! OUT!*

Missy remained on the landing of the second staircase as she explored the damage Keith had done. Her fingers found the stab wound in her back, but she was more concerned with the tear in her dress.

"He tore my good dress. I should tear his pants," Missy reasoned. That would only be fair.

Missy pulled her fingers back and saw they were smudged with fresh blood. It was her most favorite shade of red, only better because it was shiny.

"It don't hurt, so it can't be all that bad," Missy told herself, and then she shouted out, "Tickles, you used up all my Band-Aids!"

Missy made a mental note to get more Band-Aids on her trip to the Mega-Mart next Tuesday. That was a long time to wait for bandages. Luckily, Missy was a firm believer in recycling. Why, she could probably find a makeshift bandage right where she stood.

She put her resourcefulness to the test and looked around. It took her all of five seconds.

"Ha!" Missy exclaimed. She was always right.

Missy crouched and picked up a sanitary napkin that looked like it had been recycled already, many times over the years. She reached around and pressed the clotted cotton pad to her still bleeding stab wound. She pressed it hard until there was a twinge of pain that made her wince.

That Keith had left a real smarty on her. After holding the pad in place for a few moments, she let it go. The unsanitary napkin remained stuck to her stab wound, sucking up her blood like a leech.

Missy thought she might not need to buy those Band-Aids after all, although if they were on sale she might not be able to help herself. She would have to find a needle and thread as well to fix the rip that bad boy had left in her good dress.

Only finding a needle in a hoard was harder than a haystack, and Missy's promise to sew her clothing would never come to fruition. She had never sown a stitch in her life. But in Missy's mind, she always sewed her damaged clothing and returned them to perfection. Her intent always procured the desired results.

23

After setting glitter cat free, Ian vacated Missy's bedroom and continued up the hall. His exposed forearms were itchy where they had crawled over the covers of Missy's bed, on blankets he assumed had never been cleaned. There were a million things under Missy's roof, but a working washer and dryer were obviously not among them. Looking at his forearms, he was alarmed by the hives and redness that had quickly taken root on his delicate skin. He wasn't surprised that his body should react with such a severe rash anywhere he was caressed by Missy's rotten things.

The brown lit bathroom only got the most cursory glance as Ian held his breath and hurried past, before he could get a rancid lungful of fecal air. 2000 Flushes wasn't going to fix Missy's bathroom, but 2000 matches might.

Ian approached the cracked door on the right and had much the same reaction as Dani before him. He saw the doorknob and hesitated in opening it. The smell that came from the room was different than the others, although it contained traces of many stinks he had already encountered, old standbys like spoilage, mold, and shit. Somehow this room's reek was worse than all of those. Nearing the crack in the door was like getting a whiff of bleach and ammonia intermingled. It smelled dangerous, a poisonous cocktail.

Ian christened this mystery room the *Rot Room.* His every cell revolted at opening that door, but Ian had a mission to get through. Dani or Keith could be behind that door, so the room could not be avoided. All he had to do was open the door and look inside. He wouldn't have to enter the noxious interior if his friends didn't need his assistance.

Ian looked over his shoulder, took a deep breath, and reached for the doorknob.

A falling box from the end of the hallway grabbed Ian's attention. The door to the Rot Room was abandoned.

Somebody was in the room at the end of the hallway, and Ian approached to find out who it was. He heard talking, the pitching of products from a commercial sponsor. No live voices. Still, it hadn't been a professional pitchman who knocked over that box. He could see light shifting on the hoard through the door. Whether that was the television's reflection or somebody's shadow, he wasn't sure.

Ian clutched his kitchen knife tightly as he counted down his steps to the open door: three, two…

Ian didn't finish his count, since Keith stepped into the doorway before him. The handle of the butcher knife sticking out of Keith's chest was less than two feet from him. What Ian heard at that moment was cruel and surreal, the thunderous applause of a studio audience behind his brother, cheering him on. Ian looked from the knife handle up to Keith's face, his eyes already filling with tears.

Ian forgot all about keeping quiet and inconspicuous, and his emotion was let loose in heart-wrenching shouts.

"Keith! No!"

Keith looked directly into his brother's eyes, but the connection wasn't entirely there. Ian saw no recognition at all. When Keith spoke, he could have been addressing a stranger, or his reflection in a mirror.

"She took my bike." Keith's voice sounded watery, but it wasn't water that was steadily filling his lungs, it was his blood.

Keith stepped around Ian into the hall, their arms brushing together in the cramped corridor. He remained on mortally wounded autopilot, and escape from Wormwood Manor through the front door was his final goal for tonight's rapidly deteriorating mission. Unlike his trek across the bedroom, where he watched his every step as his blood pattered on his shoes, Keith's eyes remained level with Ian's eye line, even after he passed him.

Keith's singular mission to escape made him forget the reality of crossing the hoard; you had to watch every step. Keith stumbled on the garbage underfoot and fell forward. Ian turned in time to see his brother land on his chest, shoving the butcher knife in deeper. Keith's last thought was of his killer, his location, and his final state: *Wormwood.*

Ian was not one for screaming. In fact, his shock had a silencing effect. Ian's jaw dropped, his breath hitched in his chest, and he froze.

Keith had one last movement left in him. He rolled onto his side on the garbage packed floor, pulling his knees up and his upper half down in a primal return to the fetal position, as though he wanted to exit the world in the same pose he'd entered it in.

When he rolled, Keith's handheld camera slipped out of his front pocket and filmed in close-up the mess on the floor.

Ian couldn't speak, couldn't even breathe, until he heard movement, the shifting of garbage, in the room behind him. He knew he had only seconds, and he knew there was nothing he could do to help his dying brother at his feet. But he could help his legacy. Ian squatted and grabbed Keith's fallen camera. He let it continue recording.

Ian heard heavy steps in the doorway behind him and felt a blast of hot breath on the back of his neck that smelled really bad, which was not a surprise. Ian turned, knife in one hand, Keith's camera in the other, and stood face to face with Missy for the first time.

She was way too close for his comfort.

24

Missy's personality matched her massive size, and the diminutive doorframe could barely contain both. Missy was positively giddy with excitement.

"Oh lookie-lookie-loo! And who are you?"

Ian suddenly remembered what he was holding, and he whisked his right hand with the knife behind his back. It wasn't wise to make an introduction holding a deadly weapon. Missy wasn't looking down low, so he didn't think she noticed it. She was completely captivated by her new guest's face, as creepy as that was.

"I... my name," Ian stammered.

"You're with production, aren't you?"

Missy's delusion gave Ian a pre-made history to latch onto, and he seized it. Better to go along with her version of their story than flounder for a fiction that might not add up in her fractured mind. So if this was a production, and it kind of was considering the number of cameras in play, he should assume a role of authority. Ian also noticed the camera cap on Missy's head, pushed away the knowledge of who she had stolen it from, and made a mental note to get it back from Missy before the night was through.

"Yes, I'm the director," Ian responded with confidence. He had to be as convincing as possible if he wanted to lead Missy on and get himself out of her house. He would direct his way out.

"And your name?" Missy inquired again.

"Chad," Ian replied. Missy accepted Ian's pseudonym, much to his relief. Ian didn't know any Chads, did not even know why that name had leaped out of his mouth. He would have to be careful and remember to respond to his unexpected new name. *I am Chad. I am Chad.*

"Well my name is Missy, but you know that already, don't you, Mister Director? It's my show after all!" Missy exclaimed with delight, basking in an invisible spotlight.

Ian forced a smile to match his subject's. "Yeah, it's your show," he confirmed to her.

Missy snapped out of her exalted pose. "Wait! What's the name of my show?" Missy asked the last part in a nervous whisper, as though the crew might laugh at her for having forgotten this simple fact.

Ian had to think up a good answer, and quick. He didn't have the luxury of sitting around a table in a studio office, bouncing title ideas off of other creative executives.

"*Missy's House*," Ian made up on the spot. He grinned because he kind of liked it. It summed up the subject and her location, if not the bad air they produced.

Missy squealed. Ian knew he had picked the right title.

"Ooo, I like that! *Missy's House*! My name comes first!"

Missy winked at Ian. Ian grinned, although he didn't like that attention from her. When Dani winked at him, he was elated. When Missy winked at him, it was supremely unsettling. Her wink was dangerous and not to be trusted. She used it as a hook, like a fishing hook tearing through your cheek. He couldn't let himself get reeled in.

Missy lunged forward, tickling Ian's midsection with her hard hands. She was far from gentle, and Ian feared she might pinch him and rupture some crucial internal organ. He gasped, backed out of her hands, and bumped into something. Ian looked back at his dead brother lying across the ground, blocking him.

Ian feared Missy would look down at Keith, too, and he whipped his head around, looking into her eyes to seize her attention. Then he did what his new job title entailed, he gave direction.

"Wait! You can't be that close to the camera."

Missy stopped in mid-lunge, her open hands eager to grab and fondle.

Ian held up Keith's handheld camera, brandishing it like a cross before a vampire.

Ian's makeshift cross had the desired effect. Missy took a step back with a frumpy look on her face. "Oh. Well, make sure you get my best side."

"Every side is your best side, Missy." As the director, Ian knew he'd get the performance he wanted out of his actress if he lavished her with compliments.

Missy's reaction to the compliment scared Ian. She squealed again, the kind of shrill sound that painfully pierced his eardrums like hot needles, and she reached for him with wiggling fingers. Suddenly remembering her direction, Missy shifted back onto her heels away from the camera, which Ian was holding up before his right eye, checking his angle. She smiled for the lens.

"I love the red light!" Missy said.

Ian knew she referred to the record light on the front of the camera. He would have to remember that compliments posed their own danger and would have to be minimized. Also, holding the camera to his eye was a good way to get Missy back a step. The camera was less a cross and more like strong garlic. It wouldn't kill her, but it could repel her a few feet.

Missy's delight turned dour. "I am a bit ticked off with your production crew. They have been messing up my house and moving things out of place. I have a very strict order for every single thing in my house, you know."

Ian knew, all right. He knew that she must have OCD along with a dozen other mental illnesses. Where others saw a garbage dump, she saw her orderly, spic-and-span house. He might have laughed if he wasn't so terrified of her.

Missy was certainly nothing to laugh at. His dead brother and friend were enough to kill all comedy in the situation. Ian hadn't seen Missy stab Keith, but considering the limited number of players in this dark drama, it was easy enough to figure out who planted the knife in Keith's chest. Missy had murder in her. She would probably call it nurture.

"I'm sorry," Ian sincerely apologized. "But that's a small price to pay for having a whole series filmed in your house, and turning you into a star."

Missy considered her director's explanation, and Ian could see her softening. He could also see that she was having a hard time letting go of her gripe.

"The Kardashians said the same thing," Ian added.

"Oh! I'm more entertaining than those bitches," Missy confided in Ian. He couldn't argue her that.

While Missy prided herself on her classy, lady-like language, *bitch* was a regular word in her repertoire. If they said it on TV, then it must be family approved. There were other non-cuss words that qualified as offensive slurs that she used regularly, like *wetback*, *jig-a-boo*, and *faggot*. If other celebrities, politicians, and even the president (and what better president had there been than the Gipper?) used them, they had to be words appropriate of a polite lady. With the exception of Tickles, who was a prideful potty mouth, there was nobody around to hear Missy's racist slurs, or correct her from using them.

Ian smiled back at Missy. He had her on his good side again. Now he needed to lead her away from his brother. Ian didn't want Missy seeing what she had done on the floor behind him. It could put murder back in her mind. Keith had done something to make her mad, mad enough to kill one of the production crew. She might also want to replace her director if they had creative differences.

"You are," Ian agreed. "I also see that you're quite a collector. What are some of your favorite collections?"

Missy let out another shrill screech. Ian didn't know how many more of those he could handle before his ears started to bleed, or before he snapped at her to shut the fuck up.

"Ooo! My collections! I have so many, I don't know where to start!" Missy was lost in her elation.

Ian knew he had picked the right tangent to mislead Missy. He was thankful for all of the time he had spent in front of the television watching shows on Missy's ilk. Ian was the type who watched television to learn interesting things, not to veg out. He was that rare kid who would pick PBS over PlayStation. In schoolyard terms, he was a geek.

Ian had captured Missy's attention, but he could see that she was stuck in a quandary by his question and would need further leading.

"Why don't we start with this room," Ian recommended, nodding at the bedroom behind Missy.

"Okay!" Missy turned into the room. Ian followed with his

camera leading him. He glanced back briefly and saw his brother, curled up and lying on his side with his back to him. He wasn't moving.

Once Ian was inside the back bedroom, he was assaulted by the smell. It was a fragrant stew of crap, blood, and lard, and he found it obscene. Then he saw the source of the smell and had to redefine the word obscene, or at least elevate the severity of his definition.

Ian was finally introduced to the second hoarder of the house, who was nothing but a thousand pound mound of face down fat before the raw flesh upholstered sofa. The hoarder was missing skin from its neck down to its thighs. The exposed jelly of its insides was still seeping, blood staining a wide circumference of garbage around it, at least three times the blood of a normal adult. There was a lot of movement on the gore, as vermin were having a day at the new blood pool.

While Ian had every intention of destroying their footage, he aimed his camera down to film the carnage on the floor, as though an added mechanical eye would help him to process what he was seeing. He really couldn't make sense of the blob of gore and flesh (there was more of the former than the latter). He had not had the pleasure of making Tickles' acquaintance during the hoarder's life, and he figured that was for the better. Considering that Keith had just stepped out of this room and this victim was fresh, he thought Keith may have made good on his plan to murder, only he had picked a different hoarder. The flaw with that theory was he didn't think Keith had it in him to skin a morbidly obese person alive.

Ian realized he would understand it all later if he watched the footage on Keith's camera, which had been recording. Watching would be extremely difficult, since the footage would also include the stab that had taken his brother's life. Maybe the footage needed to be saved, if it answered questions that might haunt him for the rest of his life.

Missy was walking around the body like it wasn't there, but he couldn't ignore it.

"Who's that?" Ian inquired.

Missy turned back to Ian and saw whom he was filming. She didn't like that. Missy seized Ian's left wrist, and her hand squeezed like a vice. Ian had to fight the urge to open his fingers in agony, which would cause him to lose the camera. Suddenly Ian was in full movement, being yanked away from the body. His feet scrambled to find purchase on the garbage beneath him.

"That's Tickles. Never mind that camera whore. This isn't called *Tickles' House*," Missy explained, holding her director and changing his shot. Ian noticed that in twisting his wrist, she was trying to point his camera directly at her.

"It's called *Missy's House*," Ian reminded her.

In hearing the title of her show, Missy released Ian and slapped her hands together inches before his face. He had never heard flesh slapped together so loudly, and the sound had a sting that made him wince.

"That's it!" Missy exclaimed in agreement.

It occurred to Ian that Missy had lost track of her script, and he had to get her back on his page. Her scatterbrain mentality made her a frustratingly hard subject to direct.

"Your collections," Ian reminded her.

"Oh, right."

Missy looked around her hoard with uncertainty. Ian didn't doubt that she had a number of collections to show off, and she couldn't narrow it down to just one. Or maybe he was giving her too much credit. It was almost as if in trying to make a decision, the pilot light for her brain activity had gone out, and she was struggling to rekindle a spark. When the spark came, it was more of a lightening strike, because she surged with life and had to restrain herself from grabbing at the camera.

"Ooo, my clown pitchers! On the walls!"

Clown pitchers? Ian might have guessed sporks or wadded tissues or animal turds as her collections, they were the ones he could see, but he would have never guessed clown pitchers. Then he looked hard at the walls, or the limited portions visible behind the high climbing hoard. And he saw clowns.

Ian raised his camera to capture the clowniness around him. Seeing his interest in her collection, Missy stood proud.

Now that he had been made aware of Missy's clown *pictures*, they were all he could see. And they weren't actual pictures; they were paintings. On the wall to the right, a pair of crazy clown eyes peeked over the hoard beside a bookcase. On the wall to his left, a gaping clown mouth with oversize red lips, kind of like Missy's, silently laughed at him.

So Missy was a connoisseur of fine flea market art. It figured.

"Impressive," Ian complemented her. He didn't add that he

hated clowns, and found her clown pictures impressively awful.

Ian saw that Missy was also admiring her pictures, was kind of stuck on them actually. He looked around at what lay between the pictures. The majority of junk in this room was of the fast food variety, like bags, wrappers, containers, cups, and torn condiment packets. They were piled in drifts, highest around the sofa.

"You like quality restaurants, don't you?" Ian asked.

Ian saw Missy's appetite materialize like a vampire's thirst for blood when it gets a whiff of the red stuff.

"Ooo, I love me some drive-thru cuisine!" Missy agreed, and Ian thought he heard her tummy growl in agreement.

"Do you collect these containers?" Ian asked. There were so many thousands of them; he really wanted to know.

Missy threw a look Ian's way that said *Boy, are you stupid!* Ian didn't like that look, it could lead to further disagreement. It was also insulting, to be called stupid by somebody as mentally deficient as Missy. He knew he had her beat in the IQ department by a wide margin.

"Of course!" Missy exclaimed, followed by an extended pause for an implied *Duhhh!* "All these are antique original packagings. They're worth a lot of money to collectors. I can sell them on my Internet store."

Ian found this an interesting tangent to pursue. It implied that she was wired for the Internet, and he just didn't believe it. "You have an online store?"

"Yes," Missy said with complete confidence, then she got a confused look on her face. Ian and his camera were in her direct sightline, but she was seeing something else. She spoke slowly at first, looking like she was reading a teleprompter that was out of focus. "Well, no, not yet, but I'm planning to. I'm gonna make a fortune selling my treasures. Everything is valuable to someone."

Ian felt as though he could have written Missy's script. She fit the hoarder profile to a T. Most hoarders thought their stockpiles of junk were worth money, lots and lots of money, and many of them thought they could sell some of it and make bank someday. Only most never did. Many of these perceived valuable hoards ended up in dumpsters in the end. Or in those enormous junk trucks that looked more like train cars, which could roll away garbage by the tons.

Ian knew Missy would never, ever get around to selling her shit online. For one thing, he didn't think there was much of a market for used snot rags. It was a similar delusion to the hoarders who claimed they were really recycling. Recycling was work, just like selling was work. Letting garbage pile up to dangerous heights, usually through neglect and laziness, was not recycling by any definition Ian knew.

Missy and her type seemed to live by a different dictionary than everyone else, one where the definitions were based on self-serving falsehoods. Ian and Missy would never be on the same page, they belonged to entirely different libraries.

Ian decided to take Missy up on her claim about her treasures. He trained his camera on a greasy, deteriorated fast food bag, split open and spilling a half eaten cheeseburger and ketchup coated fries, sprinkled generously with rat butt seasoning, sitting on top of the television.

"Is this a collectible?"

Missy looked at the long abandoned meal with apprehension, like he might not understand. Desperate to prove herself right, she grabbed a few of the fries, shoving them greedily into her mouth. She chewed and talked at the same time, spraying crumbs of potato and poop.

"Mm-MMMM! These never go bad, you know. And they always taste good!" Proving her generous nature to him, Missy grabbed a few more fries and held them out to Ian.

"Want some?" Missy exclaimed way too excitedly. Ian saw the chunks of white potato and black feces stuck in her teeth. Those would be nice details in high definition.

"No!" Ian blurted out and drew back, fearing she might feed him the fries whether he wanted them or not. He couldn't appear rude or unappreciative, so he needed a good reason. "Not while I'm working."

Missy gave Ian a sassy look, like he was playing hard to get. "Okay, Chad, but you don't know what you're missing!"

Ian did know what he was missing, mold and fecal matter in his mouth.

Missy shoved the fossilized fries into her mouth. She looked like she had never eaten anything so delicious in her entire life. Ian could tell she was overacting for his and his camera's benefit.

The sight of Missy smacking her snack was revolting enough, and then some of those tasty morsels flew out of Missy's mouth and into Ian's face. He stepped back out of spitting distance, and his right shoe came down on top of a blue Styrofoam cup, which burst with a crunch.

Missy screamed. She didn't just spray spittle; her entire mouthful of fries was ejected in one massive, saliva slick gob, flying with surprising force.

The projectile splattered on Ian's chin. He stood frozen in the path of her rancid shockwave scream.

"You! What have you done!?"

Ian looked down as the glob of French fries dropped off his chin. He considered her question, what had he done? He had stepped back onto garbage. That's all there was to step onto, there certainly wasn't any floor to walk on. Ian had no idea what his transgression had been.

Looking down, Ian didn't see the impact coming. Missy's fist rammed into his stomach with bruising force, perhaps enough force to rupture something inside. If she had hit a little higher, she would have certainly broken his ribs. Ian stumbled back breathless, stepping on another fast food bag, which ruptured and set the refuse and a rodent inside free. He also dropped the kitchen knife that he had been hiding behind his back. The camera he thankfully held. He thought it might be his most valuable tool for saving himself.

Ian had looked away from Missy for only a few seconds and had been caught totally off guard. She had lived up to her legend. She was as powerful as an MMA fighter. Ian knew his limitations, that he was skinny, short, and lacking muscles. He didn't want to go three rounds in the ring with Missy. His brother hadn't survived round two with her, and Keith was a lot stronger than he was.

"What did I do?!" Ian shouted. Now he was asking for direction, but he need to know right away what he had done wrong, so he wouldn't do it again and get served another one of Missy's knuckle sandwiches.

Missy crouched before Ian and picked up the blue Styrofoam cup that had been flattened by his shoe. She shook the ruptured cup at Ian, and now it was spittle she was spraying into his face.

"This was part of a set of collectible cups, red, white, and blue, released last July at Chickin Grillins! The red one is over there and the white one is over there!"

Missy pointed in the direction of her red cup as she spoke, then turned her pointing finger in the opposite direction for her white cup. Ian quickly followed her finger but saw all color cups in all directions. He couldn't pick out her multi-colored Chickin Grillins' cups among the clutter if his life depended on it, which unfortunately it might. He did not think it would help him to point out that most of the cheap cups in her collection were already broken and crushed. Pointing that fact out might get him hurt.

Ian didn't doubt that Missy knew exactly what cups she was pointing at. She probably knew the layout of all of her garbage. Only where Missy saw sparkling china, Ian saw dusty turds. Part of her legend was that she spent all of her time in her house, except for her weekly terror shopping sprees and neighborhood porch raiding missions. She was always with her precious hoard. She was in love with every rotten square foot of it, and knew it all intimately.

"Now the set has lost a third of its value!" Missy seethed in Ian's face. The broken cup was crushed further in Missy's hand, and Ian saw her other hand clench into a fist. What he thought he was really seeing was a human tornado building before him.

Ian could not proceed with fear, he had to summon confidence and gain control of his star again. Not an easy task knowing his dead brother was lying outside the door, another victim destroyed and discarded by this human tornado.

"But that's the price, remember? And you can buy ten sets of these cups with the money you're making as a reality TV star."

Missy's fists stopped clenching. Ian could see her struggling with the concept, and then accepting his pitch, even though pay negotiations had never been a part of their discussion. Missy was instantly accepting of her mega-fame and fortune. And then her face soured again, into a kind of profound sadness. When she spoke, it was in the voice of a sniveling child.

"But Red Cup and White Cup will be lonely without Blue Cup."

Ian had at first felt like he was matching wits with a cunning killer, and now he had to reason with her like a spoiled child. Missy was no criminal mastermind, but she was a lethal danger in her dumbness.

"You can buy more blue cups," Ian assured her.

Ian said the right thing, as Missy's childlike sadness evaporated, and he was faced with a woman who looked like she had just won the Publishers Clearinghouse Sweepstakes, one who just might hug him to death in her excitement, or pop him like a celebratory balloon. Between her muscular thighs.

"I can!" Missy exclaimed in agreement. The loneliness of Red Cup and White Cup had been completely forgotten. "Buying is what I do best, and bargains are my specialty. You know I never buy only one, of anything! I can't, because then that one thing would be lonely and sad, and I don't want any sad-sads in Missy's house!"

Too late for that, Ian wanted to say. With Keith and Will dead, Ian definitely qualified as a sad-sad in Missy's house. He suddenly wanted to teach Missy the true definition of things.

"What about your cats? Are they friends?" Ian asked.

"Of course they're friends! But I'm besties with Booger-Snots, Albino Kitty, and Nigger-Toes." Missy said the second part in a conspiratorial whisper to Ian, his camera, and the home audience. This was a secret only to her feline friends.

Ian was glad he hadn't made a face when she rattled off the name Nigger-Toes. *Missy's House* had just earned its first broadcast bleep. She might not consider the N-word a bad word, but her ignorance did not excuse its use. Ian remembered freeing a white cat with black paws earlier in the living room and figured he had already met Nigger-Toes. Ian was happy he had freed one of Missy's besties. The rescued cat would not only benefit from a better diet, but also a new name outside of this house.

"Some of the cats I've seen are thin, and in small cages. They look sad-sad," Ian informed her.

Missy gave Ian a look like he was crazy, then shared that look with his camera with a shake of her head, knowing the audience would be as exasperated with him as she was.

"Oh no! Are you kidding? My house is like the Hilton for cats! They get to eat people food, and there's lots of mice-ies for them to play with. All the cats in town want to be at Missy's house!"

Ian thought Dani's cat Fiddlesticks might disagree. He spotted the movement of cockroaches swarming over a half eaten cheeseburger, exploring between the bun and patty. He nodded at the fattening feeding ground.

"I've noticed a few cockroaches. Are they friends?" Ian inquired.

Missy's jaw dropped in offense before she vociferously replied, "Oh no no no! I don't have roaches. Only dirty people got roaches, and I keep my house clean."

Ian knew that Missy lived in a state of constant denial, but how could she deny what was directly in front of her? He nodded at the cockroaches on the cheeseburger again. "What are those?"

"Duh!" Missy exclaimed, throwing her head back and rolling her eyes up to the heavens, asking salvation for the fool boy before her. "Those are baby butterflies, you big silly! Their wings haven't grown out yet. You can eat them, you know. They're full of protein." Missy's dietary advice was delivered in a softer register for her audience, a secret recipe shared among close friends.

To emphasize her point, Missy plucked up one of her baby butterflies and popped it into her mouth. Ian could hear the crunch of the juicy morsel between her teeth. Ian thought Missy was on the wrong TV show, she would win *Fear Factor* in a heartbeat with an appetite like that. The roach eating made him ill, but he put on a smile for Missy's sake. She was eating bugs to impress him, or anyone. It was such a pathetic sight, her desperation for acceptance.

"You want to meet them?" Missy asked.

"Meet who?"

"My friends."

"I've met your cats."

"Not my cats. My favorite collection in the whole house! My dolls! They have the biggest room to themselves, the master bedroom. You have to meet them!"

As Missy moved around Ian, she reached out to seize his left wrist. He pulled his arm away from her, and her heavy hand clenched only air. She was on a mission to show off her favorite collection, and she walked on without him, expecting him to follow. She was heading for the hallway door, and his brother's body beyond it, exactly where he wanted to keep her from going.

"Is there another way we can go?" Ian asked.

"Yes, but why go all the way through the house, up and down and loop-de-loop, when the room is right over here? Come on!"

Missy waved Ian on and didn't wait for him. Ian followed reluctantly. He gave another glance at the massive, skinned body on the floor and wondered if Tickles qualified as one of Missy's friends.

Following Missy, Ian noticed for the first time that the lower back of Missy's red dress was glistening wet with the same color.

He spotted the tear in her dress and the pad of bloody cotton stuck on it, which looked like a sanitary napkin to him (he vetoed that guess even though he had guessed correctly).

With his brother newly dead, Ian figured Missy's fresh wound could not be mere coincidence. He hoped his brother had driven the knife, or whatever weapon was responsible for Missy's injury, deep, and taken satisfaction in her wounding.

Missy plowed out of the bedroom and into the hallway. Ian stopped in the doorway behind her, wanting to watch her encounter with Keith from a distance. He feared her reunion with her victim could refuel the murderous rage that had made her plant a knife in Keith's chest in the first place.

When Missy reached Keith's corpse sprawled across her path, she stepped over him without looking down. Her right heel hit Keith's shoulder, jostling the body. Ian had expected a reaction from Missy, but not this. Keith was nothing more than additional garbage on Missy's floor to climb over.

Missy's disrespect for the dead added more fuel to the simmering anger that Ian was struggling to keep contained. It would come out, explosively and violently, he knew that now, he just had to unleash it at the right time. Ian had finally assumed his brother's final mission, to take Missy out.

Ian followed Missy into the hall, and took great care not to disturb his brother's body as he stepped over him. He flinched when he heard the clamor of a box falling over ahead. From the jingling inside the box, it was obvious the box contained glass, and the glass was long broken. Missy was knocking things over in her excitement to reach the master bedroom and her most valuable collection. For somebody who loved her stuff as much as she claimed, Ian found it ironic how much abuse she heaped on her treasures.

Missy stopped before the entrance to the master bedroom and turned eagerly to Ian. He should have figured; she was standing before the cracked door to the Rot Room that he had been so deeply reluctant to enter earlier.

It also figured that Missy's most prized collection, dolls, would be supremely creepy en masse. Most of Missy's collections rated high in the creep factor, from her clown pictures to her cat cages to her shit samples.

As Ian approached Missy, the noxious smell emanating from

the cracked door started to affect him again. His breathing slowed, so he could take in less of the air he thought might be poisonous. The hair on the back of his neck stood up in alarm. Gooseflesh broke out on Ian's arms despite the stuffy heat. Ian had to force his legs to continue toward Missy and her destination.

"You're a lucky guy, Chad. I rarely share my friends with anyone."

Ian didn't want to remind Missy that she was also sharing her friends with her show's audience. *Missy's House* would never make it to airing, but the world would know the shocking truth of Missy's collections once this night was through. Ian would make sure of that.

Missy pushed open the door to the master bedroom and climbed up into it. Ian followed her in with his camera leading him. The flip screen had acted as a minor shield to the horrors before, but it had no shielding effect now.

The Rot Room really was a poison place, and if Ian got out with serious mental scars alone, he would consider himself lucky. He also hoped that Missy would not be following him out. He would do it for Keith and Will and any others who had not survived their encounters with Missy. He suspected there were many.

25

After climbing up a few feet of soft cushioning, Ian stopped beside Missy to behold her favorite collection. First his eyes were drawn above it, at the dozens of curling flypaper strips hanging from the mold saturated ceiling. The strips were completely caked with dead flies and other flying insects, and some not so dead. Despite the many strips, the room was abuzz with hundreds of fat flies, providing a low static sound. The flies were so plentiful and busy buzzing about, Ian couldn't go two seconds without one flying into his face. It was like walking through rain with wings.

Ian covered his nose with his left forearm. What was making the flies so hungry was making his nostrils ache and sending his stomach into cartwheels.

Missy didn't so much enter the room as make a grand entrance. She threw her arms out in a wide welcome, nearly backhanding Ian beside her. He jerked his head back, avoiding impact by inches. Missy exclaimed, "Hello friends!"

Ian looked around at Missy's friends. Her doll collection numbered in the high hundreds. They were piled against every wall so their eyes faced the room's center, at any visitors. Dolls were stacked on top of each other up to the ceiling. The dolls spanned all sizes, from miniature to Barbie-size to life-size, as well as ages, from baby dolls to elderly. Some dolls didn't look so happy to be dolls, stuck with an eternity of grimacing, but the majority of them were smiling.

Ian looked down at the center of the room, which was a sea of stuffed animals. Most of the stuffies were grinning, chosen to feed Missy's endless glee. Ian spotted two shiny beanbags ahead, one red, one blue, like islands in a furry sea.

Ian found the room, with its countless eyes and toothy grins, even creepier than he had anticipated. He had always been unsettled by too many false smiles, which he remembered from both the church services during his youth and watching the last Republican National Convention on CNN. So many smiles, but they were the kind that could not be trusted, because those smiles could bite.

Dolls alone could not be responsible for the rot that Ian smelled. There had to be something within or underneath the collection responsible for the reek, and the flies. One particularly bloated fly bumped between Ian's eyes, and he fixed his vision on it, determined to follow it back to its fetid food source.

The fat fly did a lazy corkscrew to the left, heading to one of the life-size dolls. The fly alighted on the nose of a teenage girl whose head was twisted to the side at a fatally extreme angle. It was Dani.

Ian wanted to cry out, to scream and attack the monster named Missy beside him, but he was simply paralyzed by the sight of his unrequited love sitting nearby, embraced by dolls in death. He hadn't thought anything could sting worse than seeing his brother's murder before him, and yet this did. He wasn't mad at just the madder woman who had killed his loved ones. He harbored hate for the squalid location where their lives had ended. He didn't know which was the bigger vampire, Missy or Missy's house.

Now that Ian had discovered a body in the doll collection, he could see the corpses that were buried within. Many of the human sized dolls were real humans. There had to be over a dozen, and further inspection made him double that number. The corpses, like the dolls, looked toward the room's visitors, at least the ones with eyes remaining did.

The bodies ranged in age, and in freshness, from the newly dead like Dani, who couldn't have even cooled since Ian had seen her last, to mummies and skeletons with little flesh left. The worst of the bodies was bloated and blackened with rot, liquefying and roiling with maggots. The age and gender of that rot bag were indefinable.

Each body that Ian saw, he wondered who they were and what had brought them into Missy's path and wrath. He saw a spoiling pizza delivery guy, whose skin resembled the greasy cheese of a pizza. A stainless steel fork stuck out of the delivery guy's left eye. Perhaps he hadn't delivered Missy's long devoured pizza in thirty minutes or less.

Between two supremely freaky life-size girl dolls in their 1920s Sunday best dresses was a mummified Girl Scout in her uniform, empty Girl Scout Cookies boxes in her lap. Perhaps this forever young girl had run out of Do-Si-Dos, Caramel deLites, or whatever Missy's favorite cookie was and had paid the ultimate price.

Missy saw Ian gawking at the Girl Scout and became boastful.

"Look, she's laughing!"

The Girl Scout's face was frozen in a silent scream, and adding an additional dash of horror, Ian saw a cookie in her gaping mouth. It looked like a half eaten Samoas. The cookie moved and Ian looked away before he could see what it really was.

Ian looked upon a gaggle of keystone cop dolls, which sat against a dead policeman in uniform. All cops were covered in cobwebs and mold. The policeman was big, bigger than Missy, and Ian hoped he had put up a good fight. Only the clothes iron sticking out of his caved in skull revealed how the fight had ended.

Ian spotted a five-foot tall, lit up, plastic praying Jesus. Sitting to the right of the electric savior were two Mormon missionaries in their uniforms. Both were no longer in need of their garments. There was no need for modesty when there was no more flesh left to hide. There were Mormon tracts in the skeletons' laps. Perhaps Missy hadn't been down to buying the B.S. they were selling. Ian certainly couldn't see Missy embracing any religion that placed women in a subservient position, in other words, most religions.

It occurred to Ian that all of these victims were people that had likely encountered Missy at her front door. Those with something to sell, whether pizza or prophecy, and city officials, with orders to enforce. They wouldn't have been prepared for the mad woman and the hoard she was hiding, and protecting. Except for the cop, none of the victims would have been armed or expecting to fight for their lives on an ordinary suburban porch on any given morning, afternoon, or evening.

Ian wondered how many trick-or-treaters might have been snared over the years, and then he realized he was looking at one. Across the room was a tall skeleton doll that was actually a kid's plastic Halloween costume and mask set. Flies flew in and out of the mask's dark, empty eyes, giving away the meaty center.

Ian looked nearer, at a wooden crib on his left. He took a few careful steps over stuffed animals and pillows so he could look down inside.

Lying in the crib, on a dusty pink blanket spotted with rat droppings, were a baby skeleton and a rattle. Ian's first thought was that a newborn was not a victim that could come knocking on Missy's front door.

A sob turned Ian back to the star of the show. Missy had gone from happy-happy to sad-sad in a flash. She was not a good actress, and he doubted she could cry on cue. These sobs sounded heartfelt, if that horrible black beating organ inside her chest could be called a heart. To Ian, it was an engine of hate.

Missy looked into the crib with a tilted head, grabbed onto the wooden rim with one hand, and let her tears run off her cheeks and drop onto the baby skeleton's blanket. Ian bet that crib blanket had been sopping up her tears for years and years.

"That's my little Saffy. She was ten months old when crib death claimed her from me. That was twenty years ago, right after I got out of that horrible facility. We hadn't been married all that long. But after Saffy died, my husband left…"

Missy's eyes looked out of the crib and gave a cautious glance at a male mummy across the room. She had no tears for him. Ian assumed that the mummy was her former husband. For this married couple, death did not part. The deceased husband was just added to his wife's collection.

"And that's when I started to shop and buy new friends," Missy finished.

Shopping and stealing were two completely different things, but Ian knew Missy couldn't tell the difference. The end result was all she saw, more possessions in her house. Plus, you couldn't buy or steal friends. Some people did, that was the cruel reality of human history, but they were considered human traffickers, slaveholders, kidnappers, or killers. Missy was the worst kind of criminal, and it was justified as harmless collecting in her mind.

Missy inhaled deeply over the crib, savoring Saffy's scent. "It still smells like her."

Ian had to suppress a mad laugh. *Yeah, it smells like dead people*, he also suppressed adding.

With her painful, personal story told, Missy finally looked at the one she was addressing it to. Ian wore a look of sympathy. Luckily, he was a better actor than she was.

"I'm sorry," Ian consoled her.

Missy appeared touched by Ian's concern. As she wiped away her tears, Ian went over Missy's tall tale in his head. He didn't think she was lying directly, she probably believed every word she said. But her brief hard history had some glaring omissions, and he expected any original truth had been twisted in her mind to justify her current state, and the state of her house. A hoarder's history of hardships always became an excuse for their disorderly living conditions.

Ian was glad that Missy had been so forthcoming with him and his camera. He wanted his brother and friends' killer to confess herself while she was still alive to do so. He hoped she wouldn't be around much longer. She did not deserve to live, not after she had snuffed out so much life in one night, and all of these other lives over the years. She might have an idea she was a serial hoarder, but she probably had no clue she was a serial killer.

The severity of Missy's crimes against humanity and other mammals made Ian reconsider burning her house down. There were too many families missing loved ones who needed to know the dark secrets that Missy's house hid. All of this filth and waste was crucial evidence. It would provide a lot of painful closure, but that was better than never finding out a missing loved one's fate. Ian knew that all too well.

Missy's house of horrors had to remain standing until all investigations were complete. Only then could the structure be razed, like Ariel Castro's dungeon house in Cleveland. Ian wanted to be among the surviving families who would be here to cheer on the wrecking ball. He only hoped it would happen soon, before the decades of spoilage, leaking sewer pipes, and blood of the innocents turned the ground rotten, uninhabitable, and haunted.

Most interesting about Missy's condensed history was her slip about her stay in a horrible facility. Ian was sure it had been a horrible experience for her. There was no facility that would let you keep a hoard in a cell.

Missy looked back down into the crib with calm acceptance, and a small smile touched her lips.

"It's okay now. I still have Saffy, she just stopped growing."

Just like her dolls, Ian thought, except people decomposed much faster. Ian saw another cadaver beyond the crib, encircled by prince dolls. It was a city code inspector with a clipboard in his lap. He was well spoiled, a dripping feast for the flies.

Ian knew just how long dead this cadaver was, six months and five days.

"Dad," Ian barely managed to voice. No other words would come, and no other word mattered more.

Ian took back every horrible name he had called his father since his disappearance. There had been thousands, and he had meant every one. Cussing him out for his absence had been his and Keith's way of coping. They had always seen their father as a deserter. He was big and strong, curiously distant, and a loner despite the large family he had created for himself. While they knew it was a possibility, they had never truly believed him to be a homicide victim. His bank account, holding many thousands, had been cleaned out the night of his vanishing, enough to run and start a new life elsewhere.

Now it all made so much shattering sense, and he wished he had considered this possibility sooner. His father had never been one to bring his work home with him, and it was never a topic of discussion around the dinner table. But Ian knew enough about his father's duties as a senior city code enforcement officer to know that he delivered citations and condemned notices to non-code compliant home and business owners. And who was more in need of being condemned than Missy Wormwood? His father's job had unfortunately brought him right onto Missy's killing grounds, her front porch. And it was no wonder he had incurred Missy's wrath. It had been his job to make Missy remove the one thing she cared about most in the world, her hoard.

Ian's emotions spun in a cyclone, building a fury inside of him. Now he was becoming the human tornado, and he welcomed it.

Ian wasn't sure how long he had been staring at his rotting father. He was already in shock from his discovery of Dani, and the deaths of his brother and Will. Too many major shocks, too fast. Who could blame him for going a bit mad in the aftermath of so many grim discoveries? Grief was understandable, but he could not afford it. He was in mortal danger, and had momentarily lost sight and thought of the murderer beside him.

Ian turned to Missy, too fast, giving away his fear of her.

Missy looked at Ian with something like love. Or maybe she saw him as lunch.

"Thanks for your concern, Ian."

Ian froze. He wasn't Chad anymore. She knew more than he expected. She was no longer playing a charade, so neither would he.

"You know my name?"

"Yeah, I know you and Keith are Roland's boys."

Ian was deeply offended to hear his father's name spill out of her disgusting, roach reeking mouth.

"How do you know who we are?" Ian asked, although he had a clue. It would have been from the first of their family who encountered her.

Missy climbed past the crib toward Roland's corpse. Ian had to restrain the urge to lunge at her and push her away from his father. He didn't want her to touch him again, but what was one more defiling now? It would be Missy's last time; she just didn't know it yet. It also wasn't the right time to play his hand against her. Besides, he really wanted an answer to his question.

Missy leaned over Roland's corpse and stuck her hand into his front right pant pocket. Ian cringed as Missy struggled to pull his father's wallet out, joggling the corpse. Bugs crawled out of Roland's head in alarm.

With the wallet removed, Missy worked her way back toward Ian. She flipped the wallet open, went directly to the pictures in clear plastic sleeves, and flipped it to her favorite, which she held out so Ian could see. The wallet size snapshot showed Roland, Keith, and Ian together, at a back yard barbeque in happier times.

"He has your names on the back," Missy explained, flipping the picture over so the back was revealed. Ian could read their names, and recognized his father's handwriting. He hadn't even known that his father carried a picture of his sons with him, but it was a touching fact to know, and painful in hindsight.

"I have a confession to make," Missy admitted.

Ian wanted to hear her confession. Missy's behavior had been so offensive and shocking already, he couldn't imagine what other transgression she could possibly confess to. Once he heard it, he wished he had plugged his ears and shouted "*Lalalala! I can't hear you!*"

"For years I've had the hotsies for Rollie, he's just the most adorable man in the neighborhood!" Missy's cheeks rose in redness as she spoke, her blushing complicit with her overly made up lips to make her face completely red. Ian thought it was only appropriate, they painted her as the devil she was.

"So imagine my surprise that day when he finally came calling! He wanted to see my house, and he was so amazed, he never wanted to leave! We've been so happy, and now his cute-as-buttons boys have come to join us! I feel like a new woman. A new mommy!"

Missy's last word stung Ian. His mother had been a new mommy too over the past six months, one devastated by loss and daily pushed beyond her limits to cope and provide for her sons. Missy thought a family was something she could just take, like a sale item off the store shelves or a cool looking bike swiped off a porch. Missy had a lot of backwards definitions of things, but her misunderstanding of the word family was her most erroneous of all. The only family Missy deserved was her shit and mold, but she didn't even deserve those. Her shit made her happy, and she did not deserve the satisfaction of a shitty, moldy home anymore.

Ian looked back at his dead father. His plan was set. In fact, it was already in motion.

The tone of Missy's voice shifted, got a bit quieter, which made Ian nervous. "You and Keith surprised me though."

"How?"

"I didn't know you boys worked in TV land. My show will be bigger than *The Osbournes*!"

Ian almost laughed at that, but he knew better. He was lucky he hadn't falsified his fiction about the show *Missy's House* yet, and Missy was too eager for fame to let go of the fantasy. He was still the director.

"Bigger than the Manson trail," Ian corrected her.

Missy didn't see a difference between *The Osbournes* and Manson; ratings were ratings. Ian knew one other misconception Missy had about her show. She was happy to have him here to film it, but she'd never let him out to edit or release it. She had called him a part of her happy family, her happy hoard, and Missy was far too possessive of her happy things to let them out from behind her walls. She didn't have to say it, and might not even know it, but she never intended to let him out of her house again. She would be fine with him alive or dead. Preferably dead, she had a lot more control over her things that way.

Ian saw that Missy was wiping her eyes again, but these were tears of joy. It wasn't an act for the camera either. Missy was delivering another one of her honestly good performances.

"I'm just so happy today! I feel like my collection is practically complete. Until the next good sale that is!"

Missy snorted laughter, and once started, couldn't stop. She didn't see the glare that Ian was giving her, and good thing, because Ian had murder in his eyes. Ian's ultimate horror was her ultimate elation. He couldn't wait to wipe that smile off of her smug face.

Missy's chortling devolved into a series of rattling coughs that Ian thought might be bronchitis, or pneumonia if he was lucky. She might never know and would certainly deny the fact that her hoard was slowly killing her, too. He and his friends were only unlucky that the hoard had not succeeded in ending her life before tonight.

Missy looked around at all of her wonderful things. She wasn't done rubbing Ian's face in all she had taken from him yet.

"There are just so many beautiful things in the world. I want to collect them all! Under my roof. In Missy's house!"

Ian didn't doubt that Missy desired every beautiful object in the world within her walls. Only she was done adding to her collections. No more disposable cup sets. No more clown *pitchers*. No more friends.

"Thanks for being so candid for the camera, Missy. Mind if we sit together?"

Ian pointed at the two beanbags ahead.

"Sure, Mister Director."

Missy climbed with Ian toward the shiny seats. She pocketed Roland's wallet along the way, only her tight dress didn't have any real pockets, she just slipped it into a tear in her dress and the wallet remained pressed against her flesh. Ian made a mental note to take the wallet back before the night was through. He also noticed the slight grimace of pain on Missy's face as she climbed over the stuffies. Ian hoped the leaking stab wound on her back was slowly sapping her of strength and life, and he could thank his brother, or Dani, for that. He hoped the injury hurt the bitch like a bitch.

Ian went to the blue beanbag and sat cross-legged on it. Missy dropped down onto the red beanbag facing him, but her muscular thighs prevented her from crossing her legs. She sat with her legs wide open, and Ian discovered, like his brother before him, that she was not wearing panties. He thought there might be a road kill kitty on her crotch, because he saw bloody, matted fur down there. Not a very flattering position for the camera in Ian's opinion, but he kept that to himself. He wanted her to appear the fool she was. She was grinning at Ian, waiting for his direction.

This was when the show Ian was directing radically changed course. Reality was no longer the correct category for *Missy's House.* The program had changed to snuff.

26

"So we've done our tour," Ian started. "Now it's time to begin the diagnosis part of the show. This is where I talk, and ask you candid questions. And you have to answer them honestly. Are you up for that, Missy?"

"Of course, it's my show!" Missy replied with enthusiasm. She obviously thought she was a most fascinating interview. *So was Aileen Wuornos*, Ian thought but didn't add.

Missy was all smiles as Ian's diagnosis began. Her smiles did not last for long.

"Good," Ian said. "You are a hoarder. Do you know what that is?"

"That's somebody who likes to collect things," Missy answered.

Ian wasn't too surprised that Missy knew the word, but had assigned it no negative connotations. But this was the part of the show were fantasies would be shattered, and reality television would earn its name.

"Collections sometimes," Ian corrected her, "but it's usually just garbage, and huge amounts of useless waste. But you, Missy, have taken hoarding to horrific, obscene extremes. You are the first horror-der."

Ian had never heard the term before, this mating of horror and hoarder, but it rolled naturally off of his tongue, as though a new word needed to be created to define Missy and her dreadful mess.

Some, but not all, of the joy had evaporated from Missy's face. "I don't get it."

"I'm not surprised. You have had a complete break with reality, and I expect you've been that way for years, decades maybe. The skeletons in here are proof of that. In your mind, what you consider reality is actually the opposite. To you, garbage is treasure. Spoiled is fresh. Neglect is nurture. Murder is friendship. Dead is alive."

It felt so good for Ian to say these things out loud to Missy, to call her out on her lunacy.

"You're confusing me," Missy stated, and it was clear on her face.

Ian needed to spell things out for his simple subject. He wanted her to understand. "You don't even seem to notice the stink around here. I don't know how that's humanly possible."

Missy looked defensive. "My place don't stink. It smells like roses." Missy took a deep breath to verify her claim. From the look of pleasure on her face, Ian didn't doubt that the profound reek smelled like roses to her.

"You're not confused, you're delusional," Ian clarified to Missy. "Life is not like the tabloid reality shows you watch."

"Sure it is. That's why they call it reality. Your show is reality," Missy countered.

Missy had a point he had to admit. "Mine is. You're right. You know, I'm not here to say you can't be a hoarder, or watch reality TV, or believe what you want about it. The issue I have with you is you're psychotic."

Missy could not comprehend Ian's diagnosis. He noticed that these moments of confusion were the rare occasions where Missy's voice dropped down out of a sing-songy shout.

"I can't be. I'm happy and nice. I have lots of friends. Just ask them." Missy looked around at her dolls, her friends. She knew from their smiles that they agreed with her. She looked justified in her defense.

Ian looked around at the same doll collection and saw the corpses. The silently screaming cadavers could offer no opinion, although Ian was certain they would voice their disapproval if they could.

"Dolls and corpses can't talk," Ian said.

Missy leaned forward and shouted in Ian's face. "My dollies do!"

Ian wouldn't let Missy's building anger derail him from the truth. In the rage department, he thought he had Missy beat.

"And I've heard firsthand, from those who work at the store where you shop, that you are such an insufferable bitch to deal with, the employees dread your arrival. You're their legendary worst customer."

Missy thought about that for a moment, but didn't appear bothered by the information. "That's their job," Missy informed him.

"It is," Ian agreed, and then countered, "but you can drop the idea that you're nice. You're a terror, and a bully."

There was an uncomfortable moment of silence. Ian was surprised he was still being allowed to grill her. She appeared puzzled, like she didn't know who or where she was. When her speech returned, she softly said, "You're not making me look very good."

That's the point, Ian thought. He knew he was walking on a razor's edge with Missy, and he also knew she needed a bit more coddling if he was going to proceed. He loved putting her in her place, but he also had to direct her a little more.

"It's the diagnosis part of the show, so it's part of the formula," Ian informed her.

"Oh."

Missy's curious lack of emotion made Ian nervous, but he continued anyway. He had a lot left to say. This was his script.

"You have a big problem with stealing. You stole my brother's bike, right off our porch. What gives you the right to take other people's property?"

Missy didn't answer Ian's question, but she cooed about the bike. "It's a pretty bike, with those cool blue stripes. I wanted it."

Ian had to simplify his point for his dumb subject. "But it's not yours."

Ian saw both of Missy's fists were clenching and unclenching in her lap.

"It is mine. I took it," Missy corrected Ian, or so she thought.

"We took it back. My brother's bike is out of your house. It's not yours anymore," Ian informed Missy for the first time.

Ironically, the one word that ignited in Missy's mind in red neon was *THIEVES!*

Ian expected some protest from Missy. He should have expected what happened instead. Missy leaned forward on her beanbag and punched him in the chest. Her fist felt like lead, and it rattled his heartbeat. Ian fell back against a stuffed Beagle almost as big as he was and leaned right back forward.

Missy's response had been severe, but it was not a surprise. In fact, Missy's behavior completely fit the formula of the hoarding shows he had seen. The hoarders, driven to the point of cleaning their homes to avoid eviction, always acted out once the cleaning commenced. Even the nice looking old ladies turned into vicious shrews who would attack any loved one or stranger who dared to help by tossing out a piece of garbage that was inevitably invaluable to them. Ian's intervention would never be welcomed, and he knew he was putting himself in the path of attack.

They faced each other in silence. Ian tried to catch his breath, which wasn't easy after his heart had skipped a beat. Missy put her non-punching hand back behind her, to press on the sanitary napkin and lessen her growing ache.

"Don't cross me," Missy warned.

"*Cross you? I'll fucking kill you!*" Ian said, but only in his head. He tempered his actual response to, "We're just talking, remember. This isn't a hitting show like Springer's." Ian didn't add that he wished there was a big referee like Steve Wilkos between them to shield him from her attacks.

"I want my bike back," Missy demanded.

Ian ignored her demand and continued his diagnosis. "Not only do you steal property, you steal animals, and people, and lives. You neglect your cats."

"I do not!" Missy interrupted indignantly.

"Your cats are starving and diseased. They're stuffed in shit covered cages they can't move in. There are dead cats all over this house. Neglect is too kind a word. Cruelty fits better. I'm sure you beat your cats, too."

"I would never!" Missy denied, and believed completely.

"You would, you just don't see it. You keep hitting me, your director, and I don't think you even realize you're doing it. Did your stay in that horrible facility you mentioned have anything to do with violent tendencies?"

Missy's fists clenched, unclenched, clenched, unclenched.

Ian could see Missy's steam building, and knew another violent outburst was imminent, but he couldn't stop now. There were too many pages of his script left to cover.

"That person up here, Tickles, is dead or dying, and you could care less. You're only worried about getting more camera time. You're a selfish sociopath."

"I… I don't know what that means," Missy said.

"Then let me spell it out for you. You killed my father, and took him from his wife and kids, who loved him more than you ever could. He did not have eyes for your open thighs. He was probably going to issue you a citation, because the whole city wants your house condemned. And then you killed my brother and my friends. And all of these other people unfortunate enough to stumble upon Missy's house."

Missy stared at Ian without reply, trying to process all of the kid's crazy talk. She was a woman rarely criticized, at least to her face, and she did not know how to process it.

Ian felt like he was on a roll, but he was jolted to a stop when he saw a corpse's foot, nearly skeletal, sticking up out of the mound of stuffed animals behind Missy. The foot confirmed another ugly reality. He had already accepted that there were numerous dead cats hidden under the house's hoard. Who knew how many human cadavers they had been climbing over all this time? Just as Missy had crawled over Will's covered body without realizing it. Like a dog, Missy buried her bones. Except for the ones she kept out to play with.

"Who knows how many more bodies are buried under this hoard. I guess we'll find out when this house is finally cleaned out, starting tomorrow."

Missy looked around nervously, looking for an excuse. "I'm… I've had a hard time dealing with my baby's death."

Who could argue with a grieving mother? Ian could.

"I've had some hard losses, too, thanks to you, but it's never made me want to live in a garbage dump and keep the company of corpses. And by the way, they're not laughing. They're screaming!"

Missy was jolted by Ian's shout, and then she looked around at her human dolls, the Girl Scout, the Mormon missionaries, the pizza delivery guy. Their mouths (some just skeletal jaws) were all open and laughing in Missy's mind, which meant Ian was out of his mind. It was the kind of joyful laughter that always confirmed to

Missy that there was nowhere else in the world that these human dolls would rather be.

Ian also looked at the human dolls, including his father, and Dani, and those too bloated and rotten to read their faces. In Ian's mind, they were in purgatory and they were screaming. His dad was screaming. Dani was screaming. Keith was screaming from the hallway. Will was screaming from downstairs.

It was too easy to go mad inside Missy's house. The mix of death, mold, stench, neglect, and loneliness would probably drive Ian mad like Missy over time.

Seeing Missy put into prison would make him happy. Seeing Missy put in the grave might make him happier. But neither seemed punishment enough for what she had done to him and so many others. He knew a way to make her suffer, a way to pierce her vampire heart the way she had pierced his.

It was time for Ian to stop the screaming of his loved ones, no matter the cost. He was going to end it right now.

Right fucking now!

27

"I'll bet you killed your little Saffy," Ian began. "Maybe it was an accident, maybe you sat on her, or your hoard fell on her like my friend Will. But it was your fault. I'm sure of it."

"Cut," Missy said, "the show is over. I don't want this on camera. I want your crew to leave now."

If only we could leave, you stupid bitch, Ian thought as he stood. "I'll leave, because I have no intention of being trapped in here for life like these poor souls," he said as he moved his way over to the cobweb draped crib with Saffy's skeleton inside.

Missy watched Ian suspiciously from her red beanbag. She leaned forward, about to rise and follow him, when a piercing pain from her back made her sit down again. She put a hand over the bloody pad on her back, which was dripping.

Once beside the crib, Ian turned to Missy. "I'm also going to release every miserable cat and call the police. You are going to lose your precious hoard, your horrible house, and your friends. *Missy's House* is cancelled. I'll see you on your next show, *Lockup*."

From the confused look on Missy's face, *Lockup* was a show she wasn't familiar with.

Ian leaned into the crib and smashed Saffy's brittle skeleton with his fist and camera. The bones disintegrated into bursts of dust. From the ease of the bones' obliteration, he probably could have demolished them by blowing hard on them.

"NO!" Missy screamed. The pain of her stabbed back was forgotten as her adrenaline kicked in, and she launched up off of the red beanbag. She lunged for Ian, but stumbled on the floor of stuffed animals (it was Oliver the Octopus that provided the tripping tentacle). Missy fell forward and landed flat on her face, her impact fully cushioned.

A white plume of bone dust rose over the crib, nearly causing Ian to cough as he continued to pound the skeleton inside. Saffy was reduced to little more than small bone shards and a cloud, except for her skull. Adding to the desecration, Ian flipped the aged crib over. Even on a floor of furries, the crib was reduced to kindling.

As he engaged in the demolition of Saffy's skeleton and her crib, Ian offered a mental apology to the baby. He held no ill will for poor Saffy, and he even doubted whether she had been born to Missy. It would come as no surprise if he found out that Saffy had been snatched out of another shopper's cart because Missy found her too adorable and had to add her to her collection, which turned out to be pretty much the case.

The true facts of Saffy's abduction wouldn't become public knowledge until much later, after a lengthy investigation and DNA testing. And the baby's original name was not Saffy, that was a girl's name and this baby had been a boy.

It occurred to Ian that Missy's husband was probably a fiction, like his father was a man seeking her courtship in her mind. Her husband was probably just another sad victim unfortunate to be handsome enough to tickle Missy's loins.

"You don't deserve any friends!" Ian screamed at her.

Missy pushed herself up onto her knees on her carpet of stuffies and corpses.

"I'll kill you! You hurt my Saffy!"

As Missy climbed toward the shattered crib, Ian climbed toward the door. He shouted back at her, "Your little Saffy isn't laughing anymore!"

When Missy reached the overturned crib, she broke the splintered boards apart to get to the baby's bones beneath.

Ian noticed the many smiles of the stuffed animals he crawled over on his way to the door. Perhaps they were smiling because they would soon be free of this nightmare menagerie. He came upon a giant stuffed bear leg on his right, and saw the nearly four-foot bear it belonged to. Stacked on the lap, arms, shoulders, and head of the bear was a family of Puritan dolls made of porcelain.

Ian moved past the bear and turned back to it, grabbing the bear's leg and giving it a hard yank. The bear was a fluffy obstacle in Missy's path, but it was the collapsing glass dolls that would prove a better barrier. The porcelain Puritans cracked against each other and rolled off the big bear they had been mounted on for so many years.

With the crib obliterated, and with a few long splinters planted deep in Missy's fingers, she picked up half of Saffy's shattered skull, the biggest part of the baby that remained.

"My poor Saffy! What did that bad boy do to you!?"

Saffy was long past being able to answer Missy, had in fact died long before developing the ability to talk. Regardless, Saffy's half skull spoke to Missy, at least in her mind.

"Kill the punk, mommy! Crush his skull like mine!" the half skull ordered in a high-pitched scream. Missy nodded, in tears.

"I will, Saffy! I will," Missy, with all her heart, promised her daughter, who was really a dead, stolen infant boy, whom her heart had forgotten and would always deny.

"And get that bike back for me!" Saffy's half skull ordered.

My bike! Missy had momentarily forgotten the bike. Destroying Saffy and her crib was bad enough, but that bad boy and his scallywag friends had taken her favorite bike with those cool blue-striped handlebars out of her house! It wasn't just her bike; it was going to be Saffy's bike someday (never mind that nobody would ride it until the end of time if it remained in Missy's house). In Missy's mind, taking her bike was a transgression that was punishable by death.

Ian pushed up onto his feet when he was within a few steps of the door. He collided with one of the caked flypaper strips, and the gooey paper stuck to his face. He could see the little twitching fly legs between his eyes. He could smell the nutty adhesive and rotting bugs beside his nose. He could practically taste the gluey strip and its victims that ran down over his partly open lips.

Ian shifted hard to the side in the hope the flypaper would pull off of him. The strip broke off the ceiling instead, sticking firmly to his face. The flypaper was reluctant to let go of its biggest catch.

As Ian pinched the top of the flypaper strip and pulled it off of his face, he didn't see Missy pick up the wooden bottom of the crib behind him.

With the flypaper removed, glue and bugs remained stuck in a diagonal line down Ian's face. He flung the flypaper to the side, but the squirmy strip remained stuck to his fingers. Then came the blow to the back of his head as the thrown crib bottom hit him, and what he saw next was a blur as he pitched forward out of the Rot Room into the hallway.

Ian could just make out the forward leaning, three-foot tall dresser in the hall that he was falling toward. He tried to shift further right to avoid it. Ian's forehead hit the top corner of the dresser, and after an explosion of stars, he saw and thought the same thing at the same time.

Nothing.

28

Ian fell to the side of the dresser as it pitched forward, all of the packed drawers falling out, spilling junk and vermin. The dresser hit a discarded walker before it, preventing a full forward collapse.

The sound of breaking glass inside the Rot Room brought Ian back to consciousness. The porcelain Puritans were breaking, their generations stomped on by a giant, which meant Missy was on the move his way.

Ian sat up quickly and his head spun so hard, he nearly fell backward. He steadied himself and touched his throbbing forehead at the point of impact. He winced at the raw agony and indentation there, and when he pulled his fingers back, they were smudged with blood. No surprise there, he had never hit his head that hard before, or knocked himself out. He even had a new term for it, a skull-cracker.

Next he touched the back of his head where he had first been hit, by what he had no idea. This point of impact didn't feel as dented as his forehead, but he could feel a separation of skin and tissue, and when he pulled his fingers back, they were no longer smudged with blood, they were dripping with it.

Ian heard more glass breaking and a yelp from Missy. He grinned, knowing he had slowed her advance and injured her in the process.

The open door was right behind him, but he didn't dare look back and waste one second to confirm what he already knew. Ian had only two options available to him now. Left or right.

Going down the hallway to his left would take him back to the living room and the house he knew, including the front door. Only escape was no longer the next part of Ian's plan, and the tipped dresser with its extended drawers filled what little path there had been. Climbing over the tipped dresser was possible, but it wouldn't be easy. Missy would probably step right over it.

To Ian's right was the terrible bedroom with the skinned body that was not body shaped inside. But he remembered Missy speaking about another way out of that room that led down through the house, although he doubted the loop-de-loops she mentioned were real. It was the better option, only instead of a fallen dresser in his way, there was his dead brother.

Ian made his decision.

29

Missy stopped in her pursuit to pull a broken china doll arm out of her right palm. That was a real smarty, just like the poke in the back that Keith had given her in the other room. She threw the shard to the side, where it slid down out of sight between Ally the Alligator and Furry Turtle.

Missy felt bad for her broken dollies, and thought her room would feel empty without them mounted on Burly Bear. She also hoped the dollies didn't hurt from their many broken limbs. At least with the money she'd get for *Missy's House*, she could buy a whole village of porcelain Puritans. The only thing better than a family was more families. And Missy had the most family friendly house in the whole world. She had hundreds of happy families living under her roof.

Missy remembered Saffy and knew that was one thing she could not buy a replacement of. Saffy had been taken from her, again! Rage at Roland's rotten boy got her back to crawling after him. He had broken Saffy's bones, and she was going to break all of his bones in return. It was only fair.

He was also going to have to pay for the crib he broke apart. It was an antique! Missy considered her house a museum of antiques.

Roland's boys were cute, she'd always thought so (just look at their father, it was no wonder), but they had both turned out to be like stubborn jawbreakers with sour centers. They were not only disrespectful and insulting to her immaculate house, they were making a mess everywhere they went. She would soon have to make sure both boys stayed put so they couldn't run roughshod over all of her valuables anymore. She didn't just lose Saffy tonight; she also lost Blue Cup! Chickin Grillins didn't even carry Blue Cup anymore.

Because of those boys' bad behavior, Missy was going to hold out on her womanly favors for Roland tonight, maybe for a while, at least until he got his boys back in order. It might also do good to give Roland a few punches to the face, to remind him to always mind her. Only she wouldn't punch too hard, his skin was starting to feel awfully moist and soft underneath. Just hard enough to get her point across.

As Missy worked her way toward the door, she looked around at her dollies. They were all smiling and cheering her on.

Wendy the Bed-Wetter said, "*Get him, Missy! Get him!*"

Burly Bear shouted, "*Let me maul him! And eat him!*"

Despite her pulverized skull, Saffy yelled, "*Break all his bones for me, mommy!*"

Hanging from the ceiling and spinning on a string, Toots the Angel trumpeted, "*Kill him, Missy! Kill him!*"

As Missy continued her pursuit, she failed to notice the sanitary napkin had detached from the stab wound on her back. She was leaving a considerable trail of blood behind her, which was eagerly sopped up by the stuffies underneath.

The master bedroom held a bloodthirsty hoard, just like the rest of the house.

30

As Ian pushed up, he realized his hands were empty. He'd dropped the camera during his fall. He didn't see it around him, and then he discovered it between his legs. He'd landed on it, and he would find that bruise later. The red light was no longer on, but he picked it up anyway and stashed it in his front hoodie pocket. He didn't need to record anymore. He had more than enough evidence.

Ian reached the first obstacle in his escape, his brother. There was still something very important he had to give Keith. It was a promise.

"She'll regret ever taking your bike, Keith."

Ian had a much smaller cheering section than Missy, but he heard Keith loud and clear in his head. "*Kill that gluttonous bitch.*"

"I will. Love you, brother." *I love you* was a sentiment Ian had rarely said to Keith, but he had no doubt that his brother had known it. Ian told himself he'd have to start saying it more often. He would always want to be a better brother.

Ian stepped carefully over Keith's not yet room temperature body without disturbing it. A few steps beyond, Ian disappeared from view inside the back bedroom.

Fury entered the hallway first as the broken crib bottom was kicked in from the master bedroom. Missy stomped out and broke the crib bottom into pieces as she plowed over it. More of Saffy's bone dust rose into the air.

Unlike her former passage through the hallway, where she hadn't seen Keith as she passed over him, he got her attention now. He was part of that bad family of boys, and would be the recipient of her rage.

"I should have never dated your daddy," Missy told Keith at her feet. The pain he had made in her back was really starting to irritate her, and she wanted to give some of that pain back.

Missy stomped on Keith's head, onto his upturned cheek and temple, cracking his cranium in multiple places. Her second stomp went higher and managed to leave a dent in Keith's skull. A third stomp broke the skull enough to release his brains.

"See how you like it!" Missy exclaimed. By the sixth stomp, the bottom of her shoe was coated in brains. Missy was stomping in revenge for Saffy, despite the fact that the one she was stomping on had never seen or known about her child. Missy often got confused like that.

Keith's head was left nearly as separated as Saffy's skull, only a lot wetter. Missy thought that was kind of funny, and then she saw something below that earned more of her anger.

Missy squatted and pulled the butcher knife out of Keith's chest. Blood slowly drained out of the wound since Keith no longer had a pulse to propel it. She had been responsible for the knife's placement inside him, but her fractured memory was that Keith had injured himself with the blade after playing with it. That was just the kind of trouble boys were always getting into.

"I told you to put this away!"

Missy took the butcher knife with her. She would have to put it away herself, although she might find another chest to plant it in first.

As Ian worked his way through the thin passageway at the back of the room, he noticed another swarm of flies ahead, as bad as the swarm in the Rot Room. Maybe worse, since no flypaper strips hung in this room to lessen their number.

When Ian reached the landing and discovered what Keith had found before him, he stated what he saw.

"Fucking shit."

Ian regretted saying anything at all, since the air tasted like a dirty toilet.

If Ian had known the second path down was over a steep slope of shit bags, he would have crawled over the dresser in the hallway and gone the other way. These stairs made the ones in the basement and living room look like a cakewalk (these were a crapwalk). He tried to estimate how many shit bags were spread down below him and settled on innumerable.

It wasn't just the dangerously slippery surface that worried Ian. There was also the stink, which was worse than the smelliest bathroom he had ever been in (at last summer's Warped Tour, where every toilet in the stadium men's room had been backed up), times one thousand. Ian feared the air ahead was so full of fecal matter it would be like wading through mud. Butt-mud. He feared he would choke on the air, pass out, and take a header down this enormous crapper.

Ian's nose was forgotten as his ears took over, hearing Missy crashing through the bedroom behind him. Her voice boomed louder than the shouting on the television.

"Get up and help me, Tickles! He took our bike!"

Ian knew it was time to get to shit stepping. On Ian's right was a crap-smeared railing, caked from top to bottom. Ian grabbed the railing tight and took slow steps down the slope, unable to see where the steps actually were. Each step produced an audible squish, and nearly every one caused a slip. The only thing that kept Ian from repeated disaster was his white-knuckle grip on the chunky brown railing. Many of the bags under Ian's shoes burst with a wet pop, caking his shoes in whipped waste.

Ian noticed, as much as he didn't want to, that the railing didn't just have human waste on it, but also chunks of toilet paper. And the TP was transferring to his fingers. The railing was also crawling with vermin. A few roaches ran up Ian's hand, leaving little brown footprints behind them.

The shit roaches also, regrettably, startled him. Ian instinctively let go of the railing to fling his arm out, sending the roaches flying. He nearly flew with them, realizing too late the mistake he'd made (the coward's cootie dance again), and all because he'd been touched by dung bugs.

For Ian, the next few seconds seemed to slow down considerably. Every detail sharpened in his attempt to save himself.

Ian brought his right foot down hard, and only the heel of his shoe hit an unseen step before it slipped off. As Ian pitched forward, he saw the railing and knew if he didn't get an iron grip on it within the next second, he would get to know exactly what a flushed turd felt like. And tasted like, too.

As Ian's hand flew out, wide open to grip the railing, he saw a thick, seven-inch shit lying right where he was reaching. Ian grabbed the loaf for dear life. After breaking through the crusty shell, the inner cream squirted up between his fingers as they wrapped around the railing.

It was a sickening but successful grab, and it saved Ian from falling down the stairs. He let out a fecal flavored breath of relief and continued down. His mouth tasted like he was chewing Honey Bucket flavored Bubblicious.

When Ian reached the last dozen steps, the next thing that nearly made him lose his footing was Missy's booming voice behind him.

"YOU!"

Ian gripped the railing, and the sticky crap on his hand acted as an adhesive. He looked back over his shoulder.

Missy stood at the top of the stairs, her face twisted in anger. Eager to catch the dirty bike stealer in her house, she started down without grabbing the railing that was coated in her own waste, since her right hand was occupied with the knife. On her first step, her left foot slipped, and in trying to catch herself, she overcorrected and pitched forward.

Missy fell onto her belly on the slope, in her good dress no less, and slid down like a fallen log over brown snow. The log screamed all the way down.

Ian knew he only had seconds before Missy rammed into him. He let go of the railing and let his feet carry him down, uncontrollably, his arms pin wheeling as he pitched forward. Missy's scream followed at his heels.

Hitting the first floor landing at a run, Ian collided with a tall dresser that stood less than four feet from the bottom stair. The dresser tipped back until the top hit the wall behind it, a few feet back, stopping Ian's fall. Dust, cobwebs, and knick-knacks of cute animals rained down around him.

Ian rolled to the right, off of the dresser as Missy launched head first off the slope. Missy's face hit the lower dresser with a crunch, which could have been wood or bone, Ian couldn't tell. Missy's screaming had finally stopped. She was knocked out cold.

Ian saw that Missy had left a shit face print with a smear of blood in the middle on the bottom of the dresser, and he let out a triumphant laugh. "Ha!"

Ian turned away from Missy to find his way out of the alcove. He saw no way out.

Ian's surroundings consisted of three tall dressers (one tipped), two rods of hanging clothes (one above the other), and three walls. There was one way out, the shitty staircase past Missy. It had been risky enough coming down, but it would be even worse climbing up.

"No!" Ian cried in denial.

Missy moaned, eyes closed, and remained on the floor in impact position. Ian saw her legs stir and knew he had only a few more seconds to get past her and start scaling Crap Mountain.

"Fuck that." He'd find another way out, even if he had to climb the walls like a fly using the tacky shit on his fingers. Or maybe he'd find another patch of soft wall to punch his way through, made moist by years of diarrhea saturation.

In a growing panic, Ian turned away from Missy and looked more closely around the alcove, hoping to find a way out he might have missed at first glance. He squeezed around the tipped dresser and looked behind it. There was only a wall with garbage bags stacked against it.

Ian turned to the clothes hanging in two levels. He parted through the dusty, web draped wardrobe, all of it women's, and saw more clothes hanging behind the first rods. It had to be an exceptionally tall and deep closet to hold so many racks of clothing.

Ian ducked into the closet and tried to push through the second rod of clothing, which was even more densely caked in webs. The dresses and shirts were so tightly packed, Ian doubted one more hanger could be added to the rod. Ian pushed harder into the garments and saw, much to his disbelief, another tightly packed rod of clothing behind it. He also glimpsed a few slivers of light above it.

Ian had found his way out of the alcove. He was in a corridor that had been transformed into a multilevel closet. He crouched down, finding it easier to duck through the bottom of the garments. The cobwebs that had long encased the wardrobe transferred to him. He felt the passage of little legs along the back of his neck, and something else crawled over his left ear. Whether the creepy-crawlies had six or eight legs, Ian couldn't tell. The crawler he felt cross the back of his neck felt like it had a hundred legs. He forced himself not to care. He had a far larger two-legged threat close behind him. This whole house was her web, and he felt seized in it.

Ian took a moment to wipe off his poopy hands on a white dress. He hoped it was her wedding dress and she would put it on before she found his brown handprints, but he knew she would never get the chance to wear any of these clothes again. Even if he wasn't planning to stop her and she lived to be one hundred years old, all of this clothing would stay untouched. Missy might claim that every item in her collections, every piece of her hoard, was cherished and necessary, but in reality most everything was neglected and forgotten. Missy had standard hoarder-vision.

Ian could see more of an alcove ahead after passing the fourth rod of clothing. There was only one more rod of wardrobe left to push through. A hand that was more bone then flesh hung under the final fashions, and Ian ducked beneath it with a shudder of disgust. The dead fashionista helped Ian by catching hold of some of the cobwebs on his cap.

Coming up out of the final rod of clothing, Ian vigorously shook his head to throw off the crawling stowaways. He got a good look at the small alcove he stood in.

Ian's fear grew as he realized the only way out was behind him.

31

Missy moaned as she used the tipped dresser to pull herself up. She could already tell that everything on the shelves had been moved out of place, thanks to that bad boy. Bad boys deserved a spanking, and she couldn't wait to tenderize this bad boy's bottom, one swat for every item in her house he had moved out of place. Followed by a thousand more for taking her favorite bike.

Once Missy was on her feet, she looked down at her dress. It looked like her entire front side had been covered in chocolate frosting. She couldn't see that her face was equally frosted, but she figured her sexy make-up job was probably messed up. It wasn't enough of a bother for her to wipe her face off.

What did capture Missy's attention was the cool new cap she had been wearing for the last hour, at her feet. She picked it up and pulled it back onto her head. The addition of this one accessory pleased her and made her forget all about her full face and body butt-mud treatment.

Missy put one hand to her back and the other to her face as she took an inventory of her injuries. Her bruised face and nose were hollering louder than the hot jab in her back. She would have to take a few aspirin soon. She would have gobbled down a few dry ones if she had them on her, which was her favorite method for taking aspirin since she liked the chalky taste. Unfortunately, her aspirin bottle was down in her hidey-hole, a few rooms away.

Missy knew she had to get moving, she didn't want that boy to get too far ahead of her. She had seen him disappear into her clothing, which made her worry more. She wouldn't put it past him to rearrange some of her hangers of fine attire to confuse her. That was just the kind of thing that delinquents did for fun. She would have to talk to Roland later and tell him to get better control of his boys. He was the man of the house, after all. She thought Roland might be neglecting his fatherly duties lately.

She would forgive him though, the next time she sat on his face.

Missy remembered the knife she had been holding at the top of the stairs, the one she had to unfairly take back to the kitchen herself. Looking around, she didn't see the knife anywhere on the landing. She looked up the stairs and saw the blade a few feet from the top, stabbed into a waste bag, which was bleeding its viscous contents as a result.

The knife was too far up the stairs to bother getting now. She'd have to pick it up the next time she visited Tickles in the back bedroom. Just another inconvenience on a night that had been full of them, starting with the fire at the store that no good Cutter bitch had started. Honestly, if she had known how much annoyance everything was going to be, she never would have allowed the production crew into her house in the first place. If there was any good to come from this, it was that they had gotten so much good footage of her, they would have to turn tonight's episode into a two-parter. That would mean twice the money.

Missy turned to the clothing to follow Ian, saw something out of the corner of her eye, and turned back to the tipped dresser. There was something of critical importance that had to be dealt with, even more critical than the delinquent director running rampant through her house. There was an overturned glass jar on one of the shelves, and all of the colored pens that had been held inside had spilled out, lying in a chaotic pile like pick up sticks.

Missy picked up every pen, returned them to the jar, tip down, organized from lightest colors on the left to darkest on the right, set the full jar upright, and then she resumed the chase.

32

Ian was realizing far too late that the deeper he went into the house, the denser the hoard got. Missy had mentioned the other path that went through the house, but that was apparently just another one of her delusions. A rat could get through this path with ease, but Missy sure couldn't. Ian didn't think he could either.

The alcove he stood in was more the size of a closet. He could take no more than two steps in any direction. There was a corridor in front of him, nearly thirty feet long, and every foot of it was crammed with furniture, stacked topsy-turvy. Ian didn't know this was the same corridor that had stopped Dani on the other side earlier.

Ian looked back at the hanging clothes, afraid that Missy would burst through them at any moment, as Boogeymen and Boogeywomen do.

Ian reconsidered the stuffed hallway. The furniture was packed in tight, but it was not packed solid. There were crawlspaces visible through the corridor. Ian had done his fair share of climbing and crawling through perilous locations, including that black mold spotted boiler room at school. He considered himself good at it, and could see himself practicing parkour in the future. Of course, if he wanted a future, he had to get outside of Missy's house.

The corridor ahead could prove to be a death trap just as the living room had been for Will, but retreating back and facing Missy seemed a far less desirable way to die. Besides, he refused to give Missy the satisfaction of doing the same thing to him she had done to his father, brother, and friends.

It was time for Ian to act as a rat and crawl through Missy's maze. Ian hoisted himself up to the widest channel available, just over two-feet long and a foot and a half tall, between a hutch and a desk stacked on top. He squirmed his way into the furniture hoard.

Ian bumped his head on the bottom of the desk and the whole house of heavy wooden cards shifted with alarming scraping and squealing sounds. Ian continued even quicker, making himself as light as possible. Light as a feather, don't get squished by a hoard.

Ian slipped off of the hutch into a hole just big enough for him to get back onto his feet. He had a refrigerator on his left, an upended sofa on his right, and a seven-foot tall dresser directly in front of him. There looked to be maybe a foot of space between the top of the dresser and the mold saturated ceiling. It was the only space available.

Ian climbed the dresser and was startled by a cat lying on top. He quickly realized the animal was dead. He couldn't be squeamish now, and he squeezed into the space on top, sliding over it as ceiling mold smeared onto his backside. Passing the cat corpse, Ian couldn't help but feel sympathy for it. What a horrible fate to perish in this dark and lonely crawlspace. Ian had seen enough dead cats at this point to knit that terrible tapestry of cat carcasses he had imagined earlier.

Slithering through this slim space, Ian didn't notice a closed door to his right. The handle would have been inaccessible even if he had spotted the door. And good thing, too, because this long abandoned downstairs bathroom was so full of ancient shit that the trapped air would be noxious to any human or animal that inhaled it. Better that Ian didn't know the horrors that lurked just a few feet away, beyond a door that had not opened once in twenty-two years.

When Ian dropped down on the other side of the dresser, he was faced with a taller dresser that left about an inch on top, a crawlspace for creepy-crawlies only. Ian saw a small opening to his far left, but he would have to uncomfortably squeeze sideways and climb over a rickety card table to get there.

When Ian got on top of the card table, Missy's booming voice startled him into sitting up, and he knocked his head on the back of a high packed wooden rocker.

"Get off my furniture!" Missy screamed from the alcove. "They're antiques!"

Ian looked back toward the voice. He saw mostly furniture, but he could see slivers of Missy's face and an arm beyond the not so movables. With relief, he knew there was no way she could pursue through the channels he had slithered through.

Missy pulled a chair out from the furniture hoard and threw it behind her. She pulled out the desk on top of the hutch next and tossed it behind her like it weighed next to nothing. That's when the furniture before Missy began to rearrange itself.

Ian could hardly believe it. She was going to move the entire hoard to get to him. He felt the card table beneath him wobble, and then it collapsed, unable to hold his weight any longer.

Ian went down three feet with the falling table, and Missy disappeared from his view. The chairs and tables around him shifted and threatened to entomb him. Ian didn't wait to find out if they would, and he squeezed toward the next visible crawlspace.

The small alcove was quickly piled with overturned furniture, as Missy kept filling the limited space she was leaving in her wake. She grabbed a coffee table, breaking a leg off the heirloom as she yanked it out of the hall, and breaking it more when she threw it behind her. Missy was too angry with Ian for crawling on her furniture to notice she was the one destroying her precious antiques.

Ian could see the end of the hallway just ten feet away. To get there, he had to get down on his belly and squirm underneath a bed frame supporting all manner of furniture. The ground was carpeted with shockingly huge rat droppings (maybe they were raccoon droppings), dense dust bunnies, and broken glass.

Ian slithered over the mess without hesitation. A few cuts on his hands and stink nuggets up his nose were better than a hutch falling on his head. He could hear banging and breaking behind him as Missy the one woman moving crew emptied the hallway. He didn't dare waste a moment to look back at her, not that he could turn his head in the cramped underpass if he wanted to.

Ian squirmed his way out of the hallway and crawled up onto the elevated living room hoard. He finally allowed himself a moment to look back.

Ian could see glimpses of Missy behind her high-stacked stuff. She was a third of the way through the hallway. At the speed she was unpacking, he had maybe two minutes before she reached him. She looked like a giant kaiju to him, tearing down buildings as the giant monster closed in on a power plant.

Power. His monstrous image of Missy gave him an idea. He looked instinctively to the left and found the weapon he was looking for. It wouldn't kill the giant monster named Missy, but it might immobilize her temporarily.

Ian reached over and flipped down the switch to the hallway light.

The bulb inside the hallway went out, plunging the furniture hoard into darkness. Missy's screams of outright terror were immediate.

"No! Turn on the light! Turn it on!"

Missy backed out of the hallway until she bumped into her relocated furnishings. She started to throw everything back, working her way slowly toward the alcove. As she threw a chair back, she threw her voice at Ian.

"How dare you!"

"Afraid of what's lurking in the dark? You should be!"

"Ooo!"

Missy threw more furniture out of her way, breaking it if it sped up the process. Ian had reduced the big monster to a frightened child trying to flee the dark. An unnaturally massive and strong child, like Godzilla Junior.

Ian didn't wait around to watch Missy get out. There was a chance she had a light switch on her side, but that was fine. Plunging her into the dark had turned her around and bought him more time, and he'd been able to prey on her fears in the process, a psychological blow. His weapon of darkness had delivered sufficient damage.

Ian climbed around the nest, unsure what his next move should be. The front door was not an option. He could not run away with the fight unfinished. A weapon would be wise, and while he could grab blunt objects all over the place, he'd prefer a big knife, one even bigger than the blade Missy had used on his brother. Missy should pay with the same anguish that Keith had perished by. With a chill, Ian realized that Keith had chosen the knife that had eventually taken him out.

That decided it for him. Ian would make the kitchen his destination. This was going to be a knife fight.

On the far side of the nest, Ian looked back at the hallway. The banging furniture had stopped, and the hallway light remained off, which meant there wasn't a second switch or one was inaccessible. Missy had broken through her first barricade. The closet wouldn't take her long to get through, but getting back up that shit sack staircase, he hoped she'd slip and get flushed again.

Ian climbed in the direction of the dining room and was faced with the tilted, crushed pizza box and the shrouded lump of Will's hidden body. Will offered encouragement, even in death.

"*Keep it up, Squirt. Make her pay,*" Will said in Ian's head.

"I will, Will," Ian promised.

Ian spotted Will's fallen backpack, and he grabbed it, slinging it over his shoulder. The drive with their collected footage was inside, and Ian wanted control of it, to edit, release, or destroy as he saw fit. Other cameras of theirs might be left behind, but the footage was not stored on them.

Ian looked up as he heard heavy footsteps cross the floor above him. The stomps released puffs of black spores from the moldy ceiling, showing Missy's path. Ian turned his head down, not wanting to get those spores in his eyes.

Movement near the staircase made Ian spin. It was another cat, circling inside its cramped cage. The cat's tail was short, with a jagged, bloody wound at the end, having been shaved off by the corroded bars of the cage due to its incessant circling.

Ian would not let the cat suffer in captivity for one more minute, so he headed toward it, despite it being in the opposite direction of the kitchen, and near the slide that Missy would soon be coming down.

Ian felt a kinship with every trapped animal inside Missy's house. He was their liberator. Whether they were alive or dead, they deserved freedom.

Ian reached the cage and opened the door, but he didn't wait for the cat to take its leave. As Ian turned away, one of Missy's random, throwaway possessions caught his attention. It was a dirty white TV tray with a floral border design. A giant glob of ketchup remained in one corner. The condiment looked wet, not yet fossilized.

Ian thought the tray would be perfect for serving justice.

33

Missy arrived bitching at the top of the staircase to the living room. "And don't you dare turn off any more lights!"

The butcher knife had been retrieved from the waste bag on the second staircase and was held in her right hand. The blade was thickly caked with the bag's contents. Gripping the railing with her other hand, Missy easily stomped down the clothing lined staircase. She knew exactly where to step to avoid slipping. She thought of them as safe stairs, with none of the neck breaking hard edges that had killed her parents (a few extra kicks to their broken heads had helped). The clothes piled over the stairs weren't just there for safety; they were working to cover the scene of a crime that Missy didn't want to be reminded of. Thoughts of her parents were never happy-happy.

Various garments stuck to the doo-doo on her shoes and trailed behind her. This was nothing new to her. She was frequently followed by similar hoard-streamers.

Missy stopped when she reached the bottom of the stairs, scanning the room. "Where'd you go!?"

Missy was not given an answer. She came upon the cage that Ian had opened. The cat inside had not yet taken its pardon, but it had stopped circling. The emaciated animal was staring her down. She didn't think that was how friends should look at each other.

"Where'd he go, Daffodil?" Missy asked her long time prisoner.

Daffodil was not the cat's original name, and the animal had long ago grown to hate this human's high-pitched wail. Not-Daffodil leaped out of the cage with a screech at its cruel captor, clamping over Missy's head and clawing at her.

Missy dropped the butcher knife in her surprise, and she pulled the cat off with both hands. She twisted the cat's biting head until she heard its neck break, once again feeling the pleasurable snap of bones in her grip (she equated it with the satisfying cracking of her knuckles). She kept twisting until she heard the sickly skin rip, and she pulled until the cat's head ripped off of its body. Missy threw the cat's head to the left and the body to the right. Not-Daffodil's jaws were still trying to bite as the head flew.

"You ungrateful pest!" Missy screamed. And to think she had treated Daffodil like a princess inside her home! Never mind that Daffodil was a prince and not a princess. Gender was never a consideration when Missy named her cats.

Missy picked up the fallen butcher knife and moved to a dusty mirror on the nearest bookcase. She saw bleeding claw marks on her crap caked forehead and cheek. She couldn't believe that cat, making a mess of her face when she was supposed to be on camera.

"Bad cat! Bad bad bad!"

Missy abandoned the mirror and climbed toward the kitchen. Missy had a feeling Ian was raiding her yummy-yum box just to spite her. Weren't they supposed to bring craft services with them anyway? She shouldn't have to put out her good food when Hollywood was supposed to be footing the bill.

As Missy passed within a few feet of her nest, Ian leapt out of it and grabbed Missy's left leg with both hands, pulling with all his might. Missy pitched over the side, falling into the nest, screaming. The butcher knife was held out high above her.

Ian fell backward onto what he thought would be the cushioned bottom. Instead he landed on the broken mirror. Missy landed directly beside him on her side, their limbs entangled.

Ian and Missy sat up simultaneously. Ian ducked to the side as Missy thrust the butcher knife at his face. It was coming fast, but Ian could see it was caked with shit. He could smell the rancid blade as it stabbed into the cushion beside him.

Missy let go of the knife handle, and her hand clutched Ian's throat instead. Barely able to breath, Ian grabbed the knife handle beside his head, withdrew it from the cushion (the blade was much cleaner now), spun the knife around, and thrust it back at Missy. Missy's other hand grabbed Ian's wrist, squeezing with crushing force.

Ian flung the knife up, and it spun over the top edge of the nest, out of sight.

Missy's crushing hand, stained with Daffodil's blood, landed on the side of Ian's head and slammed it down onto the broken mirror, which cracked further.

"You're fucking crazy!" Ian yelled defiantly.

"I should wash your mouth out with soap, but I don't want to waste good soap on you!"

"Of course not, you cheap bitch!"

Missy couldn't believe the brat's dirty mouth. Did his father teach him to speak like that? Missy wasn't going to let this little snot talk to her that way. She was the star! She simply couldn't allow it.

"I got something to shut your dirty mouth."

Missy reached into an untied plastic bag and pulled out a used sanitary napkin that was so sopped with blood, it had yet to fully dry. Ian saw what Missy held and clamped his mouth tight a moment before she pressed the moist pad to his lips.

"Eat it! You're used to filth in your mouth!"

Irritated that she couldn't get the bloody pad into his mouth, Missy smeared it all over Ian's face. His disgust fueled his adrenaline and strength, and he pulled his head free of Missy's hand. He pushed his body back off of the mirror and kicked up into the center of Missy's face, stunning her.

Ian added insult to injury. "You eat it! You made it!"

Ian saw Missy staring at him, frozen, and couldn't resist taking another shot. He kicked her in the face again, and heard the sickening and satisfying cracks of her front teeth breaking. His shoe also hit the bill of the camera cap and knocked it off of her head, which was appropriate since it never belonged to this career thief.

When Ian pulled his foot back, he saw a couple of Missy's teeth spill out of her mouth with blood. Missy clamped both hands over her busted face.

Ian knew this was his chance to get out of the nest, and he needed that knife. First he picked up Will's backpack and slung it over his shoulder, and then he turned to where he had thrown the knife and climbed up out of the nest. He heard no sound of pursuit behind him. Ian thought he had hurt Missy pretty badly, and was genuinely happy about that.

Out of the nest, Ian searched the hoard for the knife. He thought he knew the general spot it had landed, yet the knife was nowhere in sight.

Ian sat on an uneven surface of garbage bags, boxes, and speakers. The knife could have slid out of sight into any number of dark crevices. Why waste time in search for it when the kitchen had a number of blades for his choosing? About one thousand.

As Ian decided to abandon his search for the thrown knife, Missy's bloody right hand reached out of the nest, looking for a hold.

Ian stomped on Missy's hand, and he hoped it was hard enough to break her knuckles. She wailed from below. Her bloody fingers spread wide and her hand dropped out of view.

Ian climbed toward the dining room. Getting to those knives was his singular mission now, and he did not deviate when he heard Missy grunting and climbing out of her nest. The big angry bird with a broken beak was in flight again, and it wanted the worm.

Once Missy was back atop her high living room hoard, she gasped as she saw a stranger ahead of her.

Will's body was uncovered and sitting up against the tilted bookcase that had contributed to his death. The stab wound in the center of his face was still leaking. His eyes were open but they had the glassy look of doll eyes. The TV tray that Ian had grabbed was propped on its side on Will's lap. Within the floral border and written in ketchup were four red words:

MISSY'S HOARD
KILLED
ME!

Missy was shocked at the stranger and his sentiment. She didn't even know what his message meant. Hoards were collections, Ian had said so himself, and collections couldn't kill people. That was some kind of crazy talk!

Missy caught movement to the left, and she saw Ian climbing toward the dining room. She climbed after him. Despite her stomped hand and face, which sent blood into her eyes, she could cross the hoard faster. Decades of experience gave her the legs for it, and a leg up on Ian.

Missy came upon a cage with a bouncing kitten inside. The mewling animal seemed to be worked up by all of the action going on around it. The night's surprise party had the cat dancing. Missy considered the cage, but not its contents.

Ian skidded down the incline into the dining room. He was lucky to be back in a room where he didn't have to crawl on all fours.

"Ian!" Missy cried behind him.

Looking back was Ian's big mistake. A dirty cat cage hit Ian in the head, nearly knocking him over. He saw stars, and thought of the number three. Three severe blows to his head, in the last three minutes. Or maybe in the last thirty minutes, time had an elastic quality to it. The three blows were taking their toll, making him dizzy, muddy in thought, blurry in vision, and prone to moments of freezing. Like right now. He was giving Missy time to catch up.

Ian looked upon the cage responsible for rattling his brains, and he was horrified to see a kitten alive inside. The poor animal looked in worse shape than him. One ear was torn mostly off and two of its legs were broken. How could that bitch be so cruel?

Ian willed himself back into motion, stumbling toward the kitchen. When he heard Missy's next scream, he was alarmed by its pitch and proximity.

"I want my bike back!" Missy demanded.

Ian had to look back.

Missy was in the dining room with him, a bull charging at its target. His face and hands were covered in red, and he probably smelled of fear and blood, any monster's favorite flavors.

Ian goaded her on. "You want it, come and get it!"

Ian knew Missy would never touch Keith's bike again. She just didn't know it yet. This whole big nightmare, months for him and decades for others, had funneled down to the crucial few seconds and feet between them, in a race for stabbing weapons. This was their most primal battle, and the final act, hopefully for this ruthless, lunatic killer and not him.

Ian risked another glance back and saw that Missy had stopped. He didn't know why, maybe to grab something else to throw at his head. He didn't wait to find out. The kitchen was only a few yards ahead of him, and canting to the right. His head tilted, the path threatening to spin out of control. He didn't hesitate despite his loss of equilibrium.

Missy's stop lasted three seconds. She prided herself on knowing where every item was in her house of collectibles, and that wasn't one of her delusions. Missy reached into the high-stacked kitchen table mound, stuck her hand into a mostly concealed dish strainer, and pulled out a six-inch steak knife. The knife was exactly where she'd left it. The blade still carried the residue of the steak she had used it on, which she remembered being particularly juicy and salty, her favorite Sizzler selection. There might even be a few bites of that steak left further back on the table, and she reminded herself to check for it later.

When Ian reached the kitchen's rotten interior, he risked another look back. Missy was less than six feet from him. She was drooling blood and the occasional broken tooth shard. Ian saw a glint from the dirty knife in her hand.

Ian had hoped to get to a knife first, but he was nearly in stabbing distance of Missy. He suddenly learned he was wrong about *nearly*. Her next stab plunged in deep.

Will's backpack was yanked off of Ian's arm by the serrated blade stuck in it. Missy dropped the backpack and it was forgotten before it hit the hoard.

Ian's destination was about ten feet before him, the five-foot high utensils pile. In front of it, in his way, was the slightly shorter dishes mound.

Ian was faced with a crucial decision, how to get to those utensils. He could maneuver through the cramped path that ran around the mounds, or he could go directly over the dishes, a more unstable path that would get him to the knives maybe a second or two sooner, if he didn't slip.

Ian thought those few seconds might be life-saving ones, to get a knife in his hand and keep her knife out of his back.

Ian went up onto the dishes, using his hands to climb the pile. Plates and glasses broke beneath him, more than he expected. He slipped and slid back two feet.

Two feet was one more than Missy needed.

The steak knife stabbed into Ian's right calf. Ian screamed, and then regretted that impulse. His cries would be music to this monster's ears.

Missy kept hold of the knife handle and twisted it.

Ian resisted another scream, and with his teeth gritted together, he kicked back with his left leg. Missy let go of the knife handle and caught Ian's foot before it could deliver another blow to her face. Ian pulled his left foot back, but his shoe remained in Missy's grip. His socked foot went down onto the broken dishes he was climbing, propelling him toward the utensils.

Ian's flying shoe kicked him in the back of the head. The blow nearly knocked him off of the dishes, but it didn't stop him. Missy grabbed for the handle of the knife in Ian's calf, but it pulled out of her reach.

Ian arrived at his destination, a mountain peak made of stainless steel utensils. The first handle that Ian's hand wrapped around ended up being a mirror of the one stuck in his leg, a modestly sized steak knife. Ian threw the serrated blade behind him, and it bounced off of Missy's cheek, leaving a one-inch cut which crossed a couple of the cat's claw marks. A few more cuts and she could have a tick-tack-toe grid carved into her face.

Ian used his socked foot to push a bit further up onto the utensils, not really noticing the fork that jabbed up between his toes. His hands sorted through the utensils with speed, picking out four knives and an ice pick before Missy fell on his back.

The big woman crawled up over the considerably smaller young man. "Gotcha!" she screamed.

Ian thrust a carving knife over his shoulder without looking at his target, and he was pleased when he felt it plant into the meat of Missy's right shoulder.

"I don't feel that!" Missy screamed in Ian's ear.

Maybe Missy wasn't lying, maybe she was too juiced up on adrenaline and outrage to feel any pain right now. But she would suffer its effects whether she felt it or not.

Missy's right hand closed around Ian's hood, and she pulled him back. He thrust a butter knife over his left shoulder as he came up. The not-so-sharp blade punched through Missy's brown frosted red dress and sank into her left breast easily without bone or muscle to get in the way.

Despite receiving two stabs to her torso, Missy continued to throttle Ian from behind. She leaned in as she clamped a hand over the back of his neck, where it fit all too easily for breaking his spine. In her fury, she didn't consider that her current position had gotten her stabbed twice already.

Ian countered with an ice pick thrust back over his shoulder. The steel point slid into Missy easier than the knives had. Missy's hold on the back of Ian's neck loosened. Blood dripped down onto her hand and Ian's neck. Ian turned underneath Missy, no easy undertaking considering her girth and the knife in his leg, to face his mortal foe and see where the blood was coming from.

The ice pick stuck out of Missy's left eye. She drooled blood onto Ian as she spoke.

"My… bike…"

So far as final words went, Ian thought hers were particularly greedy ones.

"It was never your bike," Ian corrected her, and hoped she understood.

Ian thrust a butcher knife that topped in length and width the one that had taken Keith's life through the center of Missy's neck. Whether this brutal stab was overkill was questionable. Missy might have soon perished from the ice pick in her eye, but he didn't care to wait and risk another blow to the head or twist of the knife. He also felt Keith guiding his final strike, felt as though his brother could see through his eyes and would find peace at seeing his killer vanquished.

Missy gurgled blood in pain and protest. Ian didn't want to hear it. He pushed himself further up onto the utensils, which didn't feel good with forks and knives jabbing his ass, but he needed to get out from underneath Missy's heavy, wavering body. She could fall either way.

Ian kicked Missy in the stomach with his leg that didn't have a knife stuck in it.

Missy fell backwards on the dishes pile, her landing shattering most of the dishes that hadn't broken already. She slid down headfirst to the bottom of the mound, her head to her hoard, and that's where she ungracefully bled out the last of her life. Hungry cockroaches were exploring her wet wounds before she expelled her last, bubbling breath.

Missy had finally become the thing she coveted most. She was just another piece of her hoard.

Ian slid down from his perch to Missy's side, barely noticing the broken glass and silver wear anymore. He tried standing with the knife stuck in his leg. It was pure agony, certainly the worst he'd ever felt, and he had to shift most of his weight to his other leg to keep standing.

Ian felt another ache, coming from his right arm. Pulling that arm in, he discovered a fork sticking out of his elbow, the prongs an inch under the skin, but luckily not in the meat. He hadn't even felt the impalement during his final fight with Missy, and he wasn't surprised. This was the price for pushing up his sleeves upstairs earlier.

Ian pulled the fork out of his elbow and discarded it. He reached for the knife in his leg to do the same, and hesitated. Ian wasn't a doctor, but he knew that a knife in this position could be a life-threatening injury, and he didn't want to risk opening an artery by removing the blade, causing him to bleed out. As agonizing as it felt, it was safer to leave the knife where it was. He could live with the pain long enough to get medical help.

Ian looked at Missy with cold triumph. "I'd burn this house down, but I don't want one more cat to die."

Ian had one final interaction with Missy before he could leave. He squatted over her, and damn did that hurt. He reached into Missy's dress where she had earlier stashed his father's wallet. Despite all of her falling and fighting, the wallet remained pressed between her dress and flesh. Ian withdrew the wallet and inserted it into his own pocket.

Ian knew his father's wallet would probably be admitted into evidence, but he remembered the picture of him, his father, and Keith in a photo sleeve inside. It was a picture he had never seen before, of a day he would always remember. He planned to take that photo out for himself before the wallet was surrendered to authorities. It had his father's handwriting on the back, and meant too much to him.

Ian knew he would need that wallet photo to heal his greatest injury of the night, his broken heart.

Ian turned away from the dead hoarder and considered the ways out. Going through the dining room, living room, and foyer seemed too long of a jaunt with his skewered leg. He didn't even know what kind of hoard the foyer held. He'd rather risk descending back down and out through the basement. It wouldn't be easy, but it was only one room instead of three, and that was the deciding factor.

Ian took a step away, and his socked foot landed on the first knife he'd thrown that had bounced off of Missy. He winced as he lifted his foot and shook the knife out of his sock. It only took a moment for Ian to locate his shoe that Missy had stripped and thrown at his head. Getting the shoe back on was another painful process, and as he struggled to tie the laces, his pulse quickened. It would take some time for the panic to leave his system. He hadn't reached safety yet.

Next, Ian retrieved Will's backpack, which had taken a knife for him. Hopefully the drive inside was okay. He would always thank his fallen friend for the foresight to bring it along.

Ian knew every minute more that he remained in Missy's house increased his exposure to its toxic atmosphere, which increased his risk of long-term side effects. He was covered in injuries in a house built with mold and shit.

Missy was dead but the other monster was not. The hoard still wanted to feed on him. He worked his way to the basement door, eager to get out of the monster's maw.

34

Six strenuous minutes later, Ian hoisted himself out of the broken basement window, groaning and sweating profusely. On the lawn, he fell onto his back and greedily gulped in the fresh air. The outdoors had never felt or tasted so good in his life. The cool night air caressed his face. The stars above reminded him that the universe remained in motion, and had other plans for him.

After a minute, the infusion of clean air gave Ian the strength to sit up. He looked down through the basement window at the hungry hoard waiting below. He hoped it was for the last time, although he knew he might have to return for the investigation. But he'd worry about that later. Ian turned away, eager to rid his vision of the obscenities inside Missy's house.

Ian grabbed the striped handlebars of Keith's recovered bike, which he had left leaning against the bushes. The rolling wheels helped in lieu of a walking stick. He walked his father's final gift to Keith up the driveway, passing Missy's car, which hadn't been parked there when they had arrived one hundred and one minutes ago. The oil slick was covered, revealing that Missy always parked in the exact same spot.

Ian looked into the windows of Missy's car and shook his head. The interior was completely packed with its own hoard of paper, stuffed animals, and food garbage. How fitting that she had a hoard on wheels. There was no seat available to anyone except for the driver. He guessed that only the trunk was empty, since she needed somewhere to store her weekly bounty of products purchased at the Mega-Mart.

Ian gave the house one final look. He knew how lucky he was to have gotten out alive, especially when his friends and family had not. Missy's house really was that mythical horror house in the woods, where fecal stains joined the bloodstains and the skeletons were out of the closet and on proud display.

Ian realized how crafty Missy had been in keeping her hoard inside, completely out of view. He knew many hoarders let their hoards spill out into their yards, acting as an exclamation of *Look at me! I need attention!* The greenery was over-run, but there were no personal belongings scattered outdoors. Missy's hoard had been a secret hidden behind decomposing walls and obscured windows, away from the public eye. Even her legendary status as the local crazy and kleptomaniac had not included hoarding. So she had not been completely ignorant of her crimes. She knew she had something to hide, namely her collection of corpses.

Ian wondered how such a nondescript dwelling could hold such a massive personality. In the end, the house had crumbled under the weight of Missy's madness. The hoard was not to blame, because a hoard could not build itself. The hoard's architect, the hoarder, warranted all the blame. The terrible place was just another victim choked by tons of garbage. In responsible hands, the house could have been a palace.

Ian knew that the house would be cleaned out (by authorities in Hazmat suits, whereas he and his friends had only hoodies for protection, which was no protection at all), but the structure was far too damaged to remain standing for long. After the shocking contents and crimes were revealed, the wrecking ball would have to move in quickly before the community, entirely justified in their outrage, converged to tear Missy's house down by hand. Ian knew it was possible; he had torn out a handful himself.

They might want to cover the neighborhood in plastic first before razing Missy's house. He feared the airborne pathogens that would be unleashed could start the next Black Death, a great plague upon humanity. The curse of Missy would drift on the afternoon air into his neighborhood to poison him and his mother first, finishing off his family. Ian shook the thought away. Missy was dead, but it would take some time to get the hoarder out of his head.

Ian pushed Keith's bike to the street, but he guessed it would be his bike now, his father's final gift to his sons. He mounted the bike carefully with the knife still stuck in his leg and pedaled away from the hoarder's house. He didn't look back.

THE END

ABOUT THE AUTHOR

Armando D. Muñoz is the award winning writer/director of a number of moist horror films including *The Killer Krapper*, *Pervula*, *Mime After Midnight*, *The Terrible Old Tran*, and *Panty Kill.* He also toils in film storyboarding, editing, scoring, make-up effects, cinematography, and acting, basically anything he needs to do to craft a bigger scare. Armando also performs as DJ Pervula, spinning an all horror themed set filled with his remixes and mash-ups.

Hoarder is his first novel. His second novel, *Turkey Day*, is also complete and nearing release.

Made in United States
Cleveland, OH
27 December 2024